What Happens in Vegas...
Stays in Vegas

A Novel by Michele Daniels

Published By Grice Publishing Company

Cover art by Deanna Cowart

Michele Daniel's World Wide Web site address is
http://www.micheledaniels.com

ISBN: 978-0-6151-4911-0

LCCN: 2004012345

Printed in the United States of America

ACKNOWLEDGEMENTS

I must first thank God for the gift he has given me to share with you. I owe a debt of gratitude to many people who helped me, believed in me and encouraged me to forge ahead to publication.

Deanna Cowart, you have done too many things to name to make this book happen. I wrote the book and you took care of all the technicalities. Your creativity has brought my vision to reality. Your hard work and dedication took this project from a word document to a book. Without you, I would still be talking about what I want to do and not knowing how to make it happen. Thank you, Deanna.

My Husband, Stan and my children Eric and Kristyn. Thanks for believing in me, it means more to me than you know. I know that I spend a lot of time in front of the computer, but when the desire to write hit me, I had to give in to it. At least you always knew where I was.

Thank you to my readers, Tina Noble, Deanna Cowart, Kim Grice and Patricia Smith for taking the time to read my stories and for giving me honest feedback.

Tina, thank you for pushing me to write more. Your encouragement is what kept me going. You convinced me that what I was writing was worth sharing with others. You have a gift for helping people realize their dreams. Keep doing what you're doing, Tina. Without you, I would have stopped at one. Thank you.

Kim, thank you for reading with so much excitement and encouragement. Every time I asked you to read for me, you were there. Your feedback always made me feel like I must be doing it right. Thanks for being there for me.

Pat, thank you and Sam for reading for me and giving me feedback as needed. You helped me more than you know.

Lynel Johnson Washington. My Editor. You are a blessing. I know that I was a little difficult in the beginning, but I finally conceded to you when

I realized that you knew better than me about what was best for this project. You've become a friend and a supporter and your encouragement has helped me move along. I look forward to working with you for many years to come. Thank you for being you!

My sister, Eva. Do you remember the day I called you at work and told you that I was writing a book? You asked me to e-mail some pages to you and you started reading for me. You encouraged me to keep typing because you were enjoying the story. If you had told me that it wasn't good, I would have stopped and that would have been the end of it. Thanks for believing in me and being proud of me.

Shywanee Manson, thanks for pushing me into that contest. Although nothing came of it, I did get the validation I needed. Shelbi Grant, you make me feel like a star. Monica Macklin, thank you for your encouragement. Rene Williamson, your support means a lot to me. Thanks for reading. Letric Watson, Angel Elliott, Annette Harrison and Marla Deloach, thank you for being a part of my inner circle. Our daily talks keep me sane. Shelton Watson, thank you for sharing your knowledge. You are truly a troubleshooter. Thanks for helping me move forward.

What Happens in Vegas...
Stays in Vegas

Prologue

Kellie, Michele, Gina and Stacey are friends from college. After graduation, they go their separate ways to begin their careers, but they talk to each other on the phone and send e-mails almost daily. They are always available for each other whenever needed no matter what is going on in their lives. It's been five years since graduation, and every year in April, they meet for a week in Las Vegas. Every year the plan is to live out their wildest fantasies in Vegas, but no one has ever followed through. Michele is the only one who has made an attempt to fulfill her fantasy. She had a one night stand with a stranger a couple of years ago, but that's it. They all promised that this is the year to make their fantasies come true.

Kellie is married with a two year-old son. She lives in Chicago. Michele has male friends, and she lives in Los Angeles. Gina is also married with two children, ages two and three. She lives in the Memphis area. And Stacey is in a committed relationship. She lives in Denver.

Kellie

Kellie is a teacher in the Chicago Public School System. She is teaching her last class of the day and can't wait for her workday to end. Tomorrow morning she will be on her way to Las Vegas.

Her husband, Craig, a Chicago police officer, has plans to spend as much time with her as possible before she leaves. Kellie and Craig met during a traffic stop shortly after Kellie graduated from college and returned to Chicago. At the time, Craig was a uniformed cop, but he's now a detective, and as Kellie calls him, "the freak of the week." The kinkier the sex act, the more it turns Craig on. Craig enjoys role playing and easily convinced Kellie to participate in his fantasies. Craig called Kellie at work during her lunch break and asked her if she is available for some fun before she leaves town. She knows what this means; she is sure he has something planned that involves restraint.

Kellie loves Craig's games. She called him from her cell phone and told him to take C.J., their two-year-old son, to his mother's house, and meet her at One Twelve in an hour. One Twelve is a hole-in-the-wall lounge on 112th and Wentworth on the south side of Chicago. They meet there on occasion because the other patrons keep to themselves, and it isn't far from their house in Beverly.

One of Kellie's favorite characters to play is known as Keisha. Whenever she and Craig meet at One Twelve, Keisha is who Craig comes to see.

When Craig enters the bar, the person he has been fantasizing about all day is waiting for him, Keisha. She is dressed just as he expects. She's wearing a short, tight, black dress, three inch stilettos and fishnet stockings, just how he likes it. He approaches her and asks, "Can I buy you a drink?"

"Sure, good looking; rum and Coke please."

"Are you here alone?"

"Yes. Is your wife joining you?"

"Naw. I was hoping to run into you, so that we can get together and do what we like to do."

"You want to go back to my place, so that we can have some privacy?"

"To be honest, Keisha, my wife will be here shortly, but I was hoping you could do a little something for me before she arrives."

"What did you have in mind, Officer?"

"Meet me in the men's bathroom."

"I'm right behind you."

After Craig walks to the back of the bar and into the men's room, Keisha waits a few minutes before joining him. Upon entry, she sees Craig leaning against one of the stall doors. She walks over to him and grabs his dick and starts massaging him. He pulls her into the stall and closes the door. Keisha turns around, leans over the toilet with her hands flat against the wall, revealing a bare ass and waits for Craig to enter her. He doesn't disappoint her. He is fully erect and fills her to capacity. While they are doing their thing, Keisha hears someone come into the bathroom. It doesn't stop them from doing what they are doing. There is a slight hesitation in step, but the visitor does his business and moves on. Once Craig and Keisha satisfy each other, Craig opens the stall door and lets her out first. Keisha straightens her clothes, checks herself in the mirror and proudly walks out of the men's room. When she enters the bar area, some of the guys are looking at her like they know what just went down. One of the other bar patrons asks her if she would like another drink. Craig walks up behind them and says, "Naw man, she's with me."

That is the thing that always kills the fantasy and brings Kellie back to reality. Once Keisha arrives in Vegas, there will be the next man, and the next man; however many she can handle, with no Craig in the way to end her fantasy.

Michele

Life in Los Angeles in April is great. Michele is looking forward to going to Vegas tomorrow to meet up with her girls and do her thing. Michele is a real estate agent who sells million-dollar-plus properties in the Beverly Hills and Brentwood areas. Not only does she work in Beverly Hills, she lives in a condo on Beverly Drive.

In her work she meets lots of celebrities and has actually dated a few. She has a free spirit and can't seem to sustain a relationship because she has no sense of commitment. Most of her friends tell her she acts like a man as far as relationships are concerned. She doesn't want a relationship, she just wants a man around to take her out and have sex with her. She is looking forward to going to Vegas and getting her fantasy on.

Her plan is to leave at six a.m., so that she will arrive in Vegas around ten a.m. While packing Michele makes sure she has the right gear, so that she can live out her fantasy the way she wants.

She packs her cat suit, thongs and other items which she plans to wear during her striptease. She has been practicing for over a year. A couple of times she slipped into strip joints and watched from afar as girls did their thing on stage so that she could get some ideas. One of the girls tried to convince her to come up on stage once, but she refused. Every time she went out to do research, she dressed in disguise. As she watched the reaction from the patrons, she was turned on. She has learned a lot from watching the other girls and can't wait to get to Vegas to do her thing.

Michele sets her alarm for five a.m. and goes to bed.

Gina

Gina is a stay-at-home mom with a loving husband who takes good care of her and their children. Marcus, her husband, is a very successful stockbroker. They live in a beautiful mini-mansion on Jenna Road in Germantown, which is outside of Memphis, Tennessee. Gina has only been sexually involved with one man, her husband. Not only is she looking to get with another man, her fantasy is to get with three men. She believes having three men take turns with her would be the ultimate sexual experience.

The name she'll use in Vegas is "Train" and she is determined to make the name fit her actions. She met two men online that she is going to hook up with and these men are both bringing two friends. She is looking forward to going to Vegas and fulfilling her fantasy.

Stacey

Stacey is an air traffic controller out of Denver International Airport. Today, she can hardly concentrate on her job, and she knows she had better get it together because if she makes a mistake, it could cause a lot of people to lose their lives. All she has been thinking about the past few days is getting to Vegas and doing her thing. She has two appointments already lined up, and she can't wait to get there and party. Her fantasy is to be a stripper at a bachelor party. She has parties to perform at on two of the seven nights that they will be in Vegas.

Her boyfriend Richard is a pilot for United Airlines and cherishes the ground Stacey walks on. She has never given him any indication that she would behave in such a manner. She is the shyest of all of her friends, and Richard is hard pressed to get her to wear sexy lingerie for him. She is shy about her body, and believes dancing in the nude for a room of men will give her the courage to be aggressive with her man. Richard is out of town and won't be back for a few days.

Her flight is scheduled to depart at nine-eleven a.m. and should touch down in Vegas a few minutes after ten. She is a little nervous about fulfilling her fantasy, but is looking forward to it. She talked to Richard about her trip and let him know how much she's missed him during his absence. After her conversation with Richard, she sets her alarm and goes to sleep.

Thursday, April 8

Michele was first to arrive at the MGM Grand where she reserved two suites for the weekend. She's sharing a suite with Kellie; Stacey and Gina will share the other. After Michele checked in, she decided to do a little people watching while waiting for the other girls to arrive. She found a seat in the hotel lobby that gave her a view of the entry door. She saw Lust, a famous rapper, and his entourage as they entered the hotel. Her mind started racing, trying to figure out a way to get his attention. While Lust was at the reservation desk, she sauntered over and asked the clerk if she had any messages. She was wearing a very revealing pair of short shorts and a halter. Lust couldn't keep his eyes off of her.

"Excuse me, Miss."

She turned his way and said, "Yes?"

"I'm hoping you're not here with your man because I would love to spend some time getting to know you."

"No, I'm not here with my man. How much time do you have?"

"Unfortunately, I'm in a hurry right now, but I would love to see you later."

"Why don't you catch my act at the Pussycat Club tonight? I'll be on after eleven."

"You're an entertainer?"

"Yes."

"I'll be there. What's your name?"

"Juicy."

"Alright, Juicy, I'm Lust, and I'm looking forward to seeing you tonight."

Michele walked away knowing that every eye in the area was on her ass. Just how she liked it.

When Kellie walked into the lobby, she saw Michele walking towards her and she noticed a group of men slobbering with their eyes plastered on Michele's ass. When Michele saw her, she broke out in a big grin. They greeted each other with a hug.

Kellie said, "Hey, Girl, you are looking hot and sexy, damn!"

"Thank you. I ain't playing with these men this time. I'm gonna get dicked down every night and into the morning. I just met Lust, and he's going to come to my show tonight. If things work out the way I plan, I'm gonna be fucking him tonight."

"You go, girl, I see you're not wasting any time getting your fantasy on."

"No I'm not, and I hope you won't either."

Kellie said, "I mapped out a couple of spots that I'll visit tonight and get my trick on."

"Girl, I can't believe you gonna be trickin'."

"I can't believe you gonna be strippin'."

"I'm gonna be getting my fantasy on, that's what I'm doing", Michele said. "Where are those other heifers? Stacey has a one-hour flight. She should have been here before I left the house this morning and Gina's ass..."

"What about Gina's ass?"

They both turned around to find Gina standing behind them. They hugged each other.

"Hey, Girl, it's so good to see you. I've really missed all you girls," Michele said.

Gina and Stacey said in unison, "We've missed you too."Just as they were getting reacquainted, Stacey arrived and they all went to their suites to get settled in. They agreed to meet in the lobby in an hour.Michele and Gina plan to begin living their fantasies tonight, and the next day will be Kellie and Stacey's turn. All the girls had dinner and drinks together to calm their nerves and to make sure they all know what Michele and Gina will be doing and where they will be before getting started. Before dinner, they rented cell phones to use for the duration of their stay, so that they could communicate with their hook-ups and not have a bunch of strange numbers on their personal phones. They didn't want anyone to be able to get in touch with them after they left Vegas.

At dinner Michele told everyone that she will be stripping at the Pussycat Club, and that she is expecting Lust to be there to see her show. Her plan is to get with him tonight. She has to call and let Stacey or Kellie know her plans before she leaves with anyone for safety reasons.

Gina is meeting a guy she met online named Vernon at Harrah's. He told her that he left a keycard at the desk for her. They are expecting her at nine o'clock.

Gina said, "Guys, don't get mad, but I'm a little nervous about this."

"Why would we get mad, Gina? If you don't want to do it, don't do it. No one will be mad at you," Kellie said.

"I didn't say that I don't want to do it. I'm just a little nervous about three men running a train on me."

Michele said, "I'm getting wet thinking about it. Anyway, I'm looking forward to some unknown dick tonight. You got your condoms, Gina?"

"Yeah, I have about thirty in my purse. I don't want to run out."

Michele said, "If you use thirty condoms, you're done for the whole trip. Your cat will be so sore; you won't want no more dick for a while."

"Well, it's better to be safe than sorry. It's twenty-to-nine, I guess I should be going," Gina said.

Michele said, "Be careful and have fun. Do you need another drink?"

"No, I'm pretty mellow now. My courage is all the way up and I have a small bottle of rum in my purse, just in case. I'll call when I'm on my way back to the hotel."

Kellie said, "Have fun!"

Michele had to be at the club at ten-thirty. The arrangements she made with the club manager would put her on stage somewhere around eleven o'clock for three nights. One show tonight, another Saturday and the last show will be the following Monday. She can't wait to get out there and put on her show. She has always been an exhibitionist and she now had an arena to put on the show she has always dreamed of.

9

Gina

Gina arrived at Vernon's hotel at five after nine. After retrieving the keycard, she sat in the lobby and had another drink before going up to his room.

When Vernon opened the door, he was surprised to see how beautiful Gina was. He got more than he expected. They hadn't exchanged pictures, so he had no idea what Gina looked like. Vernon was decent-looking in the face, and his body was tight. He introduced her to his friends, Steven and Daniel. Both were nerds who were not so good looking, but she wasn't interested in being seen with them, she just wanted them to use her.

Vernon offered her a drink, but she refused. Before any of the girls left the group to fulfill their fantasy, they discussed the rules and the number one rule is not to take a drink from anyone. Michele said to them, "If you feel like you need a pick-me-up, take your drink with you. You never know what someone might try to slip you."

Gina wore a blue jean miniskirt, three-inch stilettos, and a sheer, button down blouse that left nothing to the imagination. She also decided not to wear underwear. The men had her undressed with their eyes before the introductions were finished. She didn't want to waste time with small talk, so she walked over to an empty chair, sat down, put each leg on an arm rest and said, "Does anyone want some of this?" as she pointed to her wet pussy.

All three of them practically ran over to her. Vernon started eating her pussy, while Steven removed her blouse and sucked her breasts and Daniel stuck his dick in her mouth. They found their way over to the bed and they each took turns fucking her, having her suck their dicks and eating her pussy. They fucked her from the front, the back, on the floor, on the bed and on the balcony. Steven and Vernon both tried to get their dicks inside of her at the same time. They poured champagne all over her body and sucked it off. Then they dipped their dicks in whipped cream and she sucked them off. Vernon had a nice fat dick and he liked slamming his dick into her. Steven had a huge dick. She could tell the difference between being with her husband, Marcus, and these other men. Steven's dick was long and fat and he made her come repeatedly. Daniel's dick was kind of small, but he made up for it with his mouth. After they all busted a nut, she gathered her things and made her way back to the hotel.

Gina called when she was on her way to the hotel. Kellie and Stacey were in the lobby waiting for her return.

Michele

When Michele arrived at the Pussycat Club, the other girls were looking at her like they wanted to kick her ass. She guessed they were pretty territorial. She peeked out from backstage and saw wall-to-wall men trying to get the attention of the girl on the stage. There were men rubbing their dicks right out in the open. There were also men sitting in the back of the club beating off. Michele watched the girl on the stage dance to see if there was something she could learn from her.

Another dancer came up behind her and said, "You like what you see on the stage?"

"Naw, she ain't got no dick."

"I can make you forget about a dick with just one lick."

"I don't think so."

Michele walked away and started getting into costume. She was due on stage in thirty minutes. One of the girls came back in the dressing room and said, "Y'all ain't gonna believe who's out there."

They were all asking who it was.

"Lust. Lust is out there to see our show."

Cocoa, the dancer who is due next to go on stage said, "He won't see y'alls shows after he sees mine because I'm gonna make him forget about everyone else when I do my thang."

The other girls rolled their eyes and talked about Cocoa, but Michele didn't say a word. She continued to prepare herself for her debut.

Michele is tall and curvaceous with a medium-brown complexion and straight black hair that hangs halfway down her back. She decided to wear a clip to hold her hair on top of her head; a sheer, pull-away cat suit with the crotch cut out and holes for her nipples; a pair of three-inch, black, patent leather stilettos and a black G-string. She danced to Ludacris' "Splash Waterfalls" and it sent the men into a frenzy. She saw Lust as she walked onto the stage. The more the men were hooting and hollering, the deeper she got into her dance. When she was totally naked, she slid to the end of the stage and let a man eat her pussy. He slipped a large bill in her G-string.

When the song ended, the manager announced that Juicy will be back Saturday night, as she left the stage. When and she made it back to the dressing room, the manager met her there and asked if she could go on again. She declined because she wanted to follow the program she had laid out for herself. She didn't want to become too familiar and wanted the men to look forward to seeing her again.

It was everything she fantasized it would be. The manager also told her that Lust requested a lap dance from her.

After she put the money she had just made into her locker, Michele put on another G-string and went back out there to give Lust what he wanted. Men grabbed at her and tried to get her attention as she made her way to the front row where Lust was sitting. The girl on stage was pissed because she was doing everything she could to get Lust's attention, but his eyes were glued to Juicy as she walked towards him. She didn't say a word. She climbed on his lap and started grinding her body against his. He was fully erect and ready for some action. She did everything but fuck him in his seat. When she was done, he slipped two large bills in her G-string and she made her way back to the dressing room. The manager again appeared backstage and gave Juicy a note and a keycard. It was from Lust requesting she meet him at his room after the show. He said that he would be waiting.

After Michele was dressed, she called Kellie and told her that she was on her way back to the hotel and that her night wasn't over. She let her friends know that Lust gave her a room key and that she would be going to his room upon her return.

When Michele arrived at the hotel Kellie, Gina and Stacey were all in the lobby waiting for her. She went upstairs to her suite, took a shower and put on something sexy for her visit to Lust's room. She wore a pair of skin-tight jeans and a button down blouse, exposing her cleavage. The other girls wanted to know what happened at the strip club, but they all previously agreed that they would not talk about their adventures until everyone was back together, which meant over breakfast the next morning.

When Michele arrived at Lust's room, one of his boys answered the door and let her in. Lust was sitting on the sofa in a pair of black silk boxer shorts, no shirt nor shoes and looking as sexy as ever.

When Michele walked over to him he stood, took her hand and led her into the bedroom.

Lust said, "Can I get an encore performance?"

"Sure. You got some music for me?"

There was a CD player in the room and he put some music on. Michele started stripping for him and he was all over her. This time he was dropping bills like it was play money. She gave him another lap dance and this time she went down on him. Then he fucked her in every possible position. The sun was close to rising before Michele made it back to her suite. Kellie was waiting for her.

Michele said, "Girl, why are you still awake?"

"I couldn't sleep until you made it back safely. Was it fun?"

"Oh snap, Kellie! It was better than I dreamed. I know we are not supposed to talk about it until breakfast, but damn, I can't wait to strip again Saturday."

"What about Lust? How was he?"

"Girl, he beat my shit up. He has some serious stamina and ol' boy is packing. I hope I can get some more of that before we leave."

"Let's get some sleep. We have to be at breakfast at nine."

"Okay. Are you ready to do yo' thang tonight?"

"Yeah, I'm ready."

"Good!"

Everyone was in the lobby at nine for breakfast. Michele and Gina were anxious to tell their stories and Kellie and Stacey were anxious to hear them.

Gina went first and gave details about how everything played out. She said that her fantasy was definitely met and she hoped that her next party on Monday would be just as fun.

Michele asked, "Why do you have your dates spread so far apart?"

"Because I knew I would be sore. They tore my shit up, girl. I need a few days to recover."

Michele went next and then she pulled out a wad of money. She made over twelve hundred dollars while living out her fantasy.

Stacey asked, "How did it feel to have all of those men touching all over you?"

"I didn't mind at all. I let one man eat me while I was on stage."

"Shut the fuck up, Girl! No you didn't," Gina said.

"Yes I did. He kept slipping twenties in my band and asking me to move closer. Next thing I know, his head was in between my legs and I let him get a couple good licks and a suck before I moved him off of me."

Gina said, "Damn, Michele, you really did your thang, didn't you?"

"Most definitely. I can't wait to get back out there tomorrow. Kellie, Stacey, are y'all ready for tonight?

Kellie said, "I've been waiting for this night for years. Yeah, I'm ready."

Stacey said, "I'm definitely ready. I've got to meet with the two other strippers at three and we're supposed to be at the room at eight."

Gina said, "How many men are they expecting at this party?"

"Darryl, the guy giving the party, said they expect about twenty guys."

"You know what to do. Michele will be in the hotel lobby waiting for you to return. And Kellie, I'm going to be in the bar so that I can see who you pick up," Gina said.

Stacey said, "I need to start working on my routine and getting my outfit together."

Michele said, "Me and Gina are either going gambling or we're going to hang out. We'll see y'all later."

Stacey and Kellie went back to their respective suites to prepare for the night and Michele and Gina hit the strip.

"Michele, girl, look over there at them."

"Who? Where are you talking about?"

"Over there in the McDonald's parking lot."

"Oh. Girl, those cars got California plates. I've got to be careful with them. You never know who I might run into and those are white guys."

"Who said I only had one fantasy? Girl, come on. I want to see if we can get their attention."

Michele said, "As short as your shorts are, if you don't get their attention, they are probably gay."

"And I'm sure you know that everybody in the state of Nevada can see your ass through that short-tight dress you have on. Lie and say you don't have a thong on. I can trace it. How you gonna wear that fitted jersey dress with a thong. You are such a ho."

"Thank you."

They walked over to McDonald's and just as Gina predicted, the guys in the parking lot were trying to holla at them.

"Hey beautiful. Slow down. Let me holla at you." One of the guys said.

Both Michele and Gina stopped. Two of the four guys that were leaning against the car walked over to where they were standing.

A guy who looked like he was the ring leader said, "What y'all getting into?"

Gina said, "I'm thirsty, I'm going in here to get a drink."

"Why don't you beautiful ladies join me and my boys for some lunch at Caesar's?" the same guy said.

Michele and Gina looked at each other and nodded.

"Alright." Gina said.

"Cool. My name is Billy. This is Todd, Mark and Peter." The other two guys joined the group.

"Hi guys. I'm Train" Gina said, "and this is Juicy."

14

Billy said, "Train and Juicy. Them is some nice names."

"We like them," Gina said.

These guys looked to be in their mid to late twenties.

Billy said, "Juicy, you are one of the most beautiful women I have ever seen and that dress you're wearing was made just for your body."

"I'm glad you like it, Billy. I guess I'm getting the desired affect then."

"Y'all want to ride with us?"

"I can see the fountains from here. We'll meet you guys there."

Billy and Todd started following the girls as they began walking.

Billy said, "I can't let you ladies walk down there by yourselves. Some other man will definitely come along and try to whisk y'all away before you can make it there. So Todd and I will walk with you to make sure you get there."

Michele said, "Billy, can I ask you something?"

"Sure, what's up?"

"I was always led to believe that white guys don't like a lot of ass, but I've noticed that you can't keep your eyes off of mine. What's up with that?"

"Different strokes for different folks. You've got everything I like: big round ass, big juicy titties, small waist and a pretty face to go with it."

"That's one of the reasons they call me Juicy, Baby."

"What's the other reason?"

"I'm just as juicy on the inside as I am on the outside."

"Damn! I like you, girl. I really like you. What y'all doing this evening?"

Gina said, "We already have plans for this evening."

"How long y'all gonna be in Vegas?"

"A few more days."

Billy said, "What time are you gonna be done with what you have planned for this evening, Juicy?"

"It's going to be pretty late."

"It don't matter to me how late, I can wait. I'm sure it will be worth it."

"Give me a number where I can reach you and I'll call you when I'm done."

Michele and Billy exchanged phone numbers. After lunch, Gina and Michele did a little gambling and then made their way back to the hotel.

Stacey

Stacey left for her three o'clock meeting with the other strippers at the Venetian where the bachelor party was taking place that night. One of the other girls was black and the second was white. They were told by Darryl that Stacey is the head stripper and for them to follow her direction. Stacey and the other strippers coordinated everything that they would be doing and agreed to meet at the hotel by nine. The strippers agreed to work the party until one a.m.

Once back at the hotel, Stacey met up with Michele, Gina and Kellie to go over all of the details for her show and to bring everyone up to date on what she planned for the evening.

Kellie

Kellie was ready and dressed for her night on the town by nine o'clock. She and Gina made their way to the Hideaway, a club off the strip, which is known for prostitution.

When Kellie and Gina walked into the dimly lit club, all eyes focused on them. The men in the club were definitely looking for some action. It looked like your average club with partygoers dancing, drinking and having a good time, but the difference was that there was a price for a hook-up.

Kellie and Gina split up. Gina found a booth in the back away from everyone and let Keisha do her thing. As soon as Keisha took a seat at the bar, a good looking brother approached her and offered to buy her a drink.

The guy introduced himself as Omar. Omar is a big guy. Around 6'4", at least 240 lbs., baldhead, muscular, not hard on the eyes at all.

"How much will it cost me for your time?" Omar asked.

"Depends on how you want to spend my time. What you need?"

"I need to get up in your pussy and I need for you to suck me off."

"One hundred dollars."

"One Hundred dollars!"

"Fifty dollars for you to get up in me and another fifty dollars for me to suck you off. What's it gonna be, Omar?"

"Let's do this."

Keisha is wearing a leather miniskirt and a leather halter top. She made eye contact with Gina on her way out.

"You got a spot, Keisha?"

"Yeah, right over here."

Prior to entering the club, Kellie paid for a room at a local hourly motel around the corner from the club for the entire night.

Omar wasn't wasting any time. He undressed, sat on the bed and said, "Come on ho and suck this dick."

Keisha walked over to the bed and stuck her hand out for the money. After he paid her she got down on her knees, did an inspection of his dick, slipped a condom over it and started sucking him off. She grabbed his nuts and started massaging them too. Omar was moaning and talking.

"Suck that big dick, baby. Oh, you know how to make a man feel good. Come on up here and take them clothes off, so I can get to that pussy."

Keisha undressed as he was touching and feeling all over her body. He pulled her to him once she had all of her clothes off. He was in her within

17

seconds. He started fucking her like it was the first time he had ever had any pussy. He flipped her over and took her from behind.

Keisha returned to the bar a half an hour later. Omar talked a lot of shit, but was a minute man. Keisha made eye contact with Gina when she entered the club and then made her way to the bar. Within minutes, the next man was looking for some action. He was an average looking, older white guy, between 50-55 years old, wearing a wedding band.

"How you doing this evening?"

"I'm fine and you?"

"Good, real good. What's a pretty young thang like you doin' sitting in here alone?"

"Looking for some company."

"I think you just found him. What's your name, sweetheart?"

"Keisha."

"How much Keisha?"

"What you need?"

"Pussy."

"Fifty dollars."

"Alright. Follow me."

He took her to his car in the parking lot. He was driving a nice Lincoln with tinted windows. They climbed in the back seat. He paid Keisha and then told her he wanted to enter her from behind. He fucked her doggy style. It only took about fifteen strokes and he was done. He zipped up and she pulled down her skirt. When she got out of the car, she walked back into the club as if nothing happened. She again made eye contact with Gina and went back to the bar. By the end of the night, Keisha had been with seven different men. Omar was the only one she took to the motel. The rest of them just wanted to have sex in their cars and she had sex with one guy in the alley behind the club. They came in all sizes and colors; Black, White, Hispanic, old, and young. It didn't matter because she didn't see their faces.

When Keisha was done, she walked over to the booth where Gina was sitting and said, "Let's go."

When they arrived at the hotel, Michele was sitting at the hotel bar with Stacey.

Lust and Billy had been blowing up Michele's cell phone all night. She liked Lust a little bit and didn't want to get too attached to him. She decided not to return his calls. She wasn't sure how long he would be in town, but he knew where to find her if he was really interested in seeing her again.

Stacey

When Stacey arrived at Darryl's suite at Treasure Island, the guys were already drunk. When she walked into the room, Darryl called out to her, "Chocolick! Chocolick! Over here!"

Chocolick was Stacey's fantasy name. It fit her perfectly. She's dark brown, 5', 6", 150 lbs. and very curvaceous. There were at least twenty guys there and she didn't see the two other girls.

"Hi Darryl, are the other girls here?"

"Yeah, they are in the room getting dressed."

When Chocolick entered the bedroom, Meme and Bird were in there waiting for her. Meme looked about the same age as Stacey, 27. Bird looked to be in her early 30's and you could see each year in her face.

"You ladies look nice."

"They are both wearing too much make-up, but who am I to say anything," Stacey thought to herself.

"Thank you. What are you wearing?"

Stacey pulled out a g-string with cat whiskers and nipple tassels from her bag. She was usually shy about her body, but she got completely nude and put on her little pieces while Meme and Bird watched.

Stacey called Darryl from her cell phone and told him to put the music on. When they heard the music playing, Stacey said, "Y'all ready to do this?"

They both said, "Yeah, let's go."

When they stepped out into the living room of the suite, all of the hootin' and hollering started. They started dancing. Stacey got off into her own world and didn't let the other girls distract her from what she was there for. Guys were calling out to her, trying to flag her down with cash. She danced her way over to each one of them and let them put the money wherever they wanted to. One guy asked her to turn around and bend over. When she did, he put a $50 bill in between her legs and then said, "I'll get that out later."

Stacey winked at him and walked away. She walked over to the next guy and let him remove her tassels and suck her titties; he stuck a $20 bill in her g-string. The guys were throwing twenties and fifties around like they were one dollar bills.

Meme and Bird had been working on the groom. When they were done it was Stacey's turn. He was sitting in the chair in nothing but a pair of boxer shorts and an erection.   Stacey had gone off into Chocolick world and was in the zone.

She stopped in front of the groom and straddled him. She pushed her titties together and put both of her nipples in his mouth. His dick was so hard she couldn't wait to get it inside of her. When she first saw him sitting in the chair, she knew she was going to fuck him.

He was sucking back and forth between each nipple. Chocolick slid off his lap and slid his shorts off of him. She removed her g-string, slid a condom on him and straddled him again; this time wrapping herself around his dick. The other men in the room were screaming and slobbering. The groom stood up and Chocolick wrapped her legs around him. He pushed her back up against a wall and continued to fuck her. He then let her down and had her turn around and fucked her doggy style until he came. Once he was done, the $50 guy came over to her, pulled out his dick, slipped on a condom and started fucking her. She enjoyed fucking man after man in front of everyone.

At the end of the day, Chocolick fucked four guys, including the groom and sucked off another three. Meme and Bird were also having sex with some of the guys. Darryl paid Chocolick $100.00 to let the groom fuck her and she collected $100 each from the other three, $50 per blow job and the other money she collected dancing. She left out of there with over $1000.

When Stacey made it back to the hotel, Michele was in the hotel bar waiting for her. When Kellie and Gina joined them, Michele announced that she was going to have a nightcap with Billy.

"Where are you going to meet him?" Stacey asked.

"He has a penthouse suite at the Venetian. I'll see you guys later."

Gina said, "Don't get all caught up with this white boy, Michele."

"Girl you know me, I don't get caught up with anybody."

It was two fifteen a.m. when Michele headed to Billy's hotel room.

When she entered the Venetian Hotel, a good looking brother was checking her out as hard as she was checking him out.

"How you doing this evening?" he said.

"I'm fine, and you?"

"Fine. You in a hurry?"

"Yes, I have an appointment."

"What's your name, maybe I'll run into you again."

"Michele."

"Michele is such a beautiful name. I'm Nicholas. Are you staying at this hotel?"

"No. I'm staying at the MGM. I'm here visiting a friend."

He glanced at his watch. "Your friend is very lucky. How long are you in town? Maybe we can get together for lunch or dinner tomorrow if you're available."

"Lunch would be nice."

He handed her his card and she wrote her real cell phone number on the back of it and handed it back to him. "Call me and we'll see what we can do."

He smiled and watched her walk away. Michele was glad that she wasn't dressed too sleazy. There was something about this guy that caught her attention in a different way. He was dressed well, spoke well, smelled good and was good looking. All of the features she likes in a man. She looked forward to seeing him again.

When she arrived at Billy's room, he was high. She didn't know what he was high on, but that wasn't her thing. He offered her a drink and she told him she would fix it herself. They sat on the balcony and engaged in small talk.

Billy's daddy owns a production company in Hollywood and he's basically a spoiled rich white boy. After a half-hour or so, Michele found out what he was high on. He offered her some cocaine. She declined because she didn't do drugs. She was instantly turned off by him. He was too obnoxious. She told him that she was going to the restroom. When she came out, he had his back to the door with his head thrown back. Michele grabbed her bag and slipped out of the room then out of the hotel. When she came into her room a short time later, Kellie was still awake and waiting for her.

"That was fast."

"I know. He was high and that shit turned me off, so when he wasn't looking, I slipped out of there and here I am."

"Good. Now I can get some sleep."

"How was it?"

"You know we are not supposed to tell, but it was cool. It wasn't as exciting as I thought it would be. Men are a trip. All they want is some pussy. There were old men, young men, Black, White and Hispanic. They couldn't wait to get to the room. I was fucking in cars. One guy fucked me in the alley. It just makes you think about your man. Are all men hardup for pussy like that? Some of these guys were married, but they are still willing to pay for a few strokes in some forbidden pussy."

"Girl, I know, it's a trip ain't it."

Saturday, April 10th

The next morning they all met in the hotel restaurant for breakfast.
Gina said, "Okay Kellie, you first."
"Alright, first off, men ain't shit!"
"Duh."
"Okay, I'm sorry. That's not totally true. I don't want to put all men into one category because there are some good guys out there, but I wasn't with any of them last night. It was sad, old married men, young men, and good-looking men. All types are willing to pay for some pussy although they can probably get it at home. I guess it's the thrill of some different pussy with no attachments. Anyway, I don't know if I want to go back out there and do it again. It was okay, but it wasn't all that fulfilling for me. When I role-play with Craig, it's fun because he's familiar and there is no danger, but with the men I was with last night, I never knew what was going to happen. I felt trashy, but not in a good way. It's cool to feel trashy when you know who you are acting trashy for, but for strangers, they don't even see you, they just want to fuck you. I fulfilled my fantasy, but I don't think I'm going back out there."

"That's cool Kellie. You did what you set out to do so it's cool. We won't rag on you about it," Gina said.
"Cool."
"Alright Stacey, let's have it."
"I might be able to win the trophy for slut of the week. Ladies, Chocolick was in the house last night! I fucked the groom in front of everybody there. Then when I was done with him, I fucked three other guys and sucked off a few more. I'm not talking about going in a bedroom and doing it behind closed doors; I'm talking about right out in the open in front of everyone. The ones who weren't hitting it were beatin' off and that shit was turning me the fuck on. There was dick all over the place."
"Where were the other chicks?"
"Doing the same thing. It was a fuck-fest going on in there."
"Damn, is that what you planned to do?"
"Naw, I knew I was gonna fuck the groom, but I didn't expect to fuck all them other dudes. I was hot and the more they asked for it, the more I wanted to give. It was the shit! I've got another party tonight."
Kellie said, "You ready to do it again tonight?"
"Hell yeah! That shit turned me the fuck on!"
"You gonna be dancing with the same girls?"

"Yeah, we work well together."

Michele said, "So it's me and you tonight, Stacey. Gina's got her other hook-up Monday and after tonight it will be me and Gina on Monday finishing up."

"You ready for tonight, Michele?" Kellie said.

"Oh hell yeah! I'm with Stacey, dancing for these men really turn me on. I can't wait to get out there. As a matter of fact, I'm going to get my things together and then take a nap. I want to be fresh when I go on tonight."

Gina said, "What happened with the white boy last night?"

"Girl, he was so high on cocaine he probably didn't realize that I left before this morning. I told him I was going to the bathroom and I just left. He turned me off. He was high, drunk and getting on my nerves. I couldn't get with him."

"What happened with Lust?"

"He's been blowing my cell up, but I haven't called him back."

Kellie said, "I thought you said you like him?"

"I do. That's part of the problem. I don't want to chase him; I want him to chase me. I'll see if he shows up at the club tonight. Oh snap, I forgot to tell y'all I met this dude last night when I was going to see Billy. His name is Nicholas and he said he would call me today for lunch."

"Are you going to invite him to the show?"

"Nope. I gave him my real cell phone number."

"Why?"

"He is the shit! Well dressed, well manicured, he is all that. I might want to get to know him as Michele, not Juicy. I told him my real name too."

"He must have been a sight to see. We all know how you are."

"Let's just see if he calls."

They set up their schedules for the night before going back to their rooms.

Michele

When Michele came out of the shower, she heard her cell phone ring. She didn't recognize the number, but decided to answer it anyway.

"This is Michele."

"What's up, Michele? This is Nick."

"Hey. How you doin'?"

"I'm good. I was hoping we could get together for lunch. Are you available?"

"Yeah. What did you have in mind?"

"I'll come by and pick you up and we can take it from there."

"Okay. What time?"

"I can pick you up in front of your hotel in an hour. Can you be ready?"

"Yeah. I'll be ready."

"Which hotel?"

"MGM."

"Okay Michele, I'll see you in an hour."

"Nick."

"Yes?"

"What kind of car are you in?"

"Oh, I'm sorry, sweetheart. I'm driving a silver BMW, 750Li."

"Okay, I'll see you out front.

Kellie!"

"Yeah?"

"That was Nick. He's coming to pick me up and take me to lunch."

"Are you gonna tell him about your night job?"

"Hell no. I want to get to know him on a different level."

"Do you have any decent outfits you can wear? I've noticed that most of your clothes are pretty sleazy."

"Yeah, I know. I didn't expect to go on a real date."

They worked together to find a nice outfit. When Michele stepped outside of the hotel, Nick was out front leaning against a shiny new car.

He opened the door for her and she slid in. Michele had been considering buying this same car, but hadn't made a final decision. When Nick got in the car, he said, "You are even more beautiful in the daylight."

"Thank you, Nick. I can say the same about you."

He's wearing a pair of white linen pants and an ocean blue button down shirt. He has short, curly hair, golden brown skin and his teeth are perfect.

Michele is wearing a white cotton dress that hit every curve of her body and a pair of white sandals. It's a simple outfit and it looks sexy on her.

"I'm sorry that we are having such an early date, but I had something already planned for this evening. I hope you don't mind," Nick said.

"No, I don't mind at all."

Nick took her to Delmonico's Steak House and they got to know each other. Michele liked him and had to keep him away from her fantasy. He lives in Los Angeles and he's single. He was in a long-term relationship, but that fell apart recently because of all of his traveling and her insecurities. He works for a major record company and is responsible for promoting some of his client's gigs. He is in town because a couple of his clients are in town performing.

Michele made it back to her hotel around seven o'clock p.m. Both she and Nick had things to do, but promised to keep in touch. He is leaving the next evening and will be pretty busy all day and can't promise that he will be able to get away to see her. He told her if he can't get away this evening, for her to call him when she makes it back to Los Angeles, so that they can get together for dinner.

Michele was able to lay down for about an hour before she had to leave for the Pussycat Club. When she walked in the door, the manager came over to her and told her that Lust was in the club last night looking for her. He said that he let Lust know that she would be back tonight.

Michele thanked Lou. When she walked into the dressing room, one of the girls said, "There she is right there."

Another one of the girls said, "What's up with you, Ms. Juicy? Got rappers and shit coming in here looking for you. Dude wouldn't even hang around to see anybody else's show when he found out you wasn't here."

"You're saying that's my fault?"

"I'm not saying that. I'm just asking, what's so special about you?"

"He obviously likes something about me."

"Yeah, whatever."

Juicy was wearing an olive green satin robe and a g-string with a pair of feather slippers. She was dancing to Lil' Jon and the Eastside Boys "Ooh Na Na Naa Naa." Again, her choice of music brought the dollars out.

When she stepped onto the stage the first person she saw was Lust. He was sitting upfront and center. Juicy let her robe fall as she walked towards the pole in the center of the stage. She danced on the pole for a few minutes and then made her way over to the money. Her first stop was to Lust. He dropped a $100 bill to get things started. She walked to the side of the stage and put her ass in another man's face and made her booty clap. Men were dropping bills like mad trying to get her attention. They were smacking her ass and she loved it. When her song ended, Lou told her that she had four requests for lap dances. The first dance was for Lust. She put her robe on and walked on the floor. When she approached Lust, she straddled him, opened her robe and let him suck and feel all over her. His dick was hard as stone and she remembered how good he felt inside of her the other night and hoped to feel him again tonight. When she tried to get up, he gave her another $100 bill and said he wanted another dance. She was grinding and shaking all over him for at least ten minutes. He sat back and watched as she moved onto the next person. When she finished the next dance, Lust was gone. He told her that he wanted to see her later and she said she would come to his room after she was done at the club.

She made even more money that night. Most of it came from Lust. When Michele made it back to the hotel, she told Kellie that she was going to meet up with Lust and that she would see her in the morning.

"What's going on with y'all?"

"Nothing really. I like him and he seems to like me, too."

"Is it just sex?"

"Yeah. What kind of man would want his woman shaking her ass in front of a room full of men? I gave him two lap dances and a couple of lap dances to a few other guys. Most men are territorial. If they care about you, ain't nobody else gonna touch you if they can help it."

"Well go on and have fun then. I'll see you in the morning."

"Did Stacey get back yet?"

"No. I'm waiting for Gina to call."

"Alright. You know where I am if you need me."

When Michele made it to Lust's room, this time he opened the door. He had on a robe with nothing under it. When he sat down, the robe opened and his dick was exposed. He didn't try to cover it. Michele couldn't keep her eyes off him, so she made a move on him. She wore a sundress with nothing under it. She approached him, dropped to her knees, opened his robe, grabbed his dick and started sucking it. His boy was in the room, but she didn't care. She stood up, took her dress off and straddled him. They fucked on the couch like they were the only two in the room. When they were done, Lust took her into his bedroom where they continued where they left off.

Michele made it back to her room around seven o'clock the next morning.

Stacey

Stacey met up with Meme and Bird in the hotel lobby of the Palms. This next party was set up by Meme. When they arrived in the room, the guys were sitting around talking shit and drinking, but not really partying. Meme took Stacey and Bird into one of the bedrooms, so that they could get dressed. They planned to take turns stripping and dancing for the groom. Meme told Stacey and Bird that they could make an extra $100 if the groom requests a private dance. The host said the groom was adamant about not getting intimate with a stripper. Meme was first to go out. There were twelve or thirteen guys hooting and hollering vying for Meme's attention. When she came back in the room, Bird went out and put on her show. Next, Stacey was introduced as Chocolick as she strutted in front of the guys and started dancing to Ludacris' song "Splash Waterfalls," which she chose at Michele's insistence. In the back of the room, she saw her boyfriend Richard's best friend Charles watching. She didn't miss a beat, but she was a nervous wreck. She thought about him during her entire performance. It was too late to turn back now, so she made the best of it. After her striptease, she gave the groom a lap dance that changed his mind about getting intimate with one of the strippers. The guys were putting cash in her g-string, but Charles stayed away. She eventually made eye contact with Charles. He didn't say anything to her, he just continued to watch. When she was done, she went back into the bedroom. The host came into the bedroom and told Stacey that Roger, the groom, requested her presence in the master suite. While Stacey was walking to the suite guys were smacking her ass, which she didn't mind, but she was still concerned about Charles.

When she entered the suite, the groom Roger was sitting on the edge of the bed, nude, with a serious erection and holding his head down.

"You don't have to do this if you don't want to."

"I know, but you got my shit so hard, I've got to release some of this. Come here."

"I can suck you off; maybe you won't feel guilty about that."

"I want that pussy. I bet it's good and tight."

Stacey removed her g-string, slid a condom over his dick and straddled him. He laid back and she rode him until he came.

When they were done, he thanked her, got dressed and left out of the room. Stacey went into the bathroom to clean herself up and when she came out, Charles was sitting on the side of the bed.

"Charles!"

"Stacey. What are you doing?"

"Let me explain."

"Okay. Does Richard know about this?"

"No. Please don't tell him, Charles."

"Did you just fuck Roger?"

Stacey put her head down and looked away.

"Chocolick! Please explain, Stacey."

"A few of my friends and I came here to live out our fantasies and my fantasy was to be a stripper."

"Does that have to include fucking? I can see stripping, but you out here fucking too. That's more like being a hooker not a stripper."

"I don't have any feelings for these guys; it's just part of the job."

"These guys? How many you been with, Stacey?"

"Just this one guy." She lied.

"So if I gave you $100, you would fuck me?"

"You don't want me, Charles."

"Yeah, I do."

"It wouldn't be right."

"So you'll fuck a stranger, but I can't get none?"

"Charles. Come on. I wouldn't feel right. Would you?"

"Here's my money, Chocolick start dancing." He handed Stacey $100 and started undressing. He sat on the bed and told her he wanted his dick sucked. She gave him a blow job and then she straddled him. He flipped her and fucked her from behind. She kept her eyes closed the whole time. When he was done, he got dressed, dropped another $20 and told her, "That's for being better than I had been dreaming about" and walked out of the room.

Meme came into the room and asked her if she could come back out and dance because the guys were requesting her. After getting herself together, she went back out and danced and did a few lap dances. She headed back to the hotel about an hour later. When she came into the lobby of the MGM, Kellie was waiting. Kellie could tell that something was wrong when she saw Stacey's face.

"What's wrong, Stacey?"

"Richard's best friend, Charles, was at the party."

"What! Do you think he will tell Richard?"

"I gave him a private dance and I fucked him."

"Why did you do that?"

"I know if I hadn't done it, he would definitely tell Richard."

"Why don't you think he is going to tell him now? You know how men are. Shit Stacey, I think you made a huge mistake."

Sunday, April 11th

Everyone was at the breakfast table at nine o'clock a.m. No one had anything planned for the night and there were two more events scheduled for the next night. Gina as "Train" and Michele as "Juicy" had one more show to put on at the Pussycat Club.

Stacey said, "Y'all I think I'm in trouble."

"What kind of trouble Stacey," Michele said.

"I fucked Richard's best friend last night while I was stripping."

"What?"

"He was at the party I was working and requested a private dance. I did it, so that he wouldn't tell Richard."

"Oh shit, Stacey. I think you're going to be in trouble and then he'll tell Craig and he's going to be questioning me, asking me if I knew, and asking me what I've been doing out here," Kellie said.

"What was I supposed to do?"

"I don't know, Stacey. I really don't know. Shit!"

Gina said, "Do you think he will tell Richard?"

"Yes. I think he will. Richard called me last night when I came back to the room and asked me how it was going. He said that Charles was here for a bachelor party and asked me if I've seen him. I think Charles is going to play games with me, but I think he will eventually tell him. Fuck!"

Michele said, "See, that's why I don't want to be bothered with no damn man always in my fuckin' business. Does Charles have a wife or girlfriend?"

"He has a girlfriend."

"I'm sure he doesn't want her to know that he fucked you. You probably don't have anything to worry about."

"His girlfriend doesn't like me too much and she's Richard's cousin. He can tell her that I came onto him or some shit and she will believe it's my fault. She's dumb as a rock. He can tell her anything."

"How long is he going to be here?"

"I don't know."

"See if you can find out and I'll get him caught up in some shit that his girl will believe."

"What are you going to do, Michele?"

"Find out how long he'll be here and leave the rest to me, please Stacey. You want to save your relationship, right?"

"Yes."

"Alright then, just do what I told you."

"How was your night, Michele?" Kellie asked.

"Oh, my shit was straight. I got plenty of duckets, I was with my Boo and all is fine in the land of Juicy."

"How was your lunch with Nicholas?"

"That shit was tight. I could fall in love with a man like him."

"Does he know about your part-time job?"

"No, that's not for him. That's a different life."

Gina said," So what's up with you and your Boo, Michele?"

"Nothing. He turns me on, he is so damn sexy. It don't make no sense."

"How long will he be in town?"

"He's probably gone. They were pulling out early this morning."

"Where's he from?"

"Texas, but he is thinking about relocating to California."

Stacey was in deep thought and out of the conversation. Everyone left her alone with her thoughts.

Kellie said, "What do y'all want to do today?"

Michele said, "I'm tired from all of this dancing, I'm going to relax, go to the spa and chill."

"What about you, Gina?" Kellie said.

"Do a little gambling and people watching."

"You, Stacey?"

"Huh? Oh, I don't know. I need to find Charles and see what's up."

"Yeah, let me know as soon as possible. I want to get that taken care of," Michele said.

Stacey didn't know where Charles was staying or how long he'd be in town. She decided to bite the bullet, call Richard and ask for Charles' phone number. She told Richard that she wanted to ask Charles if he'd like to have lunch or something. Richard bought it.

She called Charles after her conversation with Richard.

He answered the phone saying, "Yeah, this is Charles."

"Charles, this is Stacey."

"Stacey. I'm surprised to hear from you. What's up?"

"If you're still in town, maybe we can get together for lunch or something."

"I'm not going to tell Richard, Stacey."

"I wasn't calling for that, I just thought that we can get a drink or something."

"Are you pushing up on me, Stacey?"

"I have always been attracted to you Charles, but after last night, I can't get you off my mind. You did something to me."

"Alright, where do you want to meet?"

"Why don't we meet at The Inn? Someone told me it was pretty cool. We can have a drink and then maybe get into something else. That's if you want to."

"Where is it and what time will you be there?"

"It's a little off the strip, but it's not hard to find. How about eight o'clock?"

"Alright, I'll be there."

Stacey called Michele to tell her what time Charles would be at The Inn. She described him as being about 5'11", 190-200 lbs. dark brown, low cut fade, goatee and well dressed with a diamond in his left ear.

Stacey stayed in her room for the remainder of the day. She wasn't able to relax until the situation was taken care of.

Gina and Kellie hung out and Michele prepared for her seduction of Charles.

Michele

When Michele arrived at The Inn, she didn't see Charles anywhere in sight, so she ordered a drink. One of the bar patrons made his way over to her and offered to pay for her drink.

"No, thank you. I'm good."

"Are you here alone?"

"I'm waiting for someone."

"Oh, I'm sorry. Excuse me."

"Thank you."

The guy walked away. After fifteen minutes or so, Charles walked in. She knew it was him. Stacey described him to perfection. He took a seat at the bar, a couple of barstools away. Michele paid for a room prior to coming into the bar. She knew if Charles didn't have a problem fucking his best friend's girl, he should be pretty easy to seduce.

When Charles ordered a drink, Michele paid for it. Charles moved down closer to her.

"Thank you for the drink, beautiful."

"You're welcome, but please call me Juicy."

"Juicy. How did you get a name like that?"

She leaned over and whispered in his ear, "All of me is juicy, inside and out. She stood up, "Come on and dance with me."

As they were walking to the dance floor, she knew his eyes were on her ass. She wore a black leather catsuit that fit like a good pair of gloves. She knew she had him when she turned around and he couldn't keep his eyes off of her body.

A slow song played and she allowed him to grind on her while they were on the dance floor. She allowed him to rub and squeeze her ass, she didn't care and he took advantage of it.

"Juicy, do you want to get out of here and get a private spot?"

"I already have a private spot."

"Cool." Before they could go any further, his phone rang. He looked at the caller ID and said, "Excuse me for just a minute.

Hello."

"Charles, its Stacey. I'm sorry, but I'm not going to be able to make it tonight. I'm not feeling too good. Maybe we can hook-up tomorrow?"

"That's alright, Stacey, I'll talk to you later."

After he ended his call, he looked at Michele with a sinister smile on his face. They danced through a few more songs, had a few more drinks and eventually left for the motel.

Once they were inside the room, Charles was all over Juicy. Michele installed a video camera earlier that day when she booked the room. Before coming to the club, she started the camera rolling with an eight hour tape. It was aimed at the bed and Juicy made sure that Charles faced the camera. He was all into Juicy. She had him screaming her name before she was done with him.

They spent a couple of hours together. Every time she thought she had him satisfied, he would come back for more. He was talking big shit and backing it up. Michele enjoyed Charles more than she'd ever admit to anyone. Once Charles was satisfied, he asked her if he could see her again and she said no. He dressed and left without saying anything else.

Kellie, Gina and especially Stacey were all waiting for Michele to return. Stacey decided to call Michele on her cell phone just as Michele came through the door. She had the camera in her hand with the evidence tape inside.

Stacey said, "Did you get him?"

"You know I did."

"Let us see."

"Y'all don't want to see this. It's me fucking this man. Take my word for it. I just want to say one thing for the record."

"What's that?" Kellie said.

"Ol' boy got big time stamina and a nice thick juicy dick to go along with it. He worked me out!"

Gina said, "How are you gonna bring this up to him, Stacey?"

"I don't know yet."

Michele handed her the tape and said, "You have everything you need. You can tell him that you have it, or you can let him know if he ever threatens to tell Richard, you will show it to his girl. Me, myself, I would tell him up front just in case he decides to tell Richard without warning. He will think twice before he opens his mouth, if he knows you have the tape."

"I'll figure something out. I'm tired and I'm going to bed."

"Well, I hope tomorrow will be a better day for everyone. We only have two days left before we're on our way out of here," Michele said.

"It sure did go by fast. After Michele and Gina do their thing tomorrow, that's it. We'll be out of here the next day," Kellie said.

Michele said, "That's why I'm trying to make the best of it. I don't want to go home saying I wish I would have. I'm just doing it."

Monday, April 12th

Michele

They agreed that there was no need to meet for breakfast the next morning because they discussed everything the night before. Michele received a call from Nicholas telling her that he was leaving in the evening and hoped they could get together for lunch in the afternoon. She agreed to meet him at the Luxor Hotel at noon.

He seemed to be everything she'd been looking for in a man. They exchanged home numbers and made plans to get together once they were both back in Los Angeles. He told her he didn't have a lot of time, but he didn't want to leave town without seeing her again.

After lunch with Nick, she made her way back to the hotel to relax before her last show that night.

Gina

Gina's final internet hook-up was with Ralph. She called Ralph, her contact, when she first arrived in Vegas to make sure they were still on. He called early in the morning to confirm their arrangements. He left a key at the front desk for her at Harrah's. She told him she would be there at eight o'clock. He said he would have two friends with him.

She had a good time with Vernon and his friends and was hoping for another good time with Ralph. When she arrived at the door, as a courtesy, she knocked before letting herself in. She was wearing a leather mini-dress which was unbuttoned half-way down the front. When she saw Ralph, she was surprised that he wasn't anything like she imagined. Ralph is about 45 years old, at least 275 lbs., around 5'10", thick glasses, balding; very hard on the eye. His friends weren't much better looking. They were slobbering when they saw her.

"You're Train?"

"Yes. You're Ralph?"

"Yeah, baby, it's me. Come on over here and give big daddy some of that sweet young pussy."

That kind of turned her on. She liked it when men talked dirty to her. She put their appearances out of her mind and fantasized about a good looking man and let them have her. They took turns fucking her. She had to ride Ralph because she didn't want him to smash her. He was breathing so hard, she thought he was going to have a heart attack. He took his glasses off, so that he could eat her pussy. What he was lacking in looks he made up for in the mouth. His friends were sucking and squeezing on her breasts. After Ralph came, he fucked her again. While he was fucking her, his friends were beating off waiting for their turn to enter her. They worked her out for four hours straight. When she finally left their hotel, she was totally satisfied. She learned not to always look past an ugly guy. Ugly doesn't mean they can't fuck.

When she arrived at the hotel, she took a seat in the hotel lounge with Kellie and Stacey as they waited for Michele to return from her last gig at the Pussycat Club.

Michele

When Michele came through the backdoor into the dressing room, one of the dancers, Gypsie, asked her if Lust was coming out again.

"Naw, he's gone back to Texas."

"I just wanted to tell you that you put on a good show. I can see why he came to see you exclusively. You're a good dancer."

"Thank you."

Michele decided to come out and get down to business. She listened to the other girls talking while they were in the dressing room and although dancing was very thrilling for her, she really liked all of the money that she was making too.

When she stepped onto the stage tonight for the last time, she decided to only wear a g-string. She worked the pole and then started collecting money. In the short time that she'd been dancing, she established a following. There were a few faces that she had become accustomed to seeing. She was surprised to see Billy and his friends there. Billy was up front grabbing and groping all over her. This was the first time since she started dancing that she felt uncomfortable. She didn't like the way Billy was looking at her and touching her.

When her dance was over, she rushed back to the dressing room. Lou came in and told her clients were requesting her for lap dances.

"Thanks Lou, I'll be out there in a minute."

She knew who made the request. Billy was waiting for her when she came out of the dressing room.

"Did you want a lap dance?"

"Yeah, I was hoping to get one the other night, but I guess I wasn't setting out no dollars. Is that why you left?"

"No. I left because you were high and it turned me off."

"I guess as long as I pay for it, I can be as high as I want to, huh?"

"You want this dance or what?"

"Yeah."

He took his seat and sat back. Juicy started by shaking her ass in his face while he was palming her ass and feeling all over her. He put a $100 bill in her g-string. She then straddled him and started grinding against his hard dick. He threw his head back and started moaning. His boys were laughing at him. After a few minutes, Juicy got up and walked away.

At the end of the night while walking to her car, Michele saw the same car that Billy was leaning against at McDonald's, sitting idle across the street. As she crossed the street, Billy got out of his car and met her at her car door.

"Why didn't you tell me you were a dancer?"

I didn't think I needed to advertise."

"Are you ashamed of what you do?"

"Not at all. Look Billy, I'm tired and I want to get home. Can I help you with something?"

"I was hoping we could keep this going."

"I don't think so. Like I said before, I'm tired and I just want to get back to my hotel and go to bed."

A couple of the girls saw her talking to Billy, but kept going. They already didn't like her and didn't bother to ask her if everything was okay.

"How much is it gonna cost me, Juicy"?

"I'm not a prostitute, Billy."

"You sure about that?"

"Yeah, I'm sure about that."

"You were shaking your ass on that stage and collecting money from strangers that you let grope all over your body for a fee, what's that?"

"I was dancing for them."

"Yeah, dancing. I'm willing to give you top dollar for some pussy and now you getting some morals? What's up with that? I'm offering you a penthouse suite for comfort, anything you want, just to get close to you. Even after finding out you're a stripper, I still want to get with you. What's it gonna take, Juicy?"

"I'm not interested, Billy."

"Alright then. You have a good night."

When Michele turned to open her car door, she felt a hand cover her mouth as she was being pulled into Billy's waiting car. She was fighting and trying to get away, but he had her in a position where she couldn't move. All of the other girls were gone and there was no one around to help. Once he pulled her into his car, he ripped her blouse open. Michele was terrified because she knew Billy was going to rape her. She was fumbling and reaching for her purse which had fallen as he dragged her into the car. She carried a switchblade since she began dancing and it was in her purse. He noticed that she was looking for something and grabbed her hands. Once he had her on her back, he fumbled with his zipper, trying to open his pants. Michele finally found a position where she was able to knee him in his groin and get out of the car. She ran to her car, got in and drove away. When she walked into the lobby of the hotel, Kellie was waiting for her. When she saw Michele, she ran over to her and asked, "What happened, Michele?"

"The white guy that I met the other day, Billy..."

"Yeah?"

"He was at the club tonight. He waited in the parking lot after the club closed and when I came out he tried to rape me."

"He didn't succeed, did he?"

"No. I kicked him in the balls and was able to get away."

"Do you want to go to the police and press charges?"

"No, I'm just mad and ready to leave. If I ever see that motherfucker again, I'm gonna do my best to kick his ass or get someone else to do it."

"Come on; let's go up to the room."

"Is Gina back?"

"Yeah. Everyone is here."

Gina and Stacey were in Kellie and Michele's room when they came in. Michele told them everything that happened and they all said that they were ready to go home.

Gina told everyone about her evening with Ralph and his friends. She told them how she was so shocked initially because they were so hard on the eyes, but after a while she didn't notice how they looked because they fulfilled her fantasy.

"I'm ready to get home to see Marcus and my babies. It's been all that and I sure did fulfill my fantasy, but I'm ready to get out of this town."

"Me too," Kellie said. "I'm sorry I punked out on y'all, but it wasn't all that I thought it was going to be. Whenever Craig and I do our thing at home, I'm so turned on when another man approaches me. I thought I was ready to be with other men, but actually doing it wasn't what I thought it would be. I'll work on something different for next year. Maybe I'll strip next year."

Gina said, "I might strip next year, it sounds like it's the bomb!"

"It is," Michele said. "What about you Stacey. Are you going to do parties again next year?"

"I don't know. I still have the Charles situation to deal with. I can't think about next year until I get this situation resolved."

"Did you tell him about the tape?"

"No. I tried to call him, but he didn't return my call. I'll deal with him when I get home."

They stayed up and talked for a while. Kellie and Gina had early flights. Stacey's flight isn't until eleven o'clock in the morning, and Michele is going to hit the road after dropping the three of them off at the airport.

Michele

The next morning after dropping Kellie, Stacey and Gina off at the airport, Michele headed back to California. Michele put on her music and thought about the events of the week. Most of it was good, but there was the incident with Billy. "What an ass!" she thought to herself.

She thought about stripping and how she felt in control of her body and the minds of the men watching. Before going to Vegas, she thought she could control who she allowed to touch her or who she touched, when, in reality, everyone in that club had access to her and it made her realize that she didn't have as much control as she initially believed.

Then there was Lust. He was fun! He brought out her wild side. She did things with him that she had never done with another man. He really helped her develop Juicy's personality. When they got together, they rarely talked. She did her thing and he loved it.

But Nick, she could change for him. She would stop seeing the other men she dated if he turned out to be the type of man she believed he was.

She arrived home around one thirty in the afternoon. She had eighty-eight messages on her home voicemail. Everyone, including all of her clients, knew that she would be out of town for the week and they all knew that she didn't mix business with pleasure.

She started cleaning out her mailbox, returning calls, opening mail and setting appointments. It took four hours to get organized, unpacked and prepare something to eat for lunch. While returning calls, she agreed to have dinner with one of her friends, Eddie. She was dressed and ready to go at eight o'clock.

Eddie is a sports agent. His clout allowed him access to almost any restaurant or club without waiting. She'd been seeing him off and on for a little over a year. They have a lot in common and they have fun together. Neither had ever said that they didn't want to be in a relationship, but they both knew it. They called each other for companionship and that's how Michele liked it.

When they were seated for dinner, Eddie asked about her trip. She told him she had a great time with her friends and left it at that.

"How often do you go to Vegas?"

"It really depends on what's going on. I go once a year to meet up with my girlfriends and if I go again, it's usually for a weekend or something like that."

43

"I'm thinking about going for a couple of days next month. I need to get away for a minute. I've also been meaning to ask you about real estate in the Bahamas."

"I've closed some deals in the Bahamas and Jamaica. A lot of my clients who have multiple properties inquire about properties in the Caribbean. If you're interested, I can pull some listings for you and if you see something you like, we can move on to the next step."

Michele looked up just as Nick was being seated a few tables away, along with a date. He nodded at her in acknowledgement and she did the same.

Eddie looked over at him, nodded and asked Michele who he was.

"I met him while I was in Vegas. His name is Nick. Do you know him?"

"I've seen him around, but I don't know him personally."

Before their conversation went any further, the waiter came to take their orders. Throughout dinner, Michele thought about Nick. She kept stealing glances at him with his date. Every now and then she would see him looking at her too. She always had fun with Eddie, but Nick could change her and she knew it.

Michele and Eddie left the restaurant before Nick and his date. Eddie took her to his house in the hills where they had a nightcap and spent the night together. Whenever they agreed to dinner, they both knew that dessert was part of the package. Eddie dropped Michele off at home the next morning at seven-thirty while on his way to work. When she checked her voicemail, she had three messages from Nick.

Kellie

Craig and C.J. were at the gate waiting for Kellie when she walked off the plane. She was happy to be home. She wasn't sure if she will be going back to Vegas next year. If she does, it will be to socialize not to live out a fantasy.

After hugging and kissing her boys, they made their way to the car.

"So how was it? Did you win any money?"

"I had a good time. No, I didn't win any money and you know how it is when I get with Michele, Stacey and Gina. It was like being in college."

"Y'all didn't get into any trouble, did you?"

"Of course not! What did y'all do while I was gone? I called the house a couple of times Saturday evening and you weren't home. Where were you?"

"I hung out with the fellas for a little while."

"Where was C.J.?"

"He was with my mother. I know you ain't trippin' about me hanging out with the fellas when you were gone to Vegas for almost a week with your girlfriends."

"Naw, I'm not trippin'. I was just wondering where you were."

Once they were in the house and situated, Craig wanted a little more detail about her trip.

"What did y'all do everyday, besides gamble?"

"We went to the spas; people watched, ate, ate and ate again. Lust was pushing up on Michele."

"The rapper Lust?"

"Yeah. He really seemed to like her."

"What were the rest of y'all doing while she was talking to Lust?"

"Nothing. What do you mean?"

"Didn't he have an entourage?"

"You're acting like you are worried about something. What is it Craig? Just say it."

"Alright. I was telling my new partner, Arthur... By the way, I invited him over for dinner this weekend, you need to meet him. Anyway, I was telling Arthur about your trip and he couldn't believe that I let you go like that. He put all of these different scenarios in my head and it got me thinking."

"What scenarios and thinking what?"

45

"He said that you could have gone there to meet someone or you could have met someone while you were there and it got me thinking that it was possible."

"Craig. Don't let someone that has never met me mess with your head like that. You know I love you and wouldn't do anything to jeopardize what we have. You knew that before I left and you knew that before Arthur put those stupid ideas in your head. So don't start thinking like that now. Baby please. We've been doing just fine up until now."

"I know baby, I'm sorry. You know I trust you, don't you?"

"Yeah, I do. I really missed you, Craig."

"I missed you too. Come here."

Kellie walked into his arms and they hugged and kissed and found their way to their bedroom.

Gina

When Gina stepped off the plane, the first faces she saw were her mother's and her two children. Marcus left for a business trip to New York the previous day and wouldn't be home until later in the evening. She was happy to see her children. Every time she made this trip, she was always anxious to get home to her family. She took a huge risk while living out this fantasy. She thought about what the consequences would be if Marcus ever found out what she'd done. She loves her family too much to lose them and when she thinks about what she's done, she gets nervous. During the flight from Vegas to Memphis she kept thinking how stupid it was of her to risk everything she has for a fantasy. She decided then and there that she would never do anything to jeopardize her family again. She hoped and prayed that what happened in Vegas would stay in Vegas.

When Marcus arrived home later that evening, Gina had an intimate dinner waiting for him. The kids were in bed, so it was just the two of them.

"Welcome home, Marcus."

He picked her up and spun her around and said, "Oohh baby, I missed you so much. It was cool having your mother here to help with the kids, but man, I couldn't wait for you to return. You're looking awfully sexy. What is it about you?"

"You just missed me. Come on and eat so you can get to your dessert."

"What's for dessert?"

"Me."

"Let's eat."

After dinner, Gina led Marcus to the family room, put on some music and did a striptease for him. He loved every minute of it. He became very aggressive with her, something he didn't do very often unless he had been drinking.

"I love when you do things like this for me."

"You do?"

"Oh hell yeah! I wanted to ask you to strip for me, but I didn't want you to think that I was degrading you."

"I don't feel that way at all. I want to do whatever I have to do to satisfy you, Marcus."

"This is it, baby. You know how you always hear that a man likes a lady on his arm, but a freak in the bedroom?"

"Yeah."

"It's true, baby. I want to see your freaky side."

"You ain't said nothing but a word, baby."

Marcus and Gina were pretty traditional when it came to sex. Missionary, doggy style and they never had oral sex. So when Gina went down on Marcus, he was blown away. He returned the favor. They explored each other's bodies for hours.

The next morning over breakfast, Marcus asked Gina if they could have a repeat of last night. With a huge smile on her face, she told him yes.

Later that afternoon, a flower delivery came for Gina from Marcus. He included a card telling her that they were going out to dinner that night, so there was no need for her to cook.

Stacey

When Stacey arrived at her house, she was exhausted and wanted nothing more than to get in bed and sleep for a few days. She always felt like this when she returned from meeting with Michele, Kellie and Gina. Richard wouldn't be back in town until the next day, so she decided to unpack, start the washing machine, eat a quick sandwich and park her body in front of the TV. Within minutes she was asleep.

When she finally woke, it was dark outside. She woke to the phone ringing, but she moved too slowly and missed the call. When she reached the phone, Richard was leaving a message for her.

"Stacey, I need to see you when I get back in town tomorrow afternoon. Will you be home? I'm going to come straight to your house."

Stacey picked up the receiver.

"Richard."

"Stacey, I was leaving you a message."

"I was asleep. I thought I heard the phone ringing, but I moved too slowly to pick it up before the call went to voicemail. I miss you and can't wait to see you."

"I'll be home tomorrow afternoon. I was hoping we can get together."

"Sure. Did you want to meet somewhere or did you want to come by here?"

"I'll come by."

"Okay baby, I'll see you then. Have a safe flight."

"Alright."

Michele

Michele waited until afternoon to call Nick. On his first message he said that ever since he saw her at the restaurant, he couldn't get her off of his mind. In the second message, which came an hour later at midnight he said, "I thought you'd be home by now, call me when you get in, don't worry about the time." The third and final message, which was at two fifteen in the morning, he said, "Hopefully, I'll hear from you tomorrow."

When she dialed Nick's number, he picked up on the second ring.

"Nicholas Malloy."

"Hi Nick, this is Michele. How are you?"

"I'm great Michele, and you?"

"Wonderful."

"I was hoping we could get together for lunch or dinner, or whenever you're available."

"How about dinner tomorrow? I have something planned for this evening."

"Dinner tomorrow will be cool. Let me get your address."

She gave him her address and they agreed on eight o'clock. She wanted to visit the spa for a manicure, pedicure, body scrub and massage, which would take hours and she would need additional hours to sit in the beauty shop getting her hair done. She called Courtney at the shop and was able to get in at ten o'clock in the morning. Between her appointments, she scheduled a visit to the spa.

She then called Gina, Stacey and Kellie on a conference call to see how everyone was doing. Gina and Kellie were both happy to be home and everything seemed to be okay, but Stacey said Richard called and said he needed to talk to her. Stacey said she would call and let them know what was going on once she found out what Richard had to say.

"Maybe he just misses you, Stacey," Gina said.

"I don't know. He just had a distant sound in his voice, but I guess I'll soon find out if I'm just paranoid."

"Let's all just hope for the best. I'll talk to you guys later, I have another appointment in a few minutes," Michele said.

She met her clients at the property. This was their third visit to the property and this time they signed a contract.

After Michele finished all of her appointments, she was able to get a facial and a body scrub, manicure and pedicure at her favorite spa.

The next morning she arrived at the shop at ten o'clock, but Courtney hadn't arrived yet. Two ladies who had appointments at nine o'clock and nine thirty were already waiting. Michele hated going there because Courtney was never on time. She never scheduled her appointments appropriately, but she was the best. Everyone always threatened to go somewhere else, sometimes they did, but they always came back because Courtney was good. There was no denying that. Everyone always sat patiently and listened to her talk about every single person who came in and out of the shop.

Courtney finally showed up at ten forty-five with no explanation or apology. She came in complaining about her kids and her problems. No one said anything because they had heard it all before.

Michele finally made it out of the beauty shop by two thirty. She had a few things that she needed to take care of in the office, but she didn't have any showings.

She wore a pale yellow dress that accentuated every curve of her body. Courtney wrapped and flat ironed her hair, and her fingernails and toenails matched her dress. She wore a pair of Stuart Weitzman sandals with a matching bag. She wanted to have it together because she could tell that Nick was the kind of guy who had his stuff together. The lady he was with the other night was impressive, but Michele wanted to look even better.

The doorman announced Nick's arrival at eight o'clock and he was allowed up to the twenty-fourth floor where Michele's condo was located. She left the door ajar while she continued to get dressed. When she heard the door close, she stuck her head out into the foyer area and told Nick to make himself comfortable and she said that she would be with him in a minute.

"Would you like a drink, Nick?"

"No, thank you. You have a nice place, Michele."

When she walked into the living room, he stood.

"You are stunning."

"Thank you, Nick. You look very, very handsome yourself."

He dropped his head and blushed. "Thank you, Michele. As I was saying, you have a nice condo. I guess you have a heads up on all of the good properties."

"I had to wait two years for this unit to become available. I lived on the other side of the building for three years before this unit went on the market. I knew the previous owners and when they were ready to sell, they called me because they knew I was interested."

"You made a wise choice. The view is spectacular."

"Thanks Nick. Are you ready to go?"

"Yes, after you."

The valet pulled up in a silver Mercedes SL600 Roadster, which was another of Michele's favorite cars and another one of the cars on her wish list. Nick opened the door for her and she slipped in. He took her to Beau Rivage, a French restaurant in Malibu. Once they were seated, Nick ordered a bottle of wine and an appetizer in French. Michele was becoming more and more impressed with him every time she saw him.

"Has everything gotten back to normal since your Vegas trip?"

"Yes, pretty much. I have to catch up on some paperwork, but everything is good."

"What's your focus area?"

"I do most of my sales in Beverly Hills, Bel-Aire, Santa Monica and in the Hills. You know how it is. Most of my clients have multiple properties and are always looking for another piece."

"You must be pretty successful."

"Yeah? What makes you think so?"

"Your address."

"I do alright."

"You're doing a little better than alright. I'm impressed with you. It's not easy to find a woman that's able to stand on her own and looks like you. You're smart and beautiful."

"Thank you, Nick. Now tell me about you. How did you become you?"

"Ha ha, me. Well, I came to this town eleven years ago from Jackson, Mississippi. I went to the University of Mississippi on an athletic scholarship and majored in communications. After I tore a tendon in my right knee and didn't recover to my pre-injury status, I had to give up my initial dream of playing in the NBA. I decided that I wanted to be a sports broadcaster. My professors always told me that I could charm the stripes off of a zebra, so I took my skills and brought them to Los Angeles and landed in the recording business. I've been here ever since and I've been pretty lucky."

"Do you get back to Mississippi often?"

"Oh yeah. My moms and pops are still there, along with the rest of my family. I'm out here alone."

The waiter came to take their dinner orders. Nick asked if she was okay with him ordering for her and of course she was, so he ordered again in perfect French.

After dinner, Nick asked her if she was interested in going back to his place. She hesitated a bit when she answered.

"Don't feel obligated, Michele. I just wanted you to see where I live. I want you to know me, where I live, how I live; that's all. I promise not to take advantage of you."

"I wasn't thinking that, Nick."

"Yeah, right."

"Okay, it crossed my mind. But yes, I would love to see where you live."

Nick has a beautiful home cut into the hills with canyon and city views. Michele did a quick appraisal and estimated that his property was worth five-million dollars. She had recently sold properties in the area and she knew how hot the area had become.

"You have a beautiful home, Nick."

"Thank you. Would you like a drink?"

"Yes, rum and coke, thank you."

"Make yourself comfortable. Would you like to sit on the deck, it's a nice evening."

"Sure."

The furniture on his deck was nicer than some people have inside their homes. They sat on the deck for hours talking and really getting to know each other. When Nick dropped her off at home, it was after two o'clock a.m. He walked her to her door and they kissed passionately before he left.

Michele went to bed with a huge smile on her face.

Stacey

When Richard arrived at Stacey's condo, she had lunch waiting for him. She hadn't resolved anything with Charles. As a matter of fact, she hadn't talked to him since she cancelled their meeting. She was a little concerned that Charles may have said something to Richard.

When the doorbell rang, she jumped. She buzzed Richard in and was standing in the door waiting for him when he got off of the elevator.

She greeted him with a kiss, but he didn't seem to be interested.

"Hey baby, you sure don't act like you've missed me."

"I'm sorry. I've got some things on my mind."

"Really, what's going on?"

"When you were in Vegas, you said you had lunch with Charles, right?"

"Yeah."

"Was he acting funny?"

"No, funny how?"

"He's trippin' or I guess he's feeling guilty and I don't know what to tell him."

"What is he feeling guilty about?"

"He said he was at a bachelor party and that he had sex with one of the strippers."

Stacey couldn't say anything, initially. She just stared with her mouth open.

Charles and Richard had been friends long before Charles started dating Richard's cousin, so he must have felt comfortable telling Richard about what he'd done.

"Why would he do something like that?"

"He said that this girl was hot and he just couldn't help himself and now the guilt is eating him up."

"Why would he tell you this knowing Carolyn is your cousin?"

"I guess he needed a friend to talk to. I was going to go to that party too, but I couldn't change my schedule."

"Really?"

"Yeah. If I had gone, I probably could have stopped him. I invited him and Carolyn over for dinner tomorrow night, if you don't mind. We can go out if you don't want to cook."

"I don't mind."

Stacey couldn't believe that Charles told Richard that story. She couldn't wait to see him. Why would he do that? She decided to tell him that she had the tape. If he wanted to play games, she could too!

The next evening, Charles and Carolyn arrived at Richard's house at seven o'clock. Stacey had been at Richard's place all day preparing dinner. When she saw Charles, she felt sick to her stomach. She couldn't believe she got herself into this mess.

"Hello, Stacey. How was the rest of your stay in Vegas?"

"It was fun, and yours?"

"I had a great time."

"Hi Carolyn. I haven't seen you in a while. Why didn't you come to Vegas with Charles?"

"It was for a bachelor party. You know how these men are about these bachelor parties."

"Yeah, I know."

"Would either of you like a drink? Carolyn? Charles?"

Charles said, "Yes, a beer for me and Carolyn will have a glass of wine."

Stacey prepared their drinks. They engaged in small talk until dinner was ready. Throughout dinner, Charles was looking at Stacey in a seductive manner. She knew she was going to have a long-term problem unless she did something about Charles as soon as possible.

It was too cold out to go on the deck, so they all went into the family room after dinner. They further engaged in small talk briefly about Vegas and Richard's upcoming flight overseas to Asia. He had been trying to convince Stacey to travel with him. She told him that she might.

Stacey excused herself to go to the bathroom. When she came out, Charles was waiting for her.

"Why did you tell Richard that you had sex with a stripper?"

"Because I did and I'm feeling guilty about it. Look Stacey, I'm sorry if I put you in an uncomfortable position although, I can't imagine flexibility being a problem for you."

Stacey started walking away. "Fuck you, Charles."

"Been there, done that. Come here, don't walk away. Let me talk to you."

She stopped. "What?"

"I'm not going to throw it in your face every time I see you and I won't tell Richard about your second job. I just want to get with you every now and then. You're good baby and you got me wanting more."

"We'll see Charles, we'll see."

She walked away and went back into the family room. She couldn't concentrate on what everyone was talking about because she kept thinking about the conversation she had with Charles. She knew something had to be done about this situation, but what?

Kellie

Kellie could hardly wait to meet Arthur. Who is he to put those ideas in Craig's head? Craig took C.J. to his mother's house for the night since Arthur was bringing a date.

Kellie heard the doorbell ring while she was upstairs. She heard voices as she put the last touches on her make-up. Kellie is wearing a pair of nice fitting low-rise jeans and a tee-shirt. Without any effort on her part, everything she wore looked sexy on her.

Craig, Arthur and his date were standing in the foyer talking when Kellie walked down the stairs. When she saw Arthur, she had to stop herself from gawking. He was gorgeous! She did an analysis of his physique in a few seconds. He was at least 6'2", 210 lbs., dark brown, with shoulder length dreads. When she made it to the landing and they were introduced, he smiled revealing perfect white teeth and two of the deepest dimples she had ever seen. Arthur was FINE.

She didn't remember being introduced to his date, but later caught on to her name. She was too embarrassed to ask her again.

They went into the family room for drinks before dinner.

"Arthur, my husband tells me that you didn't think he should let me go out of town by myself because I may have been meeting someone or that I could have met someone while I was there."

"Oh, I didn't think Craig was gonna tell you about that."

"I bet you didn't."

"I'm sorry, Kellie. I shouldn't put those types of ideas in your husband's head. I'm sure he had nothing to worry about."

"No, he didn't have anything to worry about. I accept your apology. So do you guys live around here?"

"I live in Morgan Park and Donna lives in Dolton."

"Oh, okay. Well, I hope y'all brought your appetites because I cooked up a bunch of food and it's time to eat."

After everyone was seated, they all engaged in small talk. Kellie kept looking at Arthur because he was so good looking.

They all went back into the family room after dinner and put on some music and refilled their drink glasses. Kellie and Craig started dancing and Arthur and Donna joined them. They had a great time and said that they would get together again soon.

After Arthur and Donna left, Craig said, "That was fun. So what did you think about Arthur?"

"He seems cool. As long as he has your back, he's cool with me."

"Good. I'm glad you like him because now that we're partners, you know we are going to spend a lot of time together and I don't want there to be any issues between the two of you."

"He's cool. I forgive him for putting those bad thoughts in your head. We need to make the best of our time without C.J. here. I can make you scream as loud as you want to tonight."

"Prove it."

Kellie did have Craig moaning and groaning, but he had her screaming his name over and over. They made love all over the house and slept on the floor in the family room, something they hadn't done in a long time.

Kellie had returned to work. Adjusting to the classroom had been hard, but she was back into the swing of things by Tuesday.

When Craig came in from work Tuesday evening, he told Kellie, "We're invited to Arthur's house for a cookout this coming Saturday."

All week during class, Kellie thought about seeing Arthur again. She shopped for a new outfit, something colorful and spring-like. She wanted Arthur to want her because she wanted him. She was hoping for good weather and the temperature had been in the low seventies for the past few days and was forecasted to continue in the seventies through the weekend.

When Saturday arrived, Kellie tried to conceal her excitement. She cooked breakfast, gave C.J. his bath and had him dressed by ten o'clock. She didn't usually roll out of bed until nine o'clock on Saturdays. She took her time getting dressed and made sure her hair was looking good. Craig had to run to the store to get some liquor, which he told Arthur he would bring.

Kellie was expecting to see Craig's other officer friends and their wives and girlfriends. They usually had a good time when they all got together.

They arrived at Arthur's house around one o'clock. There were quite a few people already there. They heard music playing as they parked.

They saw other people going to the backyard through the gate on the side of the house and followed them. Kellie saw Arthur as soon as they entered the yard. He was talking to a group of guys with his arm around a pretty girl.

Craig said, "There's Arthur. He has more women than any dude I know. Come on, let's go and say hi and put this stuff down."

When Arthur saw them, a smile spread across his face. He gave Craig a hug and said, "What's up?"

He said to Kellie, "It's so good to see you again. Welcome to my house. Make yourselves at home."

Craig said, "Where do you want me to put this stuff. I got a cooler in the car that I need help with and Kellie brought stuff to make a salad."

"Tony! Can you help Craig get a cooler out of his car? Kellie, you come with me and I'll show you where the kitchen is, so you can put your salad together."

He introduced Kellie to people as they made their way through the house. He showed her to the kitchen where she began putting her salad together.

"Do you have a large bowl? I don't think this one is going to be big enough."

"In that cabinet above your head, there should be a bowl there."

Kellie opened the cabinet, saw the bowl, but couldn't reach it."

"Can you get it for me? I don't think I can reach it."

He came and stood behind her, reached for the bowl and put it on the counter.

"Thank you."

In that short time, she felt the heat from his body and was mesmerized by his cologne. If she had turned around they would have been close enough to kiss. He stood behind her a second or two too long. That's when she knew that he was attracted to her too.

Throughout the day they kept sneaking glances at each other. Kellie was jealous when she saw him with his girl-friend. She thought about what Craig had said earlier about him having so many women. She didn't care because she wanted to be one of them.

Kellie took C.J. into the house to wash his hands. When they were done, C.J. ran outside ahead of her just as Arthur was coming inside.

Kellie said, "Oh, excuse me."

"I'm sorry. I didn't see you coming."

"That's okay."

"Are you enjoying yourself?" Arthur said.

"Yes, I'm having a great time. I haven't seen some of these people in a while. Where's Donna?"

He smirked. "She had to work."

"Oh. Craig tells me you're a playa."

"No, that's not true. I just like variety."

"I have a friend who I'm sure you would like."

"Does she look anything like you?"

"We favor."

"I'd love to meet her then."

Kellie smiled. "I better get back out there."

"Alright Kellie. If you need anything, let me know."

Later that evening, Craig was playing Bid Whist and C.J. was getting sleepy. Arthur told Kellie that she could lay C.J. down in his bed. She told Craig where she was going. Craig was so into the game that he barely acknowledged what she said. Arthur carried C.J. to his bedroom and laid him down in the bed. Kellie walked over to the bed and tucked him in. He was knocked out. Arthur stood in the doorway and watched. She got off the bed and walked over to the door. Arthur stepped back to let her by and she purposely rubbed her body against his. As she was walking away, he grabbed her arm. She stopped and walked back towards him.

"What are you doing, Kellie?"

"I'm not doing anything. Why? What's up?"

"You know that I'm attracted to you, don't you?"

"Yes."

"Then why would you tease me like that?"

"I'm sorry. It was wrong."

He whispered in her ear, "Tell me what you want."

She looked him in the eye and said, "It's forbidden." Then she walked away.

Gina

If Gina had known that being sexually aggressive was all it would take to bring the sparks back into her and Marcus' relationship, she would have done it a long time ago. Marcus was insatiable. He brought gifts home for her, like he did when they were first married. He planned a trip for the two of them to visit New York for the weekend. Gina continued stripping and doing all kinds of kinky things that blew his mind.

They planned to leave Thursday morning and return Sunday evening. Gina was really excited about the trip. She was enjoying their renewed love for each other as much as Marcus. She purchased new lingerie because Marcus loved when she wore lingerie and she bought a video that taught stripping because she wanted to perfect the act for him.

When they arrived in New York, they did some shopping, had lunch and planned to see a show on Broadway that evening. Marcus booked a suite in the Waldorf with a spectacular view of the city.

While they were getting dressed for the show, Marcus couldn't keep his hands off of her.

They had a good time at the show and an intimate dinner afterwards. Gina felt like her new found sexual freedom had been a Godsend for their relationship. Things had previously become mundane in their relationship and they were both enjoying the changes they were experiencing.

When they returned from New York, they fell back into their old routine with the exception of their sex life. It was still very exciting.

Gina had been corresponding with Vernon in relation to their rendezvous. She sent Ralph an e-mail telling him that she had a great time and how he fulfilled her fantasy. One afternoon while answering e-mails and doing the bills on her laptop, she received an e-mail from Ralph saying how much he enjoyed her and that his friends couldn't stop talking about it.

Gina responded by saying "I enjoyed all of you guys too. I guess I earned my name that night. And Ralph, I was truly impressed with your stamina. You have a nice fat, long, hard dick. Your wife is a lucky woman. My pussy was sore for a couple of days after the three of you got through with me. Tell Irvin and George I said thanks for a good fuck. You guys sure do know how to run a train..."

After she hit send, her doorbell rang. It was Rita from across the street. She stood on the porch and talked to Rita for a while. She was surprised to see Marcus pulling into the driveway. It was only two o'clock and he usually didn't arrive home until six thirty or later. He walked over to the porch and joined them.

"Hey baby, I'm surprised to see you this early."

"It's such a beautiful day, I just wanted to come home and spend it with you guys."

Rita said, "Oh, that is so sweet, Marcus."

"I mean it." He gave Gina a kiss. "Where are the kids?"

"Taking a nap. It's time for them to wake up."

Gina stood outside and talked to Rita for another ten minutes.

Gina said, "I'll see you later Rita, I need to get in here and start on dinner."

"Okay, Gina."

When Gina walked into the kitchen she knew something was wrong because of the way Marcus was looking at the computer screen.

"Oh, let me clean up this mess, so that I can get started on dinner."

Marcus looked up from the computer with so much sadness and disappointment in his eyes. Gina knew he saw something that she didn't want him to see.

"How could you do this, Gina?"

"What Marcus?"

"Who are Ralph and Vernon?"

Gina was at a loss for words. "Let me explain, Marcus."

"Explain what, Gina? I know everything just from reading these e-mails. You went to Vegas and fucked six different men? You let three men run a train on you two different times. That's what I'm reading here. Tell me if I'm wrong, Gina. Please tell me I'm wrong."

"I'm sorry, Marcus. I'm not having a relationship with anyone, it was just a fantasy that I had and I wanted to play it out."

"That is where you learned all of this freaky shit you've been doing with me lately?"

"I thought it would help our relationship. You know I didn't have any experience with men and I wanted to be a better lover for you."

"So you thought becoming a whore would make you a better woman?"

"I'm not a whore, Marcus."

"What do you call it? You met up with six strangers and fucked them. Did they pay you?"

"No."

"Well, that makes you a dumb whore, doesn't it? You could have at least gotten paid for it. I'm outta here."

"Marcus, please can we talk about this?"

"I've talked about it enough. I can't believe you. I give you the world. You don't have to do shit, but take care of the kids. I provide you with a fucking mansion, all the shopping money you need, trips and shit to show you how much I love you and appreciate you and you go off to Vegas, on a trip that I paid for, and go on a fuck-fest. Fuck you!"

He stormed upstairs and started packing his stuff.

Gina ran upstairs behind him and said, "Marcus, can we please work this out? I love you and I don't want to lose you."

"Listen to you. It's all about what you want."

"I love you, Marcus and I can't imagine my life without you. I'm so sorry, baby, please don't leave me. Please Marcus."

He stopped what he was doing and sat down on the bed, Why Gina? What did I do wrong? What didn't I give you? Why would you do this to me? I fucking loved you more than life. I thought you were happy?"

"You do make me happy Marcus. I was a fool. I listened to other people all of the time talking about different sexual experiences and I had never been with another man and I wanted to know if it was going to be different."

"Was it different?"

"Yes. I realized that I didn't need to be with anyone else, ever. I only want to be with you, Marcus. I love you and I don't want to lose you. I know what I did was stupid and I know it won't be easy to forgive me, but I swear I will do anything and everything to show you how much I love you and need you. One day you will be able to trust me again. Please Marcus, don't leave me."

"I guess your friends know what you did, don't they? You went out there and didn't give a shit about how you were disrespecting me in front of your friends."

"I'm sorry, Marcus. I wasn't thinking."

"No, you weren't thinking. You just wanted to be fucked by three different men, huh Train?"

"Please don't call me that, Marcus."

"Why? It's okay for the other men you were fucking to call you Train, but not your own husband."

Marcus left all of his stuff where it was and went downstairs. Gina put all of his stuff back and then went downstairs. He was sitting on the deck with a drink. Gina started dinner and woke up the kids.

Michele

After her date with Nick, Michele began thinking about being in a monogamous relationship. Nick was exactly what she was looking for in a man. She knew she should be on the road to her first appointment instead of daydreaming about Nick.

Michele had to show two properties; one in Beverly Hills, the home of a famous actor, and the other in Malibu. She believed the property in Beverly Hills was exactly what the buyer was looking for. When they arrived at the property, it was love at first sight for the buyer. They spent hours going through the house. The Buyer signed a contract to purchase the property. Later that afternoon, Michele received a call from Gina telling her that she needed to talk. Michele was in the middle of a showing and told Gina that she would call later that evening from home.

After showing the Malibu property, Michele went into her office to start the paperwork on the Beverly Hills property. She felt someone standing over her. When she looked up, Nick was there.

"Nick, what are you doing here?"

"I'm here to take you to dinner."

"Did we have a date?"

"No. If you're not available maybe we can do it another time."

"No, I'm good. Let me finish this document and I'll be ready to go."

Michele was thinking how happy she was that she had those two showings earlier. If she hadn't, she probably would have had on a pair of jeans and a tee-shirt.

Nick was driving the Beamer this time. He drove downtown to an Italian restaurant.

She could tell by his body language that he wanted to get intimate. They ate, danced and talked with their bodies. There was no mistaking what they both wanted. When they left the restaurant, Nick asked Michele if she would like to go to his place for a nightcap.

"Yes, I would love to."

He headed west on Wilshire. When he passed LaCienega, Michele thought that maybe he was going to the store or something. She remembered his bar was fully stocked.

"In case you're wondering, we are going to my condo in Santa Monica."

"Okay."

He had a corner unit on Palisades and Ocean. This condo was as stunning as the house in the hills, but this was definitely a bachelor pad; black leather and chrome. He walked over to the bar, fixed drinks and handed Michele a glass of rum and coke. He put on some soft music and joined Michele on the couch. He put his arm around her and pulled her close.

"I'm truly enjoying spending time with you, Michele. I told myself that I wouldn't call you today, but I couldn't help it. I wanted to see you. I hope you don't mind that I showed up at your business like that."

"No, I don't mind at all. As a matter of fact, I was thinking about seeing you too. I just didn't want to smother you, so I thought I would wait until I heard from you."

"I bet you didn't expect to hear from me so soon, did you?"

"No, I didn't."

"You're so beautiful." He leaned over and they kissed. Michele broke the kiss and excused herself to the bathroom.

She wanted to freshen up. She removed her panties and put them in her purse. When she felt fresh, she came back out and joined Nick.

The lights were lowered and Nick was waiting for her on the couch. She sashayed over to him. His eyes were glued to her hips as she made her way to the couch. As soon as she was seated, he picked up where they left off. His hands roamed all over her body and she did the same to him. He whispered in her ear, "Can I make love to you, Michele?"

"Yes."

He stood and extended his hand. She took it. He led her into the bedroom where he had a super king sized bed with a mirror on the ceiling. There were a few candles lit and the music was playing softly through the speakers in the bedroom. They stood by the bed and kissed and slowly undressed each other. He laid Michele back on the bed and stroked her long slender legs, arms, waistline and curvaceous ass. He enjoyed the softness and curves of her body.

"You have a beautiful body and I've fantasized about seeing it uncovered since the first time I laid eyes on you."

He took her breasts in his hands and held them like they were precious cargo and began sucking her nipples until they were hard. She felt his hard dick as it lay on her leg. She couldn't take it any longer and took his dick in her hand. She was impressed with the thickness and length. He moaned and she started massaging him. He rolled above her, parted her legs and entered her. They both let out pleasurable moans as he began to stroke her.

Michele felt like he was truly making love to her. It wasn't wild and rushed, it was slow and passionate. It was a closeness she had never felt with anyone else. When they were done, he pulled her into his arms and they fell asleep.

They were awakened the next morning by Nick's phone ringing. Michele opened her eyes to see Nick smiling at her. He reached over her and grabbed the phone. He apparently had appointments that he needed to get to, from what Michele gathered from his end of the conversation. It was seven eighteen a.m.

He wasn't greedy. He didn't try to get back into her although his dick was standing at attention. He kissed her on the forehead, got out of the bed, handed her a tee-shirt, put on a robe and told her she could use the shower in the bedroom and he would use the one down the hall.

"There is a toothbrush in the medicine cabinet."

"Thanks."

The bathroom was unbelievable. It was huge with a Jacuzzi tub and separate shower area. When she came out of the bathroom, she could smell coffee and food.

When Michele walked into the kitchen, Nick was standing over the stove fixing eggs and toast.

"Would you like a cup of coffee or some juice?"

"Some juice will be great."

He slid a plate of scrambled eggs and toast in front of her.

"Nick. You are too much."

"What do you mean?"

She just shook her head and said, "Believe me, it's a good thing."

"I have to get to the office, but I didn't want to take you home on an empty stomach." He walked over to her, kissed her on the lips and said, "I really enjoyed last night."

"So did I. Like I said, you are incredible."

"So are you. I hope we can have many more evenings like that."

"I'll do my part to make it happen."

"So will I. I have to go to New York this afternoon and I probably won't be back for a few days. I'll call you and let you know when I'll be returning, so we can get together. Okay?"

"Okay, I look forward to it."

They got dressed and he dropped Michele off at home.

She had a message from Gina. Michele forgot that she was supposed to call her last night. She called Gina immediately.

"Hey girl, what's up?"

"Michele."

"Yeah girl. Why do you sound so dry?"

"Marcus found out."

"What! How did he find out, Gina?"

"I did the stupidest thing. I had been kind of corresponding with Vernon and Ralph and yesterday Marcus came home early. I left the computer on while I was outside talking to one of my neighbors and I left my e-mail open. After he read the first one, he went on and read them all and found out what I did."

"How much does he know?"

"Everything. He knows I did it twice with three guys."

"Where is he now?"

"He went to work. He was going to leave yesterday, but I begged him not to leave and for us to talk about it. He basically shut me out. He slept in one of the guest rooms and hasn't said a word to me since."

"I think it's a good sign that he didn't leave the house. He is probably trying to figure out what to do. Give him some time. Don't bother him. When he is ready to talk to you, he will."

"I'm scared, Michele. I let this stupid fantasy destroy my marriage. I love Marcus and I don't know what I will do without him."

"He loves you too, Gina. I think he will be able to forgive you, at some point. It may just take a little time. Do whatever you have to do to keep him in the house. Don't let him move out."

"Thanks for listening, Michele. If he leaves me, I don't know what I will do."

"Let me know if you need anything. If there is anything I can do, please call me and let me know."

"Okay. By the way, he is very upset that you guys know what I did."

"How does he know that we know?"

"I told him."

"Why did you tell him?"

"He asked me if y'all know. He felt disrespected that I would do that to him and that y'all know about it. He doesn't know about anything anyone else did. He thinks it's just me and I'll keep it that way."

"Thanks Gina. I've got your back on this. Just let me know what you need."

"Okay Michele. Thanks."

After Michele's conversation with Gina, she called Kellie on her cell phone and left a message asking her to call as soon as she has a free moment.

When she was on her way out the door, Stacey called and they talked about what was going on with Gina. Michele inquired about her situation with Charles.

"Did you tell him you had the tape?"

"No. Not yet. I was thinking if I have to bring the tape out, Carolyn is the one that will be hurt and I don't want to hurt her."

"So you'll let him keep trying to get with you out of guilt? What do you think is worse, Carolyn marrying this fool who can't keep his dick in his pants, or her finding out that he fucked you?"

"I don't know. I'll tell him that I have the tape and see how that goes."

"You're going to have to do something Stacey or you're going to end up in the same situation as Gina."

"I know. I'll do something soon."

Kellie called Michele a short while later and they talked about everything that was going on. Kellie told Michele about Arthur.

"Girl, are you crazy? You were scared to get it on with a stranger, but your husband's partner is okay? I think you have lost your damn mind, Kellie. I'm all for doing some off-the-wall shit, but I don't think I would do that. Craig would kill you, Kellie. You know how protective he is over you and for you to get busy with his partner...Kellie, I'm asking you, please don't do it."

"I have never been this attracted to anyone before in my life, Michele. I'm scared that I'm going to do something stupid."

"Listen Kellie, think about what Gina is going through right now. Marcus is a mild-mannered man, but I bet he wants to kick her ass. Craig is not a mild mannered man and he legally carries a gun. Don't fuck with him, Kellie. Please don't do this."

"Okay, Michele. I'll try to stay away from Arthur."

"Don't try girl, do it!"

"Alright. How are things with you and Nick?"

Michele's tone changed to a sweet voice.

"Everything is wonderful. I slept with him last night for the first time and it was heavenly."

"If I didn't know better, I would think that you were falling in love."

"Maybe, maybe not."

"Michele. Are you falling in love with Nick?"

"I think so. Kellie, he is unbelievable. You know how hard I am to please, don't you?"

"Yeah."

"Girl, he is incredible. You know how some of these men are when you give them some pussy. They get all greedy and try to keep hittin' it like they are afraid they will never get anymore?"

"Hell yeah."

"Well, it wasn't like that. He took his time with me. He took me out on a couple of dates; you know, wined and dined me and then he made love to me, Kellie."

"There's that word love again. I think you've met your match, Michele."

"We'll see."

"I have to get back to class, but call me this weekend."

"Okay and Kellie please stay away from Arthur."

"Alright."

Stacey

Stacey stayed at Richard's house after everyone left. He knew there was something bothering her.

"What's up, Stacey? You've been distant all evening."

"I have a headache. I didn't realize that I hadn't eaten anything before we had dinner. You know how it is once you get that hunger headache; it won't go away, no matter what you do."

"Did you take anything?"

"No, I'm going to take some Tylenol and lay down."

"I've noticed lately that you haven't been feeling well. Maybe you should make an appointment to see the doctor."

"I think I will. I'm tired all of the time, I'll call in the morning."

Stacey cuddled up next to Richard all night. She barely got any sleep thinking about what she should do about Charles.

She was able to get an appointment to see her doctor the next morning because of a cancellation. She explained to the doctor that she had been feeling tired and sleepy lately. The doctor suggested a pregnancy test. The thought of being pregnant never crossed Stacey's mind. The test came back positive. Not only was she pregnant, but she was going into her fourth month. She had been getting her period regularly. It hadn't been as heavy as usual, but it had been coming on time.

Stacey left the doctor's office in a state of shock. Before her escapade in Vegas, she hadn't been with anyone other than Richard. Richard was the father, she knew that for sure. She just wasn't prepared for it.

She made it through her work day in a haze. On her way home that evening, she called Kellie. She didn't want to bother Gina, although Gina was who she usually talked with about most things going on in her life, but Gina had problems of her own.

"Kellie?"

"Hey Stacey, girl what's up?"

"I'm pregnant."

"You're pregnant?"

"Yes, Kellie. I have so much bullshit going on right now; I can't deal with this too."

"How far along are you?"

"Almost four months."

"Four months and you're just finding out?"

"Yes. Shit, Kellie! I didn't know."

"Okay! Don't bite my head off, please Stacey. What can I do to help you?"

"I don't know. I just needed to talk to someone about it. I'm scared. I'm not ready to have any children. Charles is still threatening me and I don't know how Richard is going to feel about this."

"The only way you're going to know how he feels about it is if you tell him, honey."

"I'm going to tell him today. I'm on my way over there now. I want to tell him about what happened in Vegas."

"Why do you want to do that?"

"Because I refuse to let Charles blackmail me. I love Richard and I hope that he will forgive me, but if not I'll have to deal with the consequences."

"What about your baby?"

"If he doesn't want me anymore and doesn't want to be a part of our lives, I'll deal with that. I just can't deal with the situation the way it is any longer."

"You're going to tell him today?"

"I'm going to tell him about the baby today, but I think I'll wait until we return from Asia before I tell him about Vegas."

"Good luck, Stacey. You do what you have to do to clear your conscience."

"Thanks for listening, Kellie. I'll talk to you later."

When Stacey arrived at Richard's, he had dinner waiting.

While they were eating, Richard asked Stacey if she'd made a decision about going to Asia with him. She said that she was going, but had some other news to share with him.

"What's the good news?"

"I don't know how you're going to feel about this. It may not be good news to you. I don't know."

"What is it, Stacey?"

"I'm pregnant."

Richard was momentarily speechless.

"Pregnant?"

"Yes. That's what's been wrong with me lately."

"Pregnant? Are you sure? You've been getting your period every month."

"I know. That's why it's so crazy to me. But my doctor did the test twice and she did a blood test. I'm pregnant, Richard."

"How far?"

"I'll be four months next week."

"Four months?"

"Yeah. I can't believe this. I'm not ready for a baby," Stacey said.

"Neither am I, but it's here now, so we need to prepare. Come here."

Stacey walked into Richard's waiting arms. He hugged her and said, "Don't be sad about it, we should be happy about the life we've created together. I love you, Stacey, and I love our baby."

"I love you too, Richard."

Stacey couldn't sleep. She tossed and turned thinking about how she and Richard would never be able to move forward until she cleared her conscience about what happened in Vegas. If it weren't for Charles, she would take the Vegas secret to her grave. She knew that Charles would make things hard for her once he found out that she was pregnant.

The next day she told Gina and Michele about her pregnancy. She also told them that she was going to tell Richard what happened between her and Charles while they were in Vegas. She told them that she wouldn't mention their names and that she would say that the party that Charles attended was the only party she had done. She thought it was best to tell Richard before Charles did.

Stacey and Richard agreed not to announce her pregnancy to anyone until they return from Asia, although Stacey had to tell her girls. They are leaving in two weeks. Unfortunately, Charles pushed her into telling her secret before she was ready.

One evening, Stacey and Richard were relaxing while watching a movie when Charles stopped by. When Richard let Charles in, Stacey got up and went up stairs. Charles was watching every step she took. She was lying across the bed watching a movie when Richard came in the bedroom and grabbed his wallet.

"Where are you going, baby?"

"I'm going to run to the store and get some beer. You don't mind, do you?"

"No. Of course not."

A few minutes after hearing the front door close, Charles appeared in the bedroom doorway.

"What are you doing, Charles? I thought you went to the store with Richard."

"No. He didn't need me to go with him. I was hoping you and I could get in a quick one before he returns."

"What are you talking about, Charles? I'm not having sex with you."

"I thought we had an agreement, Stacey. You don't want Richard to find out about your other job, do you?"

"I don't have another job. It was a one time thing."

"And you're damn good at it."

He sat on the end of the bed and started touching her. She jumped up and slapped him.

"Get out of here, Charles!"

"Oh, you done fucked up now, Stacey. You're going to regret doing that."

"Yeah, well add it to the list of things that I already regret."

Charles went downstairs to wait for Richard to return. When Richard came upstairs to put his wallet on the dresser, Stacey was sitting on the end of the bed, crying. He came over to her, sat down and put his arm around her and said, "What's the matter baby?"

"Richard, I have to tell you something that may end our relationship. I don't know where to begin."

She was shaking.

"What is it, Stacey? You are shaking and crying. What is it? Is it the baby?"

"No. The baby is fine."

"What is it then?"

"Charles is trying to blackmail me. He's trying to pressure me into having sex with him."

"What are you talking about, Stacey?"

"After you left, he came up here touching me, telling me he wanted to have sex with me and if I didn't he was going to tell my secret."

"What's your secret, baby? I'm gonna beat his ass, you can believe that, but I need to know what your secret is first."

"I'm so scared, Richard. It's really bad."

"Just tell me, Stacey."

"Okay. (Long hesitation) When I was in Vegas, I lived out a fantasy."

"What was the fantasy, Stacey?"

(Sniffle, sniffle – hesitation)

"I was a stripper at a bachelor party."

"A stripper!"

He stood up and stared down at her.

"What the fuck is wrong with you? Why would you do something like that?"

"I don't know, Richard. It's just been a fantasy of mine."

"What was your fantasy? A bunch of strange horny ass men groping and feeling all over you? I guess you were fucking them too, weren't you?"

She didn't say anything.

"Answer me, Stacey! Did you fuck anybody at the bachelor party?"

"Yes."

"Why, Stacey? Why would you do this to us? How many men did you fuck?"

"Just one, Charles."

"Charles! Charles!"

"Yes. He told me if I didn't sleep with him, he would tell you that I was stripping."

"That lousy motherfucker!" He ran down the stairs and grabbed Charles and started beating his ass.

When Charles was able to get away from Richard he said, "Man what the fuck is wrong with you?"

"Are you trying to blackmail my woman?"

Stacey was standing at the bottom of the stairs watching.

"Man that ho was fucking every man in the room. She freely gave it to me."

"You call her out of her name one more time and I'm gonna kill your ass."

"Richard, man, she was stripping at a bachelor party; dancing for money. She fucked at least three dudes before I got to her."

"He's lying, Richard. He told me if I slept with him that he wouldn't tell you that I was strippin'. Since we've been back this is the second time he asked me for sex and I just can't take it anymore. I know I might lose you, but I can't let him do this to me."

"Why did you fuck her, Charles? You knew she was my woman. No matter what she was doing, you should have known not to ever touch her. Then you come back here and try to get with her while you're sitting in my house drinking my beer? Get your shit and get the fuck out of my house. I don't ever want to see you again."

"I don't believe this shit. Richard, man, come on. You gonna believe this fucking ho over me?"

Richard hit him in his jaw. "I told you not to call my woman out of her name again. Get the fuck out, Charles."

"Alright, Richard. Cool. Stacey, you wrong and I hope you can live with yourself."

After he left, Richard opened a beer, drank it down, opened another one and sat on the couch.

Stacey opened her mouth to say something, but Richard put his hand up to stop her from speaking.

She went upstairs, laid on the bed and waited all night for Richard to join her, but he never did.

Kellie

The day after the cookout at Arthur's house, Arthur came by Kellie's house to return Craig's cooler. When Kellie opened the door, she was surprised to see Arthur standing there.

"Hi Arthur, you just missed Craig. He and C.J. just left. They are going to Craig's brother's house."

"I wanted to return the cooler he brought by the house yesterday."

"Okay, bring it in."

Arthur went back to the car to retrieve the cooler. Kellie waited in the door, so that she could hold it open for him.

Kellie was scantily dressed since she was in the house and not expecting anyone. She hadn't tried to cover up.

He brushed past her as he carried the cooler inside.

"Where should I put it?"

"It belongs in the garage, but you can leave it right here. Craig will put it away."

When he put it down, he got a good look at what Kellie was wearing, which wasn't much.

"How are you today, Kellie?"

"I'm good."

"What are you doing here all alone?"

"Cleaning."

"Do you need any help?"

She stared at him for a few seconds thinking how badly she wanted to get intimate with him. During those few seconds he stepped to her and kissed her. She thought about resisting, but she couldn't.

"Kellie, I want you."

"We can't do this, Arthur. It's too close. You're Craig's partner."

"I'll ask for a new partner. I need you, Kellie."

She pulled away.

"This is wrong, Arthur."

"You don't want me, Kellie?"

"You know that I do. Shit! You're all I think about."

"Why not then? Why can't we get together?"

"It's wrong, Arthur. Won't you feel guilty every time you see Craig?"

"Yeah, you're right. I'm just gonna have to control myself. Let me get out of here before I get into some real trouble."

When he left, he sat in the driveway for at least five minutes. Kellie watched him out of the living room window. She wanted to call him back in, but she knew better.

A couple of hours later, Craig called and told Kellie to get dressed. He was picking her up and they were going by Arthur's house to play cards.

"Why don't you go on and have fun, baby? I don't need to be in the way."

"You won't be in the way. I'm sure he will have one of his many women there, plus Kirk and Jackie will be there. Come on baby, we don't have anything else planned."

"Okay, I'll be ready."

Kellie wasn't in the mood to see Arthur with another one of his many women, so she decided to turn the tables on him.

When they arrived, just as she expected, Arthur was hugged up with a pretty girl, but when he saw her, his mouth dropped open.

Kellie was wearing a crocheted halter dress that caught everyone's attention. Craig kept telling her how good she looked along with the other people at Arthur's house.

Craig was involved in a card game on the deck. Kellie went into the house to get some ice for her drink. She knew Arthur would show up soon. Every time she looked up, he was staring at her. He had been trying to get close to her all evening, but she kept her distance.

She was standing over the sink when she felt him standing behind her. He whispered in her ear saying, "You are the sexiest woman I have ever laid my eyes on. Why are you teasing me, Kellie?"

She turned around when he bent down to kiss her.

She said, "Don't do this, Arthur. Anyone could come in here and catch us."

"Why did you wear that dress?"

"Why did you invite us over here this evening?"

He laughed. "You caught that, huh?"

"Arthur, we can't do this."

"Why not? You wore that dress because you knew I wouldn't be able to keep my eyes off of you. You were right. I can't keep my eyes off of you. You are sexy Kellie and you know I want you. Why are you doing this?"

"Because you know that I'm attracted to you and you knew Craig would come over here and bring me with him, so I thought I would make you suffer as much as you're making me suffer."

"What are you suffering from?"

"I want you as much as you want me."

"Let's get together then."

"When?"

A huge smile spread across his face. "I'll set something up and let you know. It will be soon, probably tomorrow."

"Okay. Let me give you my cell phone number so that you can get in touch with me."

"I already have it."

"You do?"

"Yeah, Craig gave it to me in case of an emergency, and this is an emergency."

"Okay."

Kellie went back outside. When Arthur came back out, they made eye contact. His girlfriend slid right into his arms.

The next day while Kellie was at work, during break she noticed a voicemail message on her cell phone.

It was from Arthur.

Kellie retrieved the message which said, "Kellie, I can't stop thinking about you. I need to see you. Can you get away this evening? Call me at 773-555-1234. I'll be waiting to hear from you."

Kellie knew he was on patrol with Craig, so she decided to call Craig instead.

"Hey baby. How's your day going?"

"Pretty good. How about yours?"

"The usual. You know these people in Chicago are crazy. Arthur says hi."

"Tell him I said hi. Do you mind if I go by Phyllis' house this evening? I told her I would come by and help her with her new computer."

"That's cool, baby. Tony and a couple of the guys are coming by to watch the game anyway. I'll get C.J. today."

"Alright. I'll see you when you get home."

"Okay. I love you."

"I love you too."

Arthur called Kellie while she was on her way home.

"Good afternoon, Kellie."

"Good afternoon, Arthur."

"Were you going to call me back?"

"Yes. I didn't want to talk to you while you were with my husband. Don't you think that would have been uncomfortable for you?"

"I can get away from him to talk to you. Anyway, did you make plans to be with me or with your girlfriend?"

"You."

"So you'll be there?"

"Yes. What time?"

"Six thirty."

"Okay, I'll see you then."

When Kellie arrived home, she took a shower and changed into some jeans and a tee shirt. Craig told her not to worry about dinner because they were going to order a pizza.

Kellie was dressed and ready to leave when Craig came in with C.J. It was already ten after six.

"You're looking good, baby. And you smell good, too."

"Thanks. I had to change out of my work clothes. Margaret spilled coffee all over my blouse today and it was stinking. I couldn't wait to get home to shower."

"Alright. I'll see you when you return."

They kissed and Kellie left the house on her way to meet Arthur. During her ride, she kept hearing Michele telling her not to do it, but she pushed that into the back of her mind, determined to see what was up with Arthur.

Gina

Gina sent Marcus, their son, outside to tell Marcus to come in for dinner. He came back and said, "Daddy said he isn't hungry."

Marcus stayed on the deck drinking until it became dark out. After Gina put the kids to bed, she went out and sat next to Marcus. He drank almost the entire bottle of Jack Daniels and had passed out. Gina cleaned up the mess and then tried to wake him. He looked at her with hate in his eyes when she was finally able to wake him.

She tried to help him up, but he snatched away from her. He got up, went upstairs, took a shower and slept in one of the guest bedrooms.

She heard him leave the next morning. He left earlier than usual. She tried calling him at his office, but his voicemail message said that he would be out of the office until tomorrow.

Gina called his secretary who confirmed that he wasn't in the office. Gina continuously called his cell phone, but he didn't answer. She was nervous all day wondering where he was. Just as she decided to call his mother and ask her to call him, she heard the garage door opening. It was ten thirty p.m.

Gina was waiting by the garage door when he came into the house.

"Hi baby, where have you been?"

"Out."

"I was worried about you. I called you at work and Liz said that you weren't there."

"I'm here now, so don't worry about it."

"Fine, Marcus. Look baby, I don't want to argue with you. I just want to get back what we had."

"Yeah, Gina. That should be easy. I'm sleepy, I'm going to bed."

"Okay."

He went upstairs to the guest bedroom. This time Gina had a plan. She put on some lingerie and slipped into bed with Marcus. When he felt her get in the bed, he didn't respond.

"Marcus, baby, will you make love to me?"

"Naw, Gina, I ain't feeling you like that."

She removed her lingerie and started massaging him. He tried to fight it, but couldn't help himself. He fucked her. She knew there was no passion from him. Once he was done, he rolled off of her, turned his back to her and asked her to leave.

Gina left the room crying.

The next evening he didn't return home until eleven o'clock p.m. He wasn't drunk this time. Gina was waiting for him.

"Marcus, you haven't seen your children in three days. You didn't call to say that you would be late. I had dinner waiting for you."

"I had dinner already. I'm going out of town tomorrow for three days."

"Where are you going?"

"San Francisco. I'll see the kids in the morning, before I leave."

"Marcus, can we please talk?"

"There really is nothing to talk about, Gina."

He left her standing where she was and went upstairs to their bedroom and began packing.

"Marcus."

"Yes."

"I love you. I'll do anything to show you how much I love you. Can you please give me a chance?"

"Gina, let it go, please. Maybe I'll be ready to talk about it when I return from my trip."

After he had his bags packed, he put them in the hallway and went to the guest bedroom.

The next morning Gina heard him talking to the kids and then heard the garage door go up. He didn't say anything to her. He didn't tell her where he was staying, nothing. No itinerary like he usually did. Later in the afternoon she tried calling him on his cell phone, but he didn't answer. She tried calling him again later that evening and he answered the phone.

"Hi, Marcus."

"What's up?"

"You didn't leave an itinerary and I don't know where you're staying. What if there is an emergency and I have to get in touch with you?"

"Call me on my cell."

"You don't answer my calls anymore."

In the background Gina could hear a woman's voice saying "Come on Marcus, our table is ready."

"Who is that, Marcus?"

"A client. Look, I have to go."

He hung up the phone. Gina stared at the phone for a few minutes before she set it on the table. She thought about the way Marcus had been treating her and now she was mad. She had been kissing his ass for days and he treated her like shit and now he was seeing another woman.

"Fine. Okay. If that's how he wants it to be, that's how it's gonna be. Fuck this. If he wants to leave me, I'll have to deal with it, but he is not going to disrespect me in my face," she thought.

When Marcus returned from his trip, Gina wasn't at home, but his mother was there with the kids.

"Where is Gina?"

"She went out with some of her friends. She said she didn't know what time you were returning. We were on our way to my house; I'll leave the kids here with you if you want."

"Naw Ma, I'm beat. Someone will get them in the morning if you don't feel like dropping them off."

He hugged and kissed the kids and they all left. He called Gina on her cell phone a couple times, but she didn't answer. He finally heard the garage door opening at two forty-five a.m. Marcus was waiting in the family room when Gina came in. She was wearing a revealing dress. When Marcus saw her, he was speechless for a minute.

"Oh Marcus, what are you doing up?"

"Waiting for you. Where you been?"

"Out."

"It's two fucking forty-five Gina and look how you're dressed. Did you go out with a man?"

"No."

"Why are you dressed like that?"

"Like what? I wear this dress all the time Marcus, you know that."

"That's when you're with me. Are you looking for another man?"

"No."

"Listen, Gina. I don't think I can continue in this marriage. I won't ever be able to forgive you for what you've done. I've been thinking about it all of this time and nothing has changed. I love you, I thought that we were going to be together for the rest of our lives, but I can't do it."

"Please Marcus."

"I can't Gina."

"I found a condo before I went to California. I'm going to move into it tomorrow. The kids are at my mother's house, when they come home in the morning, we'll explain to them that I'm leaving the house. I don't know if this is temporary or permanent. All I know is that I can't live with you right now."

Gina was crying, but not saying anything.

"I love you Gina and that won't just go away. I need time to sort things out without seeing you everyday. When I see you, I want to be with you. That's why I need time away from you to see if I still want to be with you. Do you understand?"

"Yes."

"Come here."

She walked over to him and they hugged for a few minutes before he pulled away.

"I'm going to take care of you and the kids. Nothing will change. I just can't be here right now. Okay?"

"Okay."

He again slept in the guest bedroom. The next morning after his mother dropped the kids off; they sat down with them and told them that daddy was going to live at a different house.

They didn't really understand, but they would eventually. He told his mother that he was moving out. Thankfully, he didn't go into detail with her as to why.

Gina took the kids to the park while he took his things out of the house. When they returned, the house seemed different. Gina went into the bathroom and cried.

Michele

Michele thought about Nick constantly while he was out of town. He called her and let her know that he would be back the next day and that he would like to see her. She asked him if he wanted to come to her house for dinner.

"I'll get a chance to taste your cooking?"

"I tasted your eggs and toast, so I think it's only fair that you see how I cook."

"Okay, I'll be there at seven o'clock and I'm looking forward to seeing you."

"I'm looking forward to seeing you too."

Michele spent the next day getting ready for her date. The cleaning lady came and changed the linens and cleaned the house until it was spotless.

Nick arrived at six forty-five. When she let him in, she said, "It's not seven o'clock."

"I couldn't wait to see you."

He pulled her to him and they kissed.

"Make yourself comfortable. Would you like a glass of wine?"

"Yes, thank you."

She fixed him a glass of wine and handed it to him and then joined him on the couch.

"How was your trip?"

"Very productive. I'm happy to be back, but it was a good trip. By the way, I want to steer some clients your way."

"Really?"

"Yes. I have a client that is looking to buy some property here. He currently lives in Texas, but is spending a lot of time out here and would like to have a permanent spot. He gave me a list of what he's looking for. If you could put together a listing that he can see when he is in town next Tuesday that would be great. I'll make sure he signs the contract with you so that everything will be on the up and up and you can get paid."

"Thanks, baby. I really appreciate this."

After dinner, they took a ride to a jazz club where they found a booth in the back and cuddled, talked, drank and enjoyed each other's company.

Nick dropped Michele off at home and told her that he would call her the next day about his clients.

One of her Beverly Hills properties was set for closing later in the afternoon and Michele had an appointment to see Courtney to get her hair done afterwards. She was already prepared to be there for four hours or more.

Michele was happy to close on that property because it put a huge commission in her pocket. She had been saving for a new car and this check would put her where she wanted to be financially. She didn't hear from Nick all day. After she left the shop and arrived home, her phone was ringing as she came through the door.

"Hello!"

"Good evening, Michele."

"Good evening. Who is this?"

"It's Eddie. You done forgot all about me?"

"I'm sorry, Eddie. I was running for the phone. I just didn't recognize your voice. How you been, baby? I haven't talked to you in a while."

"I've been good. I've been in New York for the past few weeks. Have you missed me?"

"You know I have."

"Can I see you this evening?"

"Yeah, I'd like to see you."

"Alright. You want to hang out at my place or did you want to go out?

"We can stay in and get caught up."

"Okay, I'll be by to pick you up in an hour. Will you be ready?"

"Yeah, I'll be ready. You don't have to pick me up though, I can drive over."

"I'm out already and I'd like to ride with you, I'll see you shortly."

"Alright, Eddie."

Michele took a shower and changed into a sundress and sandals. She still hadn't heard from Nick. He said that he would call, so she decided to wait for him to call.

While riding down Melrose, Michele saw Nick's car in front of a restaurant and him helping a young lady out. There was nothing she could say, she was on a date too. Eddie stopped to pick up Chinese food. She turned her phone off so that she could enjoy her evening. She thought about Nick every now and then, but they never said that they were a couple, so they both had the right to see whomever they wanted to see.

Michele told Eddie that she was seeing Nick and that she really liked him. He told her that he thought it was a good idea for her to settle down. He said that he often sees Nick around town and that they run with basically the same crowd.

"Nick is a name to know in this town. He would be good for you, Michele."

Eddie told Michele that his girl was upset with him because she was ready to take their relationship to the next level and he didn't know if he was ready for that, so she wouldn't sleep with him. As far as Michele was concerned, Eddie was her best friend in Los Angeles. Michele could talk to him about anything and they had a great relationship. Eddie's girlfriend knew that Eddie and Michele were friends; she just didn't know that they slept together.

The next morning when Michele arrived home, her phone rang before she could put her purse down. It was eight forty-five and the only people who called her that early were Gina and Kellie. They were usually up with their kids by then. She didn't bother to check the caller ID because she knew it was one of them.

"Hello Kellie or Gina, what do you have a camera on me or something? How did you know I just came in?"

"I guess that's why you weren't answering your phone last night."

"Ooh, who is this?"

"It's Nick."

"Oh, hey Nick, what's up?"

"You. I called you last night and again last night and again last night and now I'm calling again. I wanted to know if we could get together for lunch today. I was busy yesterday, but I have that list I was telling you about and I was hoping we could go over it."

"Okay. Let's meet at Fatburger on Wilshire at noon."

"Fatburger?"

"Yeah. I'm hungry."

"Your date didn't feed you?"

"Yeah, we ate."

"Alright, Michele, I'll see you at noon."

Michele had to laugh at Nick. He wanted her to know that he knew she was on a date last night, but he didn't know that she knew he was on one. She got some sleep because she was tired from being up all night with Eddie. He's having problems with his girlfriend and because of their problems, they hadn't had sex in over two weeks and Eddie was super horny.

Nick was at Fatburger when Michele arrived. When she pulled up he walked over to her car and opened the door for her. He extended his hand and helped her out.

She smiled at him and said, "Hey Nick."

"Michele."

"Let's eat, I'm starving."

They ordered burgers, fries and drinks. Nick was picking at his food, but Michele was doggin' hers.

"So where were you last night?"

Michele stopped chewing and looked up at him. He was so cute and for him to be insecure made her like him even more.

"You were right earlier, I had a date."

"You didn't return from your date until this morning?"

"Let's not do this, Nick."

"Alright, I'm sorry. Do you have a date this evening?"

"No."

"Can I see you this evening? We can grab something to eat, see a movie, whatever you want to do."

"Okay, that should be fun. Let's see a movie; I haven't been in a while."

"Seven o'clock?"

"I'll be ready. Did you bring that list?"

"I forgot. I'll bring it when I pick you up this evening."

"Okay. So what have you been up to? I didn't hear from you all day yesterday, you must have been pretty busy."

"Yeah, I was. I had some business to take care of. I'm free this evening, so I look forward to spending time with you."

"Cool."

He started eating his food.

"Yesterday I had to bail one of my clients out of jail."

"For what?"

"Excuse my language, but this fool was fucking on the beach in broad daylight."

"You're kidding, right?"

"No. I wish I were. What's the wildest thing you've ever done?"

Michele started smiling.

"This must be good."

"I don't know if I should tell you this. You may see me differently after I tell you."

"Nothing will change my opinion of you."

"We'll see. Actually it was very recent. My friends and I met in Vegas, when I met you, to live out our fantasies."

"Really? What was your fantasy, Michele?"

"I wanted to be a stripper at a strip joint."

"Did you succeed?"

"Yes. I did it three nights while we were there. It was fun, but I would never do it again. After we came home and I thought about what I did, I felt ashamed of my behavior. I felt like I prostituted myself. Now, two of my girls are in trouble with their men because of their Vegas fantasy. We should not have done it."

"You didn't have a husband to answer to. Don't feel ashamed. You did it and it's over. It's just another experience to put under your belt."

"I'll try to see it that way. Now you know my fantasy and secret, you tell me yours."

"I want to see you strip, that's my fantasy."

"If you're good, I may give you a private show."

"I'll be good," he said, looking hopeful.

"We'll see. Have you done anything that you shouldn't have?"

"Yeah. When I was in college, I had sex with my teacher to get my grade raised."

"Really?"

"Yeah. She was older and married and she started sweatin' me afterwards. That was one of my biggest regrets."

"Your secret's safe with me."

"I've got to get back to the office. I'll see you this evening at seven o'clock."

"Okay. I'm finished. I'll walk out with you."

They kissed briefly at the car and then went their separate ways. Michele didn't get any work done that day. After lunch with Nick, she stopped by her office and tried to work but she couldn't concentrate. She then went home and messed around until it was time for her date with Nick.

Nick arrived at seven o'clock. Michele left the door ajar after the doorman announced that Nick was in the lobby. She heard the door close when he came into her condo.

She stuck her head out of her bedroom door and said, "I'll be out in a minute, Nick."

"Take your time. I'm going to get a drink, if you don't mind."

"Not at all, help yourself."

Michele was wearing a pair of jeans and a tee shirt. Since they were going to the movies, she didn't want to overdress. Nick was also wearing jeans.

"You know this is the first time I've seen you in jeans and you look damn good, baby."

"Thank you, Nick. I wear jeans all the time. You ready to go?"

"Yeah. The movie starts at eight o'clock unless you want to get something to eat first. Although, I can't imagine you being hungry after that Fatburger today."

"I can wait until after the movie."

Although the movie was action/adventure, Michele fell asleep on Nick's shoulder. He had to wake her when the movie was over.

"Wake up sleepy head. It's over."

"I'm sorry, Nick. I didn't realize that I was so tired."

"It's alright. Let's get out of here."

When they got in the car Nick asked her, "How many other guys are you dating, Michele?"

"One."

"Is that who you were with last night?"

"Yes."

"Is he someone you can't stop seeing?"

"He's a friend. We get together every now and then for dinner, but it's not a serious relationship. I'm picky. Eddie keeps me company until I meet Mr. Right."

"So you're saying it's just sex?"

"We're friends and we take care of each other when we need to."

"Anyone else?"

"No."

"What about you?"

"I was seeing a couple of ladies. One I was kind of serious with, but I saw her yesterday and told her that I couldn't see her anymore. I was hoping that you and I could just be you and I?"

"We can. I don't have to see Eddie anymore since I have you."

"You've got me."

"Okay and you've got me."

"Okay." He leaned over and they kissed briefly.

He pulled the list out of his jacket pocket and handed it to her.

"This list has the must haves that my client is looking for."

Michele scanned the list and thought about a property that she just listed in the hills.

"Do you think your client would like to live in the hills?"

"Yeah, that would be perfect. Not close to my house though."

"Who is your client?"

"His name is Kevin Jasper."

"I don't think I know him."

"He'll be in town the day after tomorrow, so if you have something, you can show him at that time."

"Okay, I'll put something together tomorrow. I already know of a few properties off of the top of my head. I should have at least four properties to show."

They ordered dinner to go and took it back to Michele's condo. Nick stayed overnight.

The next day, Nick called and told Michele that his client was in town and wondering if she could show him something.

"It's twelve thirty now, I can show him two properties this afternoon around three o'clock. I'm with another client right now and I have to show another property in an hour. I'll call you back shortly with the address of the first property and you guys can meet me there. How is that?"

"That's cool. Thanks, baby."

"Anything for you."

After she finished with her first appointment, she called Nick and gave him the address of the first property. When she was done with her second showing, she met Nick at the property. She didn't see anyone when she first pulled into the driveway. Two cars were in the driveway, one of which is Nick's BMW. She got out of her car and headed towards the door. She heard voices coming from the back of the house.

Michele thought she was seeing things, but there he was and smiling at her.

"Juicy! Girl, is that you?"

"What's up, Lust?"

"You baby. It's all about you."

Nick said, "Y'all know each other?"

"Yeah, man, we met in Vegas."

"Damn baby, you look even better than I remember and I remember..."

Nick said, "Come here, man. Let me talk to you for a minute."

Michele went to the door and let the other guys into the house. When Nick and Lust came in, Lust said, "Michele, it's good to see you again. Thanks for taking time to show us these properties on such short notice."

"It's good to see you again too. I hope this is what you're looking for. Do you want a guided tour or would you like to look around and let me answer any questions you may have afterwards?"

"Let me check it out first and we'll talk afterwards."

"Okay."

When Lust and his entourage left the room, Nick turned to Michele and said, "You stripped for Lust, didn't you?"

"Yes."

"Okay. That was then and this is now. It's the past and we are going to keep it there. Okay, baby?"

"Yes."

"Remember, what happened in Vegas, stays in Vegas."

"Okay."

"Okay. Let's sell this property."

Stacey

The next morning when Stacey came downstairs, Richard was passed out on the couch. She gathered her things and went home. Later, when she arrived at work, she had a message to call Richard.

When she was able to get away, she went outside and sat in her car, so that she could have a private conversation.

He answered on the first ring.

"What happened to you this morning?"

"I had to get to work and I didn't want to bother you. You didn't want to talk to me yesterday, so I thought I would wait until you were ready."

"Look Stacey, what you did, I don't know if I can forgive you for that. I know I will never forgive Charles because he knew not to touch you, no matter what. But you, you danced naked in front of a room full of men touching and grabbing all over you. How could you do that, Stacey?"

"I'm sorry, Richard. I guess I didn't think about the consequences of my actions."

"Not only that Stacey, you're pregnant and Charles fucked you while you're carrying my child. I can't handle the thought of him with you. I don't know if I can be with you again."

"I understand, Richard."

"You do? You seem to be willing to let this relationship go."

"That's not it. I know what I did was wrong and I can't expect you to just accept what I did and act like it never happened. If you can't deal with it, I understand. I just don't want there to be any animosity between us. We have a baby on the way and I want for us to get along so that we can raise our child."

"No doubt, Stacey. I'm gonna take care of my child. Look, let's just give it some time and see how things work out. I love you."

"I love you too, Richard."

"Are you going to tell Carolyn?"

"No. I don't want to be the one to hurt her like that. Charles will have to explain to Carolyn why we are no longer friends. Look, why don't we talk again after I return from Asia and see how things are going."

"Okay." That conversation told her that he didn't want her to go with him to Asia.

After a good long cry, Stacey went back inside and finished her work day. She called Gina, Kellie and Michele and told them what was going on.

Gina also gave them an update on her situation. Kellie and Michele didn't mention what was going on with them.

Gina said, "What about the baby, Stacey?"

"I guess I'll be a single parent. People do it all the time. It's not something that I want to do, but if I have to, I will. I did this and I can't expect for Richard to want to be with me if he doesn't want to whether I'm pregnant or not."

"Damn girl, you are a strong sista," Michele said.

"I'm trying to stop Kellie from getting in trouble, but she seems to be attracted to disaster like a moth to a flame."

Stacey said, "What's going on Kellie?"

"Nothing."

"Like hell. Either you tell them Kellie or I will," Michele said.

"It's really nothing. I'm kind of attracted to Craig's new partner and he's attracted to me."

Stacey said, "Don't do it, Kellie. Craig has a gun. You don't want to end up in my situation. I destroyed Charles' and Richard's friendship. I'm sure Richard's cousin, Carolyn, will eventually find out. I don't think Richard will come back to me. I'm sure that once he is away from me for a week or so he'll be able to let me go. I think the only reason he hasn't done it yet is because of the baby. I'm sure he is torn about how to handle this. Don't do it Kellie, it's not worth it."

Gina said, "If I could take back what I did, I would. I don't think I'll get Marcus back and if I do, it will never be the same."

"It will be okay." Kellie said.

"Don't say we didn't warn you," Michele said.

Stacey didn't hear from Richard for the next week. He was due to leave for Asia in the morning. Stacey decided to use her vacation time to relax. She called Gina to see if she could use some company and Gina welcomed her. She planned to stay with Gina for a week.

Richard called later that evening.

"Hi Stacey. How are you?"

"I'm okay. How are you?"

"I'm okay, I'm missing you. I've become accustomed to seeing you everyday and not seeing you is hard. How's the baby?"

"Fine. Are you ready for your trip?"

"Yeah. Tomorrow morning I will be on my way. I wish things didn't happen the way they did..."

"Don't worry about it, Richard. Things happen for a reason and you know how that goes... Anyway, have a great trip and I'll talk to you when you return."

"Alright, Stacey. I'll call you when I return."

"Okay."

She cried again after their conversation. She got up and started packing to get her mind off of her problems with Richard.

When she arrived at Gina's house the next afternoon, they hugged and cried and talked about the misery and regrets in their lives.

Gina took Stacey shopping and to dinner to help her relax. Marcus came by the house the first day Stacey was there to pick up the kids in order to stay overnight with him at his apartment.

"Hello, Marcus."

"Stacey, how are you?"

"Okay, and you?"

"Not my best, but I'll be okay."

"I hope so."

Stacey spending time with Gina helped them both. Marcus didn't seem to be coming home anytime soon and Gina was having a hard time accepting his decision. Stacey, on the other hand, refused to pine over Richard. She loved him and prayed that things work out with them, but she didn't want to live in misery everyday wondering what decision he would make.

After spending a week with Gina, Stacey was ready to return home. She still had a week of vacation and decided to use it doing things around the house and to relax.

While checking her messages, she was shocked to have a message from Charles asking her to call him. She thought about not calling, but she was curious as to what he wanted.

"Hello, Charles, this is Stacey."

"Stacey, I thought you were in Asia. I didn't expect you to get this message for another week."

"I didn't go."

"Stacey, do you think you can talk to Richard and ask him to forgive me."

"I can't put in a word for you, Charles. Richard and I broke up."

"I thought he believed you."

"He does. He just can't deal with what I did."

"Alright." He hung up the phone.

When Richard returned from his Asian trip, he called Stacey and asked if he could come by. Stacey said, "Yes."

He arrived at her house an hour later.

When she opened the door, he was surprised when he saw her because she had a little tummy. She was five months pregnant and showing.

"Stacey, you're showing."

"Yeah, I know. Come on in."

"I didn't think that would happen so fast. Can I touch you?"

"Yeah."

He put his hand on her stomach and started smiling. "Wow, this is my child growing inside of you, our child. Can we sit down?"

"Sure. So what's up, Richard? How was your trip?"

"It was good. It would have been better if you had been there, but it was still good.

Listen, I've had a lot of time to think about our situation and I still love you, Stacey. I know that it will be a while before I can stop thinking about it, but I don't want to be without you and I want us to raise our child together."

He took her hand and said, "Stacey, will you be my wife?"

She was shocked and didn't answer.

"Stacey, did you hear me?"

"Yes, I'm sorry Richard. Yes, I love you too and I would love to be your wife."

"I don't want to have a big fancy wedding. But I want to get married as soon as possible. I don't want our child to be born out of wedlock, so the sooner we do this the better."

"How soon are you talking about?"

"Tomorrow! We can go to city hall and if you want to plan a reception or something later, that would be good, but I want to get married immediately. I don't want to spend another day without you, Stacey."

"I feel the same way, Richard. I love you and I will never do anything to jeopardize our relationship again."

He stayed the night with her.

The next morning they got a marriage license and planned to return the following day to get married. They agreed not to tell anyone until after they were married. Otherwise, everyone would try to convince them to have a wedding which they didn't want.

After getting their marriage license, they got a hotel room and spent the night.

As soon as city hall opened the next morning, Richard and Stacey were married. When they returned home, they called their friends and families and told them the good news about their marriage.

Kellie

Kellie called Arthur when she was on her way to the motel. He told her which motel, the room number and said for her to knock on the door when she arrived. When she pulled into the parking lot, she drove around to the back of the motel where she saw Arthur's truck. She parked next to it. As she approached the door, she started getting nervous and feeling guilty. For a brief moment she thought about turning around and going back home. The door opened and when she saw Arthur, all of those thoughts left. He stepped aside to let her in. They stared at each other for a brief moment. When Kellie knew he was going to kiss her, she turned away and sat down on the end of the bed.

"Arthur, what are we doing? You know there is no turning back if we go through with this, don't you?"

He sat down next to her.

"I've thought about all of the consequences and I have never been attracted to anyone the way I'm attracted to you, Kellie. I'm doing stupid shit and I know it. I ain't never chased a woman before, but for you, I'm risking my life just to spend time with you, Kellie, and that's for real."

"I know it's for real. We're both taking a big chance."

"Come here."

She turned to him and they started kissing. He helped her out of her clothes and started kissing and sucking all over her body. When he stood to take his clothes off, she stood with him and helped him. She opened his pants and started massaging his dick. He was ready for her and she wanted him. He laid her down on the bed and continued with his exploration of her body. He touched and teased her until she couldn't take it anymore.

"Arthur, please."

"Please, what?"

"I can't take it anymore."

"You can't take what? Whatcha need?"

"I need you. I need you inside of me."

"Are you sure? You don't like how I'm making you feel?"

"Oh yeah, I love it, but I need to feel you, Arthur. I need you inside of me. Please Arthur, please give it to me."

"What is it you want, Kellie?"

"I want you inside of me. Please Arthur, please!"

He slid his dick inside of her and said, "Is this what you want, Kellie?"

"Yes, Arthur, yes! Oh that's good! Fuck me, baby."

"Whose pussy is this?"

"It's yours, whenever you want it. It's yours."

"Say my name."

"Oooh, Arthur, you can have my pussy whenever you want it. This is your pussy."

"Yeah, that's what I want to hear."

He worked it out! When they climbed into the shower together, it was going on ten o'clock. Kellie knew she had to get home. She was happy she pulled her hair into a ponytail because it was a mess. There was no way she would have been able to explain it if it was hanging loose.

They left the motel together. Arthur walked her to her car where they kissed for another five minutes.

"When can I see you again?"

"I don't know, Arthur. I can't get away a lot, but I'll let you know."

"Alright, baby. You be careful driving home."

"Okay."

When Kellie came in the house, it was ten thirty and Craig's friends were still there. Craig met her in the kitchen while she was getting a glass of water.

"Hey baby, did you have fun with Phyllis?"

"Yeah, we had fun. Is C.J. sleep?"

"You know it. He couldn't hang past eight thirty. The game is almost over and these guys will be gone soon."

He started kissing her on her neck.

"I'll be upstairs shortly."

"Okay."

Arthur wore her out and she knew Craig would want to get intimate. Whenever he gets with his boys and they drink, he's usually all over her.

She heard him come in the room and she faked sleep. That didn't stop him. He climbed in the bed and pulled her to him and started groping all over her. She knew what she had to do, so she turned to him and took care of him. All she thought about was what Arthur had done to her a few hours earlier.

The next morning, Craig said that he and Arthur were going with his brother Bruce to help paint and make repairs to the rental property Bruce recently purchased.

"How long are you going to be gone?"

"Most of the day, I'm sure. Why? Did we have something planned?"

"No, I was just wondering. Are you going to be home for dinner?"

"Naw, I'll probably get something to eat while I'm out."

"Okay, baby, I'll see you when you get back."

"What are you going to do today?"

"C.J. and I will do some shopping. I'll probably stop by my mom's house for a little while. That's about it."

"Alright. Call me if you need me."

"Okay."

While Kellie was out grocery shopping, Arthur called her on her cell phone.

"Hello."

"Good afternoon, Kellie. I can't stop thinking about you and I want to know when I can see you again."

"Arthur, I've been thinking about you too. I don't know when I can get away."

"What about today? Craig is over here with Bruce."

"I can't, I have C.J. and I promised him that I would spend the whole day with him. I can probably get away for a couple of hours tomorrow."

"I can't tomorrow. I already have plans."

"Okay. Well, I don't know after that. I'll let you know. Maybe one day next week."

"Kellie, you did something to me last night. I never had an experience like that and I'm craving for more of you."

"I told you already that I'm yours, baby. We just need to work on a time when we can get together."

"I'm glad to hear you say that. I was hoping you didn't just tell me that during a moment of passion and that you truly meant it."

"Yeah, I meant it. I'm yours."

"Alright. I'll see what I can work out and I'll let you know."

"Okay."

Kellie took C.J. to Hollywood Park and let him play for a while and tire himself out. Once they returned home, she gave him a bath and put him to bed. He was asleep immediately. Craig called shortly after and said that he was on his way home.

Kellie was on the couch when he came in. He sat next to her and said, "I love you, baby. You put it on me last night. Can we get a replay?"

"Sure, baby. I've got something even better."

"Better? What could be better than last night?"

"Hold tight, I'll be back in a minute."

She jumped up and ran upstairs. When she came back downstairs about ten minutes later, she wore a robe. She pulled one of the dining room chairs into the family room, turned the TV off and put on some music. She told Craig to sit in the chair. Once he was seated, she started dancing for him. Under the robe she was wearing a crotch less teddy. He loved every minute of the dance. Then she stripped to the music. Once she was nude, she walked over to him and gave him a lap dance. She opened his pants and slid onto his erect, throbbing dick. While she was riding him, she asked him, "Did you like my dance, baby?"

"Damn Kellie, what are you trying to do, kill me? Baby you look so good I thought I was gonna bust a nut just looking at you and that lap dance, damn! It was the shit!" He stood up and said, "Turn around."

He had her leaning over the back of the couch and he took her from behind. They were both worn out and crashed as soon as they hit the bed.

Monday, while at work, Craig told Arthur about Kellie stripping for him. He didn't give all of the details, but he gave a lot.

Arthur called her while she was at lunch. When she looked at the caller ID on her ringing phone, she excused herself and stepped outside.

"Hello."

"Hey, baby."

"Hi Arthur. How are you?"

"Missing you. I need to see you. Can you get away today?"

"Yes, only for a few hours though. I usually stay at work until six o'clock on Mondays."

"What time do you get off?"

"Three thirty."

"Okay, meet me at our place as soon as you can get there."

"Okay."

Kellie couldn't keep her eyes off of the clock all afternoon. As soon as the bell rang, she gathered all of her things and found her way to their spot. Arthur was already there. As soon as she came in the door they were all over each other. Again the lovemaking was exceptional. Arthur made her feel things that neither Craig nor any other man ever had. While they were lying in bed Arthur said, "You sure did make Craig happy last night."

"What are you talking about?"

"Craig never talks about any of your intimate business, but he was smiling all day today because of what you did to him last night."

"He told you about that!"

"Yeah, my dick got hard thinking about it. Can you do that for me, please?"

"I can't believe he told you."

"Listen baby, you made him feel good, I think he had to tell somebody about it."

"What else has he told you about me?"

"Nothing intimate. I told you, he don't talk about you like that. But I could picture it all as he was telling me."

"What did he tell you?"

"He said you did a striptease, gave him a lap dance and basically fucked him real good."

"Damn."

"What?"

"He shouldn't be discussing our sex life with other people."

"He was just happy, baby. That's how men are. Come here and make me happy."

It was fifteen after six when she left the motel. On her way home she decided to call Michele because she needed to talk to someone. She was falling hard for Arthur.

The call was on the third ring before Michele answered.

"Hey, Kellie. What's up, girl?"

"You sound awfully happy. What's up with you?"

"Girl, I think I'm falling in love with Nick. He is the shyzt!!!"

"Dang, Michele, I've never heard you talk about a man like this before. He must be doing something right."

"He's doing everything right. Enough about my happiness, what's up with you?"

"Girl, where do I begin?"

"I don't like the sound of this, Kellie. What's up?"

"Michele, I know we all usually share, but we have got to keep this between the two of us, okay?"

"Alright. This must be serious. You know I don't like to keep secrets."

"I know Michele, but you're the only one I can talk to about this."

"What's up, Kellie?"

"I slept with Arthur and I don't want to stop."

"I told you not to do that, Kellie!"

"I couldn't help myself. I'm so attracted to him. I ain't never been like this with nobody, including Craig and you know how crazy I am about Craig."

"How many times have you slept with him?"

"Twice. I'm leaving the motel now on my way home."

"Kellie you have got to stop seeing this man. Do you know what would happen if Craig found out?"

"Yes. I just can't resist him, Michele. He's not just good looking, he makes me feel sexy and free and I love being in his company."

"Kellie. You have got to get a grip girl. I'm all for having fun and being with the one that makes you feel good, but this is dangerous."

"I know, Michele. You're right. I'm not going to see him again. I have to be strong because I could lose my husband over this."

"And your life. Don't fool yourself Kellie, Craig will kill you."

"I know. I'm not going to see him again. Thanks for listening, Michele."

"Anytime, Kellie. I love you girl and I don't want to see anything happen to you. Okay?"

"Okay."

"Have you talked to Stacey or Gina?"

"No, but I need to check on them. I'm at my house. I'll talk to you later."

Gina

Three weeks after Marcus left the house, Gina was still having a hard time making the adjustment. She cried constantly which made it difficult for her to entertain the children. She asked Marcus' mother if she could watch the kids overnight because she needed time to herself.

Gina planned to meet one of her friends, Tiffany, for drinks at a sports bar on Beale Street. She hadn't been out in months and it felt good to be amongst other adults.

Gina waited for Tiffany at the bar. A male patron sent her a drink. She looked down the bar to see who sent the drink, so that she could thank them. She saw the guy stand and walk towards her.

"Is this seat taken?"

"No. Thank you for the drink."

"You're welcome. Are you waiting for someone?"

"Yes, my friend should be here shortly."

"Can I keep you company until he/she arrives?"

"Sure, and it's a she."

"Okay. My name is Chris."

"Hello Chris, I'm Gina."

"Gina, it's a pleasure to meet you. Are you from Memphis?"

"Yes, born and raised."

"I'm visiting from Miami. This is my first time visiting Memphis and I like it. I'm here on business this time, but I'm hoping to see more of the city during my next visit."

Tiffany called and said that she wouldn't be able to make it because her babysitter cancelled and she didn't have anyone to watch her kids.

Gina had a disappointed look on her face after her phone call.

"Is everything okay, Gina?"

"Yes. That was my friend telling me she won't be able to make it."

"Oh, I'm sorry to hear that. Since you're here, would you like to get something to eat? We can get one of these tables and continue getting to know each other."

"Okay, Chris, I'd like that."

He grabbed their drinks and they headed towards a table. After they were seated, a waitress approached their table to take their orders.

"I see you're wearing a wedding ring so I won't try to get too personal, but I did want to let you know that I think you are very beautiful."

"Thank you, Chris."

"Does your husband let you come out alone very often?"

"We're separated."

"Oh. Can I get you another drink?"

"Yes, please."

Gina knew that Chris was going to try to get her drunk and she wanted to be drunk. They talked and drank for a couple of hours before Chris invited her to his room. Gina wasn't so drunk that she didn't know what she was doing when she accepted. She just wanted some companionship. When they arrived in Chris' room, Gina became Train and took Chris on the ride of his life. He was talking dirty to her and it turned her on. She gave herself to him freely and he took all of her.

As she dressed to leave, Chris begged her to stay, but Gina wanted to hurry out of the room and hoped that she would never see Chris again.

When she arrived home, she took a hot shower, slipped into a nightgown and was sleep immediately. She was awakened by the kid's voices early the next morning. She remembered telling Marcus' mother that she would come and get them. She looked over at the clock and it was ten thirty-eight a.m. She sat up to get out of the bed and Marcus appeared in her doorway.

"Marcus, what are you doing here?"

"I was at my mom's this morning and the kids were ready to come home, so here we are."

He moved the clothes Gina had on the night before out of the chair and had a seat.

"So it looks like you had a long night. I've never known you to sleep this late."

"I know, but I didn't get in until pretty late. I met Tiffany for dinner and drinks and we talked for hours. You know what I decided, Marcus?"

"What?"

"I want to get a job."

"What about the kids?"

"They can go to daycare. I realized last night that I need adult companionship. Since you're not here anymore and I'm with the kids all day, I rarely have any adult contact."

"What kind of job are you talking about?"

"When I talked to Tiffany, she said they were looking for a staff writer at the TV station and she said that she would put in a word to the station manager for me."

"That sounds pretty demanding, Gina. I just don't want the kids to be with strangers all of the time."

"I can do it part-time until they get in school. Maybe I can hire a nanny to come here so that they don't have to go into a strange environment."

"I don't know about this, Gina. It may be too many changes for them at one time. I think they are just realizing that I don't live here anymore and then for you to be gone, too. It may be too much for them to handle."

"I can't take it, Marcus. I've got to get out of the house."

"Why all of a sudden? Being a housewife never bothered you before."

"Because I was a housewife. I'm not a wife anymore and I need to start thinking about my future."

"It's all about you, Gina. Don't you think you should be thinking about what's best for my kids?"

She got out of the bed not realizing what she had on was skimpy. She was so comfortable around Marcus that she didn't realize she was turning him on.

"I've always done what's best for OUR children, Marcus. Since I'm a single parent now, not only do I have to do what's best for them, I need to do what's best for all of us and if getting a job is what's best for all of us, then that is what I'll do!"

She recognized the look in his eyes. He wanted to have sex with her. She could also see him trying to control himself.

"I just don't want them to be raised by strangers, Gina. That's why I pay all of the bills here and give you everything you need so that you can be here with them."

"You are not giving me everything I need, Marcus."

"What is it you need that I'm not giving you?"

"Nothing, just forget it."

As she began to walk away, Marcus came up behind her and put his hands on her shoulder to stop her. When she turned around, he kissed her.

"What do you need, baby? What do you need that I'm not giving you?"

"I need you, Marcus. I need you to make love to me."

"I want you so bad, Gina. I just didn't know how to ask you."

"Where are the kids?"

"They are watching a movie that I put on for them."

He quickly undressed and was all over Gina. She didn't think that he was seeing anyone because of the way he came to her. She had been worried about him being with another woman since it had been almost a month since he left the house.

He was rushing and she made him slow down. She wanted to give him something to remember. She climbed on top of him because he loved it when she took control. She rode him and had him moaning and calling her name telling her that he loved her and missed her.

When they were done, neither one of them said anything. Gina went into the bathroom and took a shower and Marcus went down the hall to another bathroom. When Gina came downstairs, Marcus was watching TV with the boys.

"Do you guys want some lunch?"

The kids said that they wanted lunch, but Marcus said no, he had to leave. He hugged and kissed the kids and told them that he would see them soon. Gina walked him to the door. He could hardly look her in the eye.

"Bye, Marcus."

"I'll call you, Gina."

"Alright."

Marcus was a mess. Making love to Gina confused him. He enjoyed having sex with her, she made him feel good and she was a great mother and wife. He didn't know what to do. Seeing her weakened him. He knew that if he ended things with her that she wouldn't be single for long and he didn't know if he would be able to handle seeing her with another man or having another man around his children.

But, he still wasn't able to get over what she did in Vegas.

The next evening while Gina was cleaning up the dinner dishes, she received a phone call from Pamela, a family friend inquiring about what was going on with Gina and Marcus.

"Why do you think something is going on with Marcus and I?"

"I saw him on a date this evening."

Gina was stunned into silence.

"Gina?"

"Yeah, I'm here Pamela. How do you know he was on a date?"

"I know the difference between a date and business. The way the lady was dressed, their body language, it was a date. Why didn't you tell me, Gina? I'm your friend."

"I really haven't told anyone. I was hoping we could work things out but if he's dating, I guess that isn't going to happen. Thanks for calling Pamela."

Gina went into the bathroom and started crying. After she pulled herself together, she called Tiffany and asked Tiffany to give her resume to the station manager. She knew that Marcus was not coming back now that he was dating and if he were coming home, he would have done so after they made love yesterday.

The next day Herbert, the station manager from the news station called Gina and asked her if she could come in for an interview. Marcus' mother stayed with the kids while she interviewed. Her mother-in-law was very supportive and believed it was a good idea for Gina to get out of the house. Gina didn't give her all of the details, but she did tell her the reason she and Marcus were separated was her fault.

When Herbert saw her, he asked if she had ever done any on air broadcasting.

"I did some radio in college, but no video."

"Tiffany says you're interested in one of the writing positions?"

"Yes, I'm looking for something part-time."

"Do you have any writing samples?"

She handed her portfolio to him. He was nodding as he read some of her articles. "We have a position for a writer in our sports department. Are you interested in sports?"

"Pretty much."

"Okay, come on. Let me introduce you to the people you will be working with. Have you done any interviews?"

"Yes, while I was working at the radio station."

"How did you like it?"

"I liked it a lot."

"Good. You may have to do some interviewing. You don't mind do you?"

"No. Not at all."

Herbert walked around the station with her, introducing her to people, people she'd seen on TV and the people she would be working with. He asked if she could start the following morning. She said that she couldn't, but would be able to start Monday. He agreed.

Gina called a child care agency when she returned home and asked to see applicants for the nanny position as soon as possible. She then called Marcus and told him that she would be starting a job Monday and that she would be interviewing nannies for the next two days and would like for him to interview the applicants with her.

"I thought we agreed that it wouldn't be a good idea for you to work."

"No, we didn't agree on that. That's what you want, but I think it will be a good idea for me to work."

"What kind of work will you be doing?"

"A writer for the sports department."

"Sports? Surrounded by a bunch of men."

"Women play sports too, Marcus. Do you want to participate or not?"

"I don't have a choice. I asked you not to work but you're going to do it anyway. What about my kids?"

"Why don't you get your girlfriend to watch them?"

"What are you talking about, Gina?"

"I know you're dating, Marcus. You could have had the decency to tell me."

"Tell you what?"

"That it was okay to see other people."

"I'm not seeing anyone, Gina. It was one date."

"Why did you sleep with me, Marcus?"

"Because I can't resist you."

"So I guess it's okay for me to date too, right?"

"Hell naw, Gina. We're still married and you have two young children at home. I don't want another man over my kids."

"I don't fucking believe you, Marcus. It's okay for you to date, but I have to wait until what...when the kids are grown and out of the house?"

"Naw, I'm just saying. I went on one date. That's it. That doesn't mean that you should start dating, plus we are still married."

"You were married when you went on your date. Did you sleep with her, Marcus?"

"No."

"The first applicant will be at the house tomorrow morning at nine o'clock. Can you be here?"

"Yeah, I'll be there. How many hours do you plan to work?"

"It's a part-time position. I guess when I go in Monday we'll talk about the schedule."

"Alright, Gina, I'll see you in the morning. Does this mean that you are going to start dating too?"

"What does one have to do with the other?"

"You'll be meeting a lot of new people."

"Should I start dating other people, Marcus?"

"No."

"How long do you think is a sufficient amount of time for you to decide if you want me or not. After your fifth or sixth date?"

"It was one date Gina. ONE! We'll talk about it soon. Okay?"

"Yeah, okay."

Michele

After looking at both properties with Nick and Lust, Lust put a contract on the first property. Lust was in town for a label party that was taking place that evening. Nick invited Michele to go with him.

Nick told Michele that he would need to mingle because it was a company function, but he would try to spend as much time with her as possible.

The party was being held in a Mansion in Beverly Hills. When they arrived, the party was in full swing. One of the first people Michele saw was Lust. He came over and greeted them at the door. He had that lustful look in his eyes. She never asked Nick what he said to Lust, but whatever he said stopped Lust from talking about Vegas. He came over and gave Michele a kiss on the cheek and shook Nick's hand. As they were walking around and Nick was introducing Michele to everyone, as his woman, Michele noticed the hard stares she received from a lot of the women in the room.

Nick told her he had to take care of a little business. He asked her to mingle and that he would be by her side shortly. Michele decided to walk around and check out the house. She found herself outside around the pool when a young lady approached her.

"So you're Nick's latest."

"Latest? What does that mean?"

"You're the latest to get his attention. You won't last for long sweetie, they never do."

"And you are?"

"The one before you. Look, honey..."

"Michele."

"Michele, I know you're attracted to Nick. I was too. But don't get too caught up with him. He still loves me and he'll be coming back to me. I'm just warning you so that you're not surprised when it happens."

"Thanks for letting me know, uh..."

"Lindsey."

"Thank you Lindsey for letting me know. By the way, did you get a warning from the one before you?"

"No."

"Good looking out."

Nick walked up on them.

"Lindsey, how are you?"

"I'm fine Nickey, missing you."

"I see you've met Michele."

"Yeah. When you're done playing with her give me a call, Nickey, you know I'll be waiting."

"This is the real thing, Lindsey." He leaned over and kissed Michele. "This is what it's supposed to be like."

"I'll be waiting to hear from you." She walked away.

"Are you enjoying yourself?"

"I'm seeing a lot of celebrities here and as long as I watch my back, I should be okay."

"What does that mean?"

"How many of the women here have you dated?"

"Only Lindsey, why?"

"Because these women are cutting their eyes at me like I stole you from them."

"You know how it is out here, Michele."

"Yeah, I know."

Someone called Nick from across the room.

"I'll be back shortly, baby. Are you okay?"

"Yeah. I'm fine."

While Michele was sitting on the patio waiting for Nick to return, one of the guys from Lust's entourage came and sat next to her. He was the same guy who was in the hotel room with them while she and Lust did their thing.

"Hey, Juicy. Can I get a private dance?"

"That was a one time thing. I don't dance anymore."

"It's really not the dance I'm interested in. I'm talking about me and you getting busy. I still remember how you can ride a dick. How much is it gonna cost me?"

"I'm not a prostitute and I'm not going to get with you."

He put his hand on Michele's thigh and was moving it up her leg. She slapped his hand off of her and started getting up when Nick appeared.

"Man, what the fuck are you doing?"

"Hey Nick man, what's up? This you?"

"Yeah."

"Oh snap, I was just trying to get a little action. I didn't know she wasn't dancing no more."

"Naw, she don't dance no more."

"That's a damn shame man cause she put on a better show than Lust."

Nick took Michele's hand and they headed inside. He seemed a little irritated, but Michele didn't say anything. He took her into a private room and closed the door behind them. He turned to her and said, "Did you sleep with Lust or any of his friends?"

Michele put her head down and said, "Yes."

"Shit!"

"Who, Michele?"

"Lust."

"What's up with his boy?"

"He was in the hotel room both times."

"You slept with him twice?"

"Yes."

"What about the other guys?"

"NO, I didn't sleep with anyone else. Shit, I knew I would end up regretting what I did."

"I just don't want everywhere we go to hear someone calling you Juicy, that's all baby."

"I'm sorry, Nick."

"Don't be sorry. This happened before we got together and what you did before won't change the way I feel about you now. I just need to know how far things went with these guys so that I'll know how to handle them. Is there anything else I should know?"

"No. I only slept with Lust. He gave me his contact information but I never contacted him. Everything that happened with us happened in Vegas. Once I left, I thought I put it behind me."

"Everything will be fine. Come on let's get back out there. We can leave soon, okay?"

"Yeah."

When they stepped back out into the party, a young lady walked up to Nick, put her arms around him and said, "Nick, where have you been? I've been calling you for the past two weeks, but you're never around anymore. What's up? I need you baby." She had a South American accent.

He pushed her away and said, "Valencia, this is Michele. Michele, Valencia."

She stepped back and looked at Michele like she was nobody and turned back to Nick and said, "Nickey, I need you baby. Who is this?"

"Michele is the woman I love. I'm sorry, but I can't be there for you any longer. I am officially off the market."

"Nicky, you used the L word referring to this woman. You said you never told anyone that you loved them and you said you would always be there for me."

"Things change, you know that. Come on, be a big girl and let it go."

She looked at Michele with hate in her eyes. She rolled her eyes, kissed Nick on the mouth and walked away.

"I'm sorry about that, baby."

"Who am I to say anything?"

"Let's get out of here."

They went to Nick's place in the hills. His phone was ringing as they were coming through the door.

"Hello; what's up Valencia? No, Michele is here with me and like I told you before, I'm off the market. I've got to go."

He hung up the phone.

"Come here, Michele."

She walked over to him and they sat on the couch.

"I have a past, just like you. Some of these women are very persistent and they will keep trying to get me back. I'm not saying that I'm all that, but you know how it is?"

"Yeah baby, I know how it is. I know it must be hard to let a man like you go, but I've got something for you to make the time you spend with me memorable."

"Yeah, what's that?"

She pulled a chair from the dining room and put it in the middle of the floor and told him to have a seat. She then walked over to his stereo, found Ludacris Splash Waterfalls and started dancing for him. The dress she was wearing was easy to remove. She danced for a while and then started stripping. He was undressing himself along with her. By the time she was totally nude, so was he. She walked over to him and gave him a lap dance and they had sex in the chair in the middle of the floor. When they made it to the shower, Nick was ready to go again. He had been so gentle with her the previous times they had sex, but that striptease she did for him opened him up.

After they had sex again in the shower and were lying in bed, Nick said to Michele, "Earlier when we were at the party and I told Valencia that you were the woman I love, I meant it, Michele. I'm in love with you. I don't know how you feel about me, but it doesn't matter right now. I know I love you and want to be with you and hopefully you'll grow to love me too."

"I do love you, Nick. I fell in love with you on our first date. I know it's soon, but I guess it doesn't matter how long it takes to happen."

"Michele?"

"Yes, Nick?"

"I've never been in love before and I finally understand the saying about how love makes a man do stupid things. I can't stand to see another man near you. I've never been possessive or jealous or anything like that, but with you it's different."

"Don't worry about another man Nick, I'm faithful. I'll never do anything to jeopardize what we have."

"Promise?"

"Yeah, I promise."

The next morning Nick had to run to his office to get some papers, but he told Michele that he wanted to spend the day with her and that he would be back shortly.

She was lying in his bed listening to music when the doorbell rang. She slipped on his shirt and went to the door. When she opened the door, Valencia was standing there with a jacket on. She pushed her way past Michele.

"Nickey, it's me baby, where are you?"

"Excuse me Miss, Nicky isn't here. Can I help you with something?"

"Oh, it's you again. Look honey, why don't you gather your things and go. I'm here to give Nick what he needs."

She opened her coat and was naked under it.

"Honey, cover yourself. You don't have anything I need. Look, I've been nice because Nick and I are just getting started, but I have a feeling I'm gonna have to kick your ass. I never thought I would see the day that I would be fighting over a man."

"We don't have to fight over him. Why don't you just go away and let us get on with our relationship?"

"Are you retarded or something? I clearly heard Nick tell you to go the fuck away, but like he said, you're persistent. Like I said, I've been nice. I'm giving you this last chance to go the fuck away or I promise you, I will beat your ass."

"Look bitch." Her accent was gone. "I've been with Nick off and on for the past two years and I'll be damned if I sit back and let your nobody ass come in and try to take my man."

"You phony ass, bitch. What happened to your accent?"

"Don't worry about it. What you need to be worrying about is what's going to happen to you if you don't stay away from my man."

"Why don't we take care of this now because I'm not going away and for the record, you don't scare me. I don't feel the least bit threatened by you. If you're going to do something, let's do it."

"I'll deal with you later. Tell my Boo I came by to see him." She turned and walked out the door.

When Nick returned, Michele told him what happened and how Valencia lost her accent when she got mad and had to get street. He told her not to worry about Valencia and that she would eventually go away.

They stayed in all day listening to music and making love. Nick took Michele home early the next morning. When she checked her voicemail, she had messages from Stacey, Kellie and Gina. She called Stacey first.

Stacey

After telling Kellie, Michele and Gina about her marriage and convincing them that she didn't want to have a wedding, she gave them the details surrounding the make-up and proposal.

Stacey and Richard planned a reception in September and invited everyone to come.

Stacey moved into Richard's house until their house is completed. They were having a new house built that would be ready by August.

Carolyn called Richard and asked what happened between him and Charles. Richard told her to ask Charles. She said she asked him and he wouldn't say. He told her that he was sorry, but he couldn't tell her and that it was up to Charles to clear his conscience.

Richard and Charles had not spoken to each other since the incident at Richard's house and Stacey asked him to forgive his friend and put it all behind them. She told him that she was not asking for them to be best friends again, but for him not to carry around the burden of a grudge and to let it go. He agreed that he would forgive Charles, but insisted that that forgiveness did not include an invitation back into his life.

Kellie

When Kellie made it home, Craig and C.J. weren't there. Kellie started dinner and then called Craig.

"Hey baby, where y'all at?"

"We stopped by my mother's, but we're on our way. What's for dinner?"

"I'm cooking spaghetti. How does that sound?"

"That sounds good. I'm hungry. We'll see you in a few. I'm just around the corner."

"Alright."

During dinner, Craig told Kellie that Arthur invited them to join him and one of his girlfriends for the weekend in Wisconsin.

"Do you want to go?"

"Yeah, it sounds like fun. We can use a little get away. Arthur said that he goes to this spot often and they have cabins for rent and it's real romantic."

"When is he talking about going?"

"He said at the end of the month, the weekend of Memorial Day."

"Okay, if you want to go then we can go. Are we taking C.J.?"

"I really didn't want to. I thought it could be just you and I. I'm sure my mother won't mind hanging out with C.J. for a few days."

"Alright. Tell him that we'll go."

Kellie tried to keep her distance from Arthur, but she couldn't stop thinking about him. He had been calling her cell phone constantly, but she never answered his calls. After a week of avoiding him, he showed up at her job after work one day.

When she saw his truck she couldn't believe it. When she walked over to the truck, he rolled down the window.

"Arthur, what are you doing here?"

"I had to see you, Kellie. I want to know why you're avoiding me."

"I can't see you anymore, Arthur. What we are doing is wrong and I can't do it anymore. Look, I can't stand out here and talk to you."

"Okay, meet me at our spot so that we can talk."

"I can't, I've got to get C.J.."

"Meet me tomorrow then."

"Arthur, let's not do this. I can't see you anymore."

"Meet me tomorrow and tell me why and then I'll leave you alone."

"Okay, I'll be there at three forty-five."

"I'm looking forward to seeing you."

During her drive home, Kellie kept thinking about Arthur. She knew, as well as he did, that she would not be able to control herself if she was in a room alone with him.

The next day after school when she arrived at the motel, she saw Arthur's truck in the parking lot. He sent her a text message earlier with the room number.

When he opened the door and they made eye contact, she knew she was in trouble. She missed him. She didn't realize it until that moment, but she missed him and wanted him. Once the door closed, they were drawn to each other instantly. No words were spoken. They quickly undressed and satisfied each other.

After making love, Kellie asked Arthur why he invited her and Craig to the go to Wisconsin with him and one of his girlfriends.

"I want to see you in a bathing suit and I want to spend time with you outside of this motel. If I have to deal with Craig being there, I will. I just want to be with you."

"How do you think I will feel with you having one of your many women there, knowing when you close the door to your cabin, you'll be making love to her."

"But I'll be thinking of you."

"I've got to get home, Arthur."

"Kellie, please don't cut me off like that again. I was going crazy not being able to see you or talk to you. I already told Craig that I am having a little something at my house this weekend, so I'm sure he'll be asking you if you want to come. I had to find a way to see you."

"I guess I'll see you this weekend."

They kissed and went their separate ways.

The day before the gathering at Arthur's house, Craig came home and said that it was cancelled. "Arthur has to go out of town for the next few days to his aunt's funeral and won't have time to put it together. He is rescheduling for next weekend."

Kellie's period due date came and passed over a week ago, but she tried to ignore it. Craig asked her about it and she pretended to be on it last week. She was terrified at the thought of being pregnant because if she was, she didn't know who the father was. She had been sleeping with Arthur and Craig regularly. With Craig, they didn't use condoms every time. With

Arthur, the condom broke once or twice and on another occasion, they were so into each other that they didn't use any at all.

The next morning, after Craig left for work, Kellie called Michele.

"Girl, do you know its five fifteen a.m.? This had better be an emergency."

"I think I'm pregnant."

"What! C.J.'s finally going to get a brother or sister."

"No, Michele. If I am, I don't know who the father is."

"What! Kellie what are you doing?"

"I don't know anymore, Michele. I can't stay away from Arthur and I had unprotected sex with him and Craig. Now I think I'm pregnant and there is no way I can say who the father is."

"When are you going to find out for sure?"

"I'm going to pick up a test on my way to work and take it as soon as I get there. If I'm pregnant, I'm gonna need you to come here and go with me to get rid of it, Michele. I can't have this baby."

"Let's just find out if you're pregnant first, Okay?"

"Okay. I'll call you in about an hour."

"I'll be waiting. Kellie!"

"Yeah?"

"You have had a period since Vegas, haven't you?"

"Yeah. That's not the problem."

"Alright. I'm just making sure."

When Kellie left work and after picking C.J. up from the sitter, she headed to McDonalds. She called Craig to let him know that she will be arriving home a little later than usual.

"Hey baby, I was just about to call you."

"Oh yeah, what's up?"

"I just wanted to remind you that it's my night to host the game and to find out if you remembered to pick up the chips and stuff."

"Yeah, I got everything over the weekend."

"Thanks, Kellie. You're the best wife a man could have."

A tear fell out of her eye when he said that.

"I just wanted to let you know that I stopped by McDonald's to let C.J. play for a little while and I got him a happy meal."

"Okay, I'll see you when you get here."

"Okay."

She called her OB/GYN and made an appointment, but couldn't get an appointment to see her until the following Monday.

120

When Kellie arrived home, all of the guys were there, including Arthur. When he saw her coming in the door he came over and helped her with C.J. and all of her bags. Craig must have been in another room.

He discreetly whispered to her, "I miss you."

She looked him in his eyes and he could see that she missed him too.

"What's wrong, Kellie?"

"Nothing. I'm just a little tired."

"Please call me."

Craig came in. "Hey baby." He walked over to her and they kissed. He grabbed C.J. and started playing with him. When Arthur and Craig went back to watch the game, Kellie and C.J. went upstairs.

Later when Kellie came downstairs to get a drink of water, Arthur was in the kitchen. When she saw him she hesitated and thought about turning around, but he saw her before she could move.

"Kellie, why have you been avoiding me?"

"No reason. I've just been busy, Arthur."

"Will I see you this weekend at the cookout?"

"Yeah, I'll be there."

"Can I see you before then?"

"I don't think I can get away before then, but I'll let you know."

"Alright."

Kellie didn't call Arthur, but he kept calling her. When he saw her Saturday he wanted to know what was going on.

When they were alone in the house, Arthur said, "Kellie, I call you constantly and you don't answer or return my calls. Did I do something wrong?"

"No, Arthur, you didn't do anything wrong. I just needed a little time to think about what I was doing. I tried my best to stay away from you, but I can't."

"Does that mean that we can get together?"

"Yes. When?"

"Tomorrow. Maybe we can see a movie, get something to eat, something. I enjoy making love to you, but I would like to spend time together outside of the bed."

"We can't do that, Arthur. It's too dangerous. I would love to spend time with you outside of the bed too, but we can't take that chance."

"I want more, Kellie."

"No Arthur, don't do this."

"I want you to be my woman."

Before she could respond, one of his girlfriends emerged.

"There you are, baby. I've been looking for you. I'm sorry I'm so late getting here, but I had to go back home and get that item you like for tonight."

She walked up to him and kissed him.

"Hey, Kellie. It's good to see you again."

"Hi, Lauren. It's good to see you too. Let me get back out there and see about C.J."

The next day Kellie told Craig that she was going to hang out with Phyllis, but she was on her way to meet Arthur. She was still carrying around the pregnancy test in her purse because she forgot to throw it out. She didn't want to throw it out at work because someone could find it and would keep digging until they found out who it belonged to. She didn't want to toss it at home because Craig might find it. She knew she had to get rid of it soon.

She told herself that she was going to break things off with Arthur because her feelings were getting too strong and now that she is pregnant, she is an emotional mess. When he opened the door and she saw that beautiful smile, she was putty in his hands. After they made love, he told her that he wanted to talk.

"What's on your mind, Arthur?"

"I'm in love with you and I want to be with you."

"Arthur, you knew how it was when we started out. I'm married and I do love my husband."

"How do you feel about me?"

"I'm in love with you, but I know I can't have you, Arthur, so I'm trying to stay away from you."

"You can have me, Kellie. The problem is I can't have you."

"When I first met you, I was physically attracted to you. I had no intention of falling in love with you and now, I can't stay away from you. But we have to stop, Arthur."

"Why do we have to stop, Kellie? I love you, you love me, and I want to be with you. I'll ask for a transfer to another district, that way I won't be Craig's partner anymore and it will be easier for us to work this out."

"I can't do that, Arthur. Craig hasn't done anything to deserve this. I still love him. And what about C.J.? I can't do it, Arthur."

When Kellie arrived home after meeting with Arthur, Craig's car was blocking the garage door, so she parked her car behind his. The next morning he got her car keys out of her purse, so that he could move the car.

While Arthur and Craig were on patrol, Arthur could sense that something was wrong with Craig.

"What's up man? You're quiet and you're never quiet."

"Man, I've got shit on my mind."

"What's up? You can talk to me. You know you can talk to me about anything."

"Alright. I found a positive pregnancy test in Kellie's purse, but she hasn't mentioned it to me. I needed her keys to move her car and there it was in a drugstore bag. The receipt said she bought it last week, but she hasn't said a word about it to me and I want to know why."

"She's pregnant?"

"According to the test she is and then I remember asking her about her period and she said she was on it. We had sex one of the days that she was supposed to be on her period, and she wasn't."

"Why wouldn't she tell you if she was pregnant?"

"I don't know. I don't know what's going on."

"Talk to her man. Ask her about it. I'm sure there is a good explanation."

"Yeah, we'll see."

Kellie's phone was blowing up while she was in class. She had to excuse herself to see what the problem was.

He answered on the first ring.

"Hello."

"Arthur, you know I'm in class. What's going on? Did something happen to Craig?"

"No. He's fine. I need to see you as soon as possible."

"I can't Arthur. I was with you last night. I told you I can't get away like that."

"I need to see you, we need to talk. I need fifteen minutes of your time. I'll meet you in the parking lot of your school. I'll be there at fifteen after three."

"No Arthur, No. Don't come here."

"Well, where then?"

"Meet me in the drugstore parking lot down the street from the school."

"Alright. I'll see you there."

Arthur was waiting when Kellie arrived. She hopped in the car with him.

"What's up, Arthur?"

"Are you pregnant?"

She gasped. "What!"

"You are, aren't you?"

She started crying.

"Are you carrying my baby, Kellie?"

"I don't know."

"You don't know if you're pregnant or not?"

"Yes, Arthur, I'm pregnant but I don't know if you or Craig is the father."

"Damn, Kellie. If it's mine, I want it."

"I can't keep this baby, Arthur."

"Craig already knows."

"How did y'all find out?"

"He said he had to get your keys out of your purse to move your car and he found the test in there."

"Shit!" She pulled the test out of her purse, so that she could throw it away.

"That's it?"

"Yeah."

She couldn't stop crying.

"What am I going to tell Craig? I can't tell him that I don't want it when we talked about having another baby this year. I've got to go, Arthur. I'll talk to you later."

She got out of his car and walked over to the dumpster in the parking lot and threw the test out. She got back into her car, not once looking back at Arthur and drove herself home. When she arrived home, Craig was cooking chili.

"Hey baby. I thought I would give you a break and cook for you tonight."

"Thanks, baby. You are so thoughtful."

"Anything for you. Why don't you relax and I'll let you know when it's ready."

"Okay."

"Michele called. She wants you to call her back."

"Thanks baby, I will."

She decided to wait until morning before calling Michele. She could talk freely after Craig leaves for work.

While they were lying in bed later that evening, watching TV, Craig said, "Is there something you want to talk about, Kellie? You seem so distant lately."

"No. I guess I've just been a little tired. There's a lot going on at work and I've been trying to wrap up the school year. I can't wait to be home for the summer.

"Kellie, what's up, baby? We don't keep secrets and it's scaring me that you won't talk to me. I need to know why?"

"I'm talking to you, Craig."

"Are you pregnant?"

"Yes."

"Why didn't you tell me? I thought that this is something we both want."

"I thought we wanted to wait until the end of the year and I guess with it happening sooner, I wasn't ready."

"Why didn't you tell me? Why did you lie when I asked you about your period? Are you thinking about not having this baby?"

"I'm sorry I lied, I was just so caught off guard, I didn't want to say anything about it until I took the test and then after I took the test, I just wasn't ready to deal with it."

"Are you thinking about not having the baby, Kellie, because I thought we agreed that we would do this? I'm happy about it and I want this baby."

"I'm going to keep it Craig, you know that. I just wasn't ready to acknowledge it, but now that you know, I'm happy."

"Good. Come here."

They hugged and kissed and made love. The next morning Craig woke Kellie up with breakfast in bed.

"You're so sweet, Craig."

"Anything for my babies."

After Craig left, Kellie called Michele.

"What's up, Kellie?"

"They both know that I'm pregnant and I'm caught up now. Craig is so happy and he wants the baby and Arthur is going to be sweating me because he thinks the baby is his and he wants it too."

"This sounds like a soap opera. This doesn't happen in real life."

"Yes it does because it's happening to me."

"What am I going to do, Michele?"

"Pray that Craig is the father."

"I need help for real, Michele. Do you think I can get rid of it and tell them both that I had a miscarriage. Do you think they would believe me?"

"Doesn't that require a hospital visit?"

"Yeah, but I can come out there with you and say it happened while I was there."

"And you don't think Craig would be on the first flight out to see about you? Come on Kellie, you are going to have to go through with this."

"Michele I need you. Can you please come and visit me? I'm a mess."

"Alright, girl. I'll be there tomorrow, but I can only stay for a few days. I have a closing Monday, so I need to be back for that. Three days should be enough, right?"

"Yeah. Thank you."

"Alright. I'll see you tomorrow. I'll call you this evening with my flight information."

"Okay."

Kellie called Craig and told him that Michele was coming the next day to spend the weekend with her.

When Craig got off of the phone with Kellie, Arthur asked him if he talked to Kellie about the test he found.

"Yeah man, she's pregnant. Looks like we're going to have an addition to the family."

"Congratulations."

"Thanks. She said one of her girlfriends is coming in from Los Angeles tomorrow to spend the weekend. You may want to check her out. Maybe I'll put together a cookout or something Saturday. Why don't you come by the house so you can meet her?"

"What does she look like?"

"She's good looking. Your type, you know."

"Alright, I'll come by and check her out."

Kellie called off work Friday morning and went to the airport to get Michele.

Gina

Marcus was at the house by eight thirty. Gina was still upset about Marcus dating. When he came in she barely acknowledged him. He talked to the kids and then went into the kitchen to talk to her.

"How are you, Gina?"

"I'm fine, Marcus and you?"

"Fine. Look, I'm sorry about going out with someone else. I shouldn't have done it, but when I was with you the other day it confused me and I thought that being with someone else might help me keep the focus off of you."

"Maybe I should go out with someone to keep my mind off of you."

The doorbell rang and Gina went to answer it. The first applicant was an older woman, around fifty years old, all of her children were grown and out of the house and she loved children.

After seeing five applicants that day, Gina and Marcus decided that they liked the first lady, Mrs. Carver. Gina called the agency and told them that she didn't need to see anymore applicants at the moment and they would like to have Mrs. Carver come back and spend some time with the children the following morning, if that was possible.

They received a call a half hour later saying that Mrs. Carver would be at their home at eight o'clock in the morning.

Marcus said that he would be back in the morning and then left for work. Gina spent the remainder of the day preparing for her new job.

The next morning, Marcus was at the house at six thirty. When Gina came out of the shower, Marcus was sitting on the bed.

"Marcus, you scared me. What are you doing here?"

"I miss you. I was hoping that we could get together before Mrs. Carver gets here."

"I don't think so, Marcus."

"Why, Gina?"

"You're dating, Marcus, fuck your girlfriend."

"She's not my girlfriend. I need you."

"You're horny, Marcus. I'm good enough to fuck, but you can't say if I'm good enough to be your wife any longer. So since you can't make the decision, I'll make it for you. I don't need to be married to you any longer. If you loved me, you would forgive me and we would get on with our lives, but you're dating Marcus; that tells me a lot. I understand that you can't forgive me and I accept it, but don't think you're going to keep sleeping with me

127

under the pretense that you are considering working things out when you know you don't want to. I'm not gonna be here to satisfy you until you start fucking someone else."

"That's not it, Gina. I do love you and I'm trying to get past what happened, but in the meantime, I do need sex baby; and I was hoping I could get it from you so that I don't have to turn to anyone else."

"You do what you have to do, baby. If I'm not good enough to be your wife, then you don't need to have sex with me."

"Fine, if that's how you want it."

He went downstairs and watched TV until Mrs. Carver arrived. When she arrived, Gina explained to her that she and Marcus were separated. Mrs. Carver spent a couple of hours with the kids while Marcus and Gina were there and then a couple more hours with them while they were gone. Mrs. Carver came back again the next morning at six o'clock and went through the routine with Gina.

Monday morning Mrs. Carver was at the house at six o'clock and she took over as nanny. Gina was out of the house and on her way to work by eight o'clock. When she arrived in the office, Herbert was waiting for her.

"Gina, I hate to do this to you, but I don't have anyone else to do this. I need you to interview Rick Winters."

"The baseball player?"

"I'm so happy that you know who he is. Tommy, the sports guy had an emergency and there is no one else to interview Rick and he's already here. If we don't do this now, he'll never come back."

"Is this an on air interview?"

"We'll be filming, yeah. Don't worry about it. We'll film it now and edit later. Right now all you have to do is talk to him. Tommy left some questions for you to ask."

"Okay, Herbert. Where is he?"

"You are the absolute best, Gina. I will never forget this. Come on."

When Gina walked into the studio, Rick stood up to be introduced.

Herbert said, "Rick, I'm so sorry, but Tommy had an emergency. Gina Gibson will be interviewing you. Gina, this is Rick Winters, Rick, Gina Gibson."

"It's a pleasure to meet you, Gina."

"And you too, Rick."

"I'm going to leave you two alone to get to know each other before we start the interview. I'll be back in about a half hour or so," Herbert said.

"Rick, I'm sorry that Tommy isn't here and you got stuck with me, but I'll do my best to make it as comfortable as possible for you. I guess the question that everyone wants to know is when will you be back in the lineup? I understand that your injury isn't as bad as originally thought and you are healthy enough to play."

"Herbert said that Tommy left questions for you to ask and that this is your first day working here. You seem knowledgeable, do you follow baseball?"

"Some. I've always been a fan of the Generals. I've been to a few games in the past couple of years, so I guess I can say I know a little something."

They talked about baseball and other sports and life in Memphis. Herbert reappeared a short time later.

"Are you guys ready? Gina I need you to go to makeup so that we can get this show on the road."

"Where is makeup?"

One of the stagehands showed her where to go. Twenty minutes later Gina was back on the set and ready to interview.

The interview went better than everyone expected. Rick and Gina had a chemistry that everyone on the set could see. The interview was carefree and informative like old friends talking. Afterwards, when the cameras were off, Rick asked Gina if she was available for lunch.

"Yes, I would like that. Let me talk to Herbert for a minute and then I'll be ready."

"Herbert, if it's okay with you, I'm going to grab some lunch with Rick. I'll be back shortly."

"Sure Gina, enjoy. Thank you so much for doing a great job. See me when you return, we need to talk."

Gina and Rick went to a local restaurant and had lunch. She found out that Rick was married, but in the process of divorcing. She told him that she was married, but separated and things didn't look good.

"Do you have any children, Gina?"

"Yes, two sons. They are two and three. Do you?"

"Yes. One son and a daughter. My son is four and my daughter is three."

"We're both divorcing with young children. I just hope my children aren't affected negatively because of this."

"That's what I was thinking, too. Can we get together again for lunch, dinner or coffee, something? I would really like to see you again."

"I'd like that, Rick. Look, I'd better get back to work since this is my first day."

They started walking towards the station.

"Are you working because you're separated?"

"Yes, but it's not because I need the money, my husband is maintaining the household. Since he isn't there anymore, I needed to get out of the house and have contact with other adults."

"Can we have dinner tomorrow?"

She wrote her cell phone number on a piece of paper and handed it to him and said, "Call me later this evening and I'll let you know. I need to see what's going on with this job and I also need to know how things are working out with the new nanny."

"Okay, Gina, I'll talk to you soon."

When she went into the station she saw Tiffany.

"Girl, whatever you did, you definitely found a friend in Herbert. He said you did a great job on that interview and that he may have other plans for you. He's waiting for you in his office."

"Alright. Let me see what he has to say. I'll talk to you later, Tiffany."

She knocked on his door. He stood up and said, "Gina, come in, come in and have a seat."

After she was seated he said, "That was a great interview you did with Rick Winters. The cameramen and everyone else on the set agreed that you have great stage presence and they thought that you did one of the best interviews they had seen in a long time."

"Thank you."

"I was wondering if you are interested in doing more interviews. It will be a huge increase in salary and a promotion. It may require a little more of your time. I know you said you wanted to work part-time and it can remain part-time, but instead of three days, can you work four?"

"Can I give you my answer about this tomorrow, Herbert? I'm already making an adjustment from housewife to the workforce and I had no intentions of being on air, so this is a big adjustment. I'll have to see what I can work out and I'll let you know tomorrow."

"Okay, Gina that sounds good. I look forward to working with you in which ever capacity you decide. You really came through for me this morning and I'll never forget that."

Marcus' car was in the driveway when Gina arrived home. Mrs. Carver was gone and Marcus and the kids were in the yard in the pool. When

Marcus saw Gina standing on the patio, he waved her over. She gave the boys a kiss and spoke to Marcus.

"Mrs. Carver is gone?"

"Yes. I told her she could leave since I was here."

"I wanted to talk to her and see how things went."

"She said the boys were very well behaved and she didn't have any problems out of them. She also said that Marcus seemed to be quite advanced for his age and that she is looking forward to spending more time with them."

"That's great. I was worried all day about them."

"Maybe you should stay home with them, so that way you won't have to worry."

"Don't start, Marcus."

"So how was your first day?"

"Busy. I was offered a promotion into a new position."

"What! After the first day? Who's trying to get with you, Gina?"

"No one is trying to get with me, Marcus. I did an interview with Rick Winters this morning and they thought I did such a great job that they want me to do more interviews."

"Rick Winters?"

"Yes. I was looking at the schedule and there is an interview scheduled with Jeff Lee."

"The quarterback?"

"Yes. I guess they are getting ready to start training."

"I don't like this, Gina. You said you were going to be a writer, but now you're around all of these men."

"I never knew you were so insecure Marcus. It's a job and I liked doing the interview today and I think I'll enjoy doing more. I was originally scheduled for three days a week as a writer, but Herbert told me that he would need me four days for this new position. I really don't want to leave the kids so much, but until I get established, I'll have to do the four days."

"I guess Mrs. Carver will be raising the kids then."

"You know how you found your way over here to spend time with them today? You can do that more often. Just because I'm not here all of the time doesn't mean that you can't be. We have to work together, Marcus, and if you see that I'm not around enough then you can step up."

"How much is the job paying?"

"I'll know tomorrow and I'll let you know then."

"Why don't you put on your bathing suit and join us."

"Okay, I'll be back."

Gina joined them a short time later. They had an enjoyable time together in the pool, relaxing and they later ordered a pizza. Once the kids were in bed, Marcus again tried to get intimate with Gina, but she again rebuffed his advances.

The next day, Gina accepted the position. She'd do one interview a week and also some writing. Tommy was back in the office and thanked her for filling in for him while he was out. Herbert called her down to the editing room to look at the film from yesterday. They were all impressed with the way she handled herself on camera and the way she was able to get Rick to open up and talk to her.

She was given an office and an assistant. Later that afternoon she received a call from Rick inquiring about dinner.

"I won't be able to go this evening. How about Friday? My soon-to-be ex will have the kids for the weekend and I'll feel more comfortable not worrying about getting home to them."

"Okay, Gina. I look forward to seeing you. I'll call you Friday afternoon with the arrangements."

"I'll be waiting to hear from you."

When she came in from work, Mrs. Carver was there and they were able to talk and get an assessment of what was going on. Mrs. Carver liked the kids and they liked her and were getting along very well.

Gina was getting accustomed to the station and her new position. She happily prepared for her interview with Jeff Lee which was set for the following Monday. He was twenty eight years old, single, a known playboy and he was ranked number one quarterback in the NFL. Tommy helped her put together some questions and made sure she was well informed. She had lots of reading materials to go over before the interview. Tommy did a mock interview with her to make sure she was able to cover all the bases.

Marcus began calling more often, not saying that he wanted to come home and resume being husband and wife, but instead inquiring about her job, who she'd met and other questions she found ridiculous.

When Friday arrived, Gina was excited about her date with Rick. He told her that he would pick her up at eight o'clock. Marcus was getting the boys at four o'clock on his way home from work.

Marcus was at the house when Gina arrived at home. The boys were packed and ready to go.

"I wanted to give them a chance to say bye to you. What are you going to do all weekend with no kids?"

"I have to prepare for this interview Monday. I'll probably have lunch with Pamela tomorrow. Who knows?"

"Well, enjoy yourself and we'll see you Sunday evening."

"Okay."

After they left, Gina prepared for her date with Rick. She didn't want to under dress and look sleazy. She called Michele for some advice.

"Hey Gina, long time no hear."

"I know I've been pretty busy. I started a job Monday at a TV station."

"A job? We really haven't talked, have we? How did this come about?"

"I needed to get out of the house. I'll call you tomorrow with all of the details, but I have an emergency now and I know only you can help me."

"I'm in Chicago with Kellie right now, so call me at home Sunday evening. What is the problem you need help with?"

"What's up with Kellie?"

"Long story, we'll talk. What do you need help with?"

"I have a date."

"A date? What is going on with everyone? You have a date; Kellie and Stacey are pregnant..."

"What! Did you say Kellie was pregnant?"

"Shit! Yeah. She wasn't ready to tell everyone yet. We'll talk later. So you have a date. With who?"

"His name is Rick Winters. I met him while I was interviewing him at work."

"We really need to talk about this job, but what's the problem. I can't believe you are going on a date."

"I don't know what to wear, Michele."

"What kind of man is he?"

"He's a professional baseball player. He's a starting pitcher for the Generals. He's tall, dark, muscular and handsome."

"How did you pull that off?"

"I had to interview him and we hit it off and he asked me out."

"What about Marcus?"

"Marcus went on a date last week. If he can date, so can I."

"Be careful, Gina. Listen, you don't want to look easy on the first date. Wear something dressy, but not suited up like you're going to work. Do you have a little black dress?"

"Yes."

"Wear that, wear your hair down, nice pair of pumps, nice jewelry. Pearls look good on you, wear your pearl necklace and earrings. You don't want to look like a slut nor do you want to look like you're going to work. You want him to respect you."

"Okay, I'll wear the dress. I'll talk to you Sunday, Michele. I've got to get in the shower. He's going to be here at eight o'clock and I want to be ready."

"Okay, I can't wait to hear about this job, this man, everything. Have fun girl and I'll talk to you later."

Rick was there at eight o'clock on the dot and Gina was ready. He took her to a downtown restaurant and afterwards they went on Beale Street to listen to some blues. Gina found out that Rick's wife was contesting the divorce and had unbelievable demands to stall the divorce. He said that he caught her cheating. She had gotten his schedule mixed up and he came home and found her in their bed with another man.

Gina didn't give the details about her separation. She just said that they were not getting along anymore. She told him that Marcus started dating, so she thought it was time that she did too.

Rick dropped Gina off at home at one o'clock a.m. They shared a brief kiss and he was on his way, promising to call her the next day.

Marcus called Gina first thing the next morning. When she answered the phone he said, "How was your date, Gina?"

"What are you talking about, Marcus?"

"Bob said he saw you last night with Rick Winters at a club. Is that true, Gina? Are you dating Rick Winters?"

"He took me to dinner, Marcus, that's it."

"Did you sleep with him?"

"Fuck you." She hung up the phone. Marcus called back immediately.

"Does that mean yes, Gina?"

"No, it doesn't. Just because I went to dinner with him doesn't mean I slept with him."

"You didn't have any problem sleeping with those men in Vegas, so I just assumed since you were dating a big famous baseball player, you would definitely let him hit it. I'm your husband and I can't get none, but everyone else can."

"Marcus, you can kiss my ass. Don't call me again!"

She hung up again. He called back, but she didn't answer the phone. Instead, she showered and dressed and went shopping. She wanted new clothes for work and the way she was feeling, she was going to burn up Marcus' black card. She went to Peabody Place and spent seven hundred dollars at Victoria's Secret alone. She then went to Wolfchase Galleria and went into Goldsmith's and spent another five thousand dollars on clothes and accessories. It took four trips from her car to get all of these items into the house. She had a hair appointment in thirty minutes so she left everything in the middle of the floor in the familyroom and ran out of the house for her appointment. Marcus had been calling her on her cell phone for hours, but she ignored it.

The phone was ringing as she came in the door from her hair appointment. She saw that it was Marcus again and let it go to voicemail. Rick called during the time that she was ignoring calls. He left a message saying that he enjoyed her company last night and hoped that they could get together again soon.

She called him back.

"Hello."

"Good afternoon Rick, I'm sorry I missed your call."

"Pretty busy today, huh?"

"Yeah, I had to do some shopping. I need some work clothes and I can't think of another time when I'll get a chance to shop. How are you today?"

"Okay, thinking about when I'll get a chance to see you again. I'm leaving for a road trip this evening and I wanted to talk to you before I left town."

"I'm glad you called. Maybe when you're back in town we can get together."

"How about you come to my next home game? I would love to look in the stands and see you."

"Okay, I'll do that."

"Alright Gina, I'll call you soon. I'll be on the road for the next six days, but I'll call you while I'm out."

"I look forward to hearing from you."

"Feel free to call me if you want to talk."

"I will."

Marcus continued to call all afternoon. Gina finally answered the phone.

"Hello."

"Where have you been, Gina? I've been calling the house and your cell phone. Why didn't you answer?"

"Because I didn't want to argue with you."

"I just want to know what's going on. I didn't know that we agreed to start dating other people."

"You've been dating Marcus, so why shouldn't I?"

"I guess you don't want to work things out with me then?"

"We're not going to be able to work things out, Marcus. If you wanted to be with me, you would be with me. I've accepted that this marriage is over and yes it's my fault and I've come to terms with that too. I'll be filing for divorce next week. I've already called Megan to get the paperwork started."

"You're filing for divorce?"

"Yes. I don't want to live like this. You moved out of the house and we are not working towards being together, we are growing further apart."

"Are you doing this so that you can be free to date?"

"I went on a date while we're still married, Marcus, so being married or divorced doesn't make a difference. You should know that."

"You're right. I just don't want to rush into a divorce, Gina. I'm not ready for that yet. I know that I still love you and I loved the life we were living. Please don't file yet, give it some time and let's see how things go in the next month or so, okay?"

"Okay, Marcus. I won't file yet."

"Are you going to continue to see Rick Winters?"

"I don't know. We just went to dinner, that's all."

"Look, I have to take the kids to the movies. They are waiting for me. We need to finish this conversation soon."

"I agree."

Michele

When Michele finished her call with Stacey, Kellie called with a big problem. She's pregnant and don't know who is the father. She asked Michele to come and visit her for the weekend. Michele made arrangements and told Kellie she would be there the next day.

When she arrived at the airport in Chicago, Kellie was outside waiting for her. She put her bags in the the back of the car and hopped in. They briefly hugged.

"What's going on, Kellie?"

She looked at Michele with tears in her eyes.

"I'm scared, Michele. I don't know whose baby this is. Craig will kill me if this isn't his child."

"Have you stopped seeing Arthur?"

"I haven't seen him in a few days. He wants the baby too. He wants me to leave Craig. It's all a big mess, Michele."

When they arrived at Kellie's house, Arthur was there helping Craig with something in the garage.

"That's Arthur, Michele."

"Damn girl, he is fine as hell!"

"I told you that. I'm so nervous when he's around Craig. I'm so scared that he's going to tell him something."

"Have you talked to Arthur about terminating the pregnancy?"

"No. I haven't talked to him since I confessed to being pregnant."

"Come on, let's get out of the car."

Craig and Arthur met them at the car.

Craig said, "Michele, it's so good to see you again. How are you?"

"I'm good, Craig. How are you?"

"Good, real good. I'm sure Kellie told you our good news."

"Yes. C.J.'s going to have a sibling."

"Yeah, hopefully we'll get a girl this time. I'm sorry, Michele this is my partner Arthur, Arthur – Michele."

"Nice to meet you, Arthur."

"You too, Michele."

Craig said, "Let me get your bags."

He took her bags in and put them in the guest room. They hung around for a little while and socialized, but Craig and Arthur had to go back to work. They were still on duty.

Once Michele and Kellie were alone again, Michele said, "Damn Kellie, you have a big mess on your hands honey and I don't know what to tell you that will help."

"I know, Michele. You told me not to do it, but I couldn't control myself. What if it's Arthur's baby, Michele? What am I supposed to do? Arthur will tell Craig if it's his."

"Stop worrying about it right now. You'll find out when the baby is here. When are you due?"

"I don't know, I have an appointment with my doctor Monday. I'll find out everything then."

Michele stayed with Kellie until Sunday afternoon. Craig tried to get her to hook-up with Arthur, but she wasn't interested and neither was he. He couldn't keep his eyes off of Kellie. Arthur was in love with Kellie and Michele could see it and was wondering why Craig couldn't. She was sad for the situation her friend was in, but there was nothing she could do to help her at the time.

When Michele arrived home, she had a message from Gina and called her immediately.

"Gina, girl what is going on with you having a job and dating? What is Marcus saying about all of this?"

"You know he is not happy and the only reason I felt it was okay for me to date is because he went on a date."

"What!"

"Yes. One of my friends saw him out with some chick and I confronted him. He tried to downplay it like it was nothing. I slept with him that morning and later that evening he took someone else out, so fuck it Michele, I'm through. I love Marcus, but he's not going to get over what happened. He keeps trying to get with me for sex, but he can't decide if he wants to be married to me anymore. So I asked him for a divorce."

"A divorce? Isn't that jumping the gun?"

"I don't think so. Why drag it out? I'm not going to sit back and watch him date other women and fuck around for a while and then try to come back to me. I'm letting go now."

"Does he know that your date was with Rick Winters?"

"Yeah and he was furious. He's mad that I'm working in the sports department at the station. He has the nerve to act jealous, but he doesn't want to be with me. He wants to have his cake and eat it too, but I'm not having it. If he can date, so can I."

"I heard that, girl. So what's Rick Winters like?"

"He's real cool. I had a lot of fun with him. He's easy to talk to and he's going through a divorce too. His wife is trying every trick in the book to stop the divorce, but he doesn't want to be married to her anymore. Maybe we'll be divorced at the same time."

"Wouldn't that be convenient?"

"Guess who I'm interviewing tomorrow?"

"Who?"

"Jeff Lee."

"Number twenty eight?"

"Yes girl. I'm a little nervous. What if I make a fool of myself?"

"You'll be fine. You sure did get lucky with this job. What if Jeff asks you out, will you go?"

"I don't know. I don't want to be known as the station slut. They know I went to lunch with Rick already. I can't go out with every person I interview. Plus, who said he would even ask?"

"Girl, you know you look good, so does Marcus, that's why he's clowning."

"Looks ain't everything, Michele. Because if we went by looks and Marcus thought I looked so good, he would be at home with his family and I wouldn't be talking about dating other people."

"You're right, Gina."

"What is going on with Kellie?"

"You are not going to believe this. Don't say anything to her about this because she doesn't want anyone to know, but you know she's pregnant, right?"

"Yeah, you told me that."

"Well, she don't know who the baby daddy is."

"Get the hell outta here, Michele. Are you for real?"

"Yeah. She started messing around with Craig's partner and now she don't know which one of them got her pregnant."

"She's keeping it?"

"They found out before she could do anything about it."

"They?"

"Yeah. Both of them know she's pregnant and they both want her to keep it. And Craig's partner, Arthur, besides being fine as hell, he's in love with Kellie. He wants her to leave Craig so that they can be together."

"Girl, shut up! I don't believe this soap opera. What is she going to do?"

"She gonna have the baby and hope and pray that Craig is the daddy because if he ain't, there's gonna be some real trouble in that delivery room."

"I don't believe this Michele. How did she get caught up like that?"

"Lusting."

"Speaking of Lust, have you seen him since Vegas?"

"Girl, that's another story. It turns out Nick is Lust's manager. I made that discovery while trying to sell Lust a house. Nick squashed any communication about Vegas so we're cool now. I had to tell Nick what happened and he told me what happens in Vegas, stays in Vegas."

"I heard that. I can't wait to meet him in September. When is Stacey due, before or after the reception?"

"I think she is due in August. She should have already had the baby before the reception."

"Good. I won't have to make two trips. Well, it was good catching up with you, Michele. I'll talk to you soon. I need to start getting ready for work tomorrow. I went to the mall this weekend and charged about six thousand dollars worth of clothes and stuff on Marcus' card. He's gonna be pissed, but I'll deal with him when the time comes."

"You are crazy. I'll talk to you later."

Michele started spending more time with Nick. One evening over dinner, Nick asked Michele if she would like to go to Hawaii for a week or so.

"Yes, I would love that Nick. I need to get away for a while."

"Do you have a travel agent?"

"Yes."

"Can you check on some packages for September? Is that good for you?"

"I'm going to Denver for a few days in September, to my friend's reception, and I was hoping you would be able to go with me."

"What days?" He pulled out his Blackberry.

"Friday the 3rd returning the 5th."

"I can do that."

"Great. Why don't we make it all one trip. When we leave Denver, go on to Hawaii?"

"Okay, I'll call my travel agent and see what I can set up. Seven days in Hawaii?"

"How about ten? I really need to get away and I want to relax and not rush back."

"Okay. I'll call her tomorrow."

Michele made the reservations for their trip to Denver and Hawaii. Nick gave her his credit card to pay for the entire trip.

Over the following months Michele had to continuously fight off the females that were trying to take her man while she and Nick grew closer. She told him everything about herself that she thought was important enough for him to know and he did the same. She had never been this close to a man and he confessed that he had never had a relationship with any woman like the one he was having with Michele and he was very happy. They were both looking forward to their vacation which was coming up in two weeks. Michele had been shopping for herself and Nick all summer getting ready for their trip.

When Friday September 3rd arrived, Nick had a limo pick them up from Michele's house. They arrived in Denver and went straight to their hotel. Michele called Stacey and told her that they arrived safely.

Stacey

Stacey and Richard were decorating the baby's room when she felt her first labor pain. She tried to continue putting the baby's things away. They moved into their new home three days ago and were still trying to get organized. The baby wasn't due for another two weeks, but when Stacey's water broke, she knew the baby would be born within a matter of hours.

Stacey gave birth to Robert Kenneth Phillips at twenty three minutes after eleven that night. Richard called everyone and told them about the baby and that Stacey would call them the next day to talk.

Stacey didn't talk to Kellie, Gina or Michele until she was home and they got on a conference call.

They all were looking forward to getting together next month so that they could get caught up and for everyone to see Robert.

Kellie told everyone that she was pregnant. She didn't mention Arthur. Gina told everyone that she was getting divorced and that she had a job. Michele told everyone that she was deliriously happy in her relationship with Nick and that she was bringing him with her to Denver to meet everyone.

Stacey and Richard had less than a month to finalize the reception, but they were looking forward to the party and for everyone to see Robert.

The morning before the reception, Stacey received a call from Michele saying that she and Nick were in town and that they would be at Stacey and Richard's house in a couple of hours. Kellie and Gina were expected to arrive shortly.

Kellie

After circling around the airport twice, she saw Michele as she approached the United Airlines pick-up area. Michele hopped in the car; they hugged and got right to it. She told Michele everything that was going on and felt so much better to be able to talk about it with someone.

When they arrived at the house, Craig and Arthur were in the garage. It was the first time Kellie had seen Arthur since he found out that she was pregnant. He kept staring at her. While Craig and Michele were upstairs putting her bags away, Arthur wrapped his arms around Kellie and put his hands on her stomach and said, "I've been missing you, Kellie. I don't know if this is my baby or not, but I want to be a part of his life if he's mine. I can't be without you, baby, I miss you so much. Don't you miss me?"

She didn't pull away because she couldn't. She was where she wanted to be.

"Yes, I miss you, Arthur."

"When can I see you?"

"Not until after Michele leaves."

"Does she know about us?"

"Yes."

"Does she know this might be my child?"

"Yes."

They heard Craig and Michele coming down the stairs. Kellie sat down.

Michele stayed until Sunday. Craig kept trying to get Arthur and Michele together, but they both knew what was up. After Michele left Sunday afternoon, Kellie concentrated on getting the year-end closed out at work and looked forward to going to Denver in September.

Kellie continued to see Arthur and she was becoming more attached to him and was entertaining the idea of leaving Craig, if she was indeed carrying Arthur's baby.

When September arrived, Kellie had a little tummy, nothing that couldn't be covered, but enough for Craig and Arthur to feel.

Arthur would be transferred to another district when Craig returned from Denver. He put in a request a month ago and it finally came through. He didn't tell Craig, he thought it best that he told him after the transfer took effect while Craig was out of town.

After dropping C.J. off at Craig's mother's house for the weekend, Kellie and Craig made their way to the airport to catch their flight.

Kellie and Craig arrived in Denver the day before the reception. They checked into their hotel and then found their way to Stacey's house. There were a couple of cars in the driveway of Stacey and Richard's beautiful home.

Stacey saw Kellie and Craig as they were getting out of the car and met them at the door. After hugging everyone, they all made their way into the great room where Michele, Nick and Richard were oohing and ahhing all over the baby. Richard greeted Kellie and Craig and Michele introduced them to Nick.

They were all taking turns holding Robert. He was a beautiful baby. Just as Stacey began a tour of the house, Gina and Jeff arrived.

Gina

When Marcus brought the kids back after their weekend together, he and Gina sat down at the kitchen table and had a heart to heart.

He began, "Gina, I love you and I don't think I'll ever be as in love with anyone again the way I'm in love with you. I've tried to get past what you did in Vegas, but I can't. This is hard for me, but I can't continue in this marriage. I know that I may regret it down the line, but it's unfair to you to keep you hanging on, wondering what I want. Like I said before, I don't want to rush into a divorce. I was hoping that we can continue with the separation for now. What do you think?"

"I knew when you left that you weren't coming back, Marcus. I know you and I know that you will never be able to get over what I've done. I never dreamed this day would come. I never dreamed that we would raise our kids separately. I never dreamed that I would live my life without you, but here it is. I'm a big girl, Marcus and I'll be strong for my kids. We'll be okay. I'm not mad at you because it's not your fault. I did this and I accept it. So let's do what we have to do to move on to the next step."

"I wanted to tell you that I'm going to see Miranda again. She is the lady that I had dinner with last week. I don't want someone calling you again telling you they saw me on a date. I think we should be honest and upfront so that we can get through this as easily as possible. Are you going to continue to see Rick?"

"Yes."

"Are you going to have a relationship with him?"

"I don't know, Marcus. We went to dinner. I'll see him when he comes back from his road trip. I'm not trying to get involved in a relationship with anyone right now. I need to resolve things with you before I can move on to another man."

"So you're going to date a bunch of different men?"

"I may not date for a while, Marcus. It's not about me dating anyone. I've lost you, Marcus. I need to deal with that. I don't understand why you are so concerned with me dating. We are over. It shouldn't concern you any longer."

"Gina, I love you and I always will. I guess the thought of you being with another man hurts. I can't stand the thought of it. Although I don't think I can be in a relationship with you, I can't stand the thought of you giving yourself to another man. I guess I'm selfish."

They hugged and promised to keep things civil for the children's sake.

When Gina walked into the station Monday morning, Tiffany was waiting for her.

"Girl, Jeff Lee came in this morning and I swear he is better looking in person than he is on TV. Oh, my God!"

"Really, Tiff? I hope I can do this interview without drooling."

"You look just as good as he does. You are wearing the shit out of that dress."

"If these interviews are going to be shown on television, I need to have my hair and wardrobe together. Girl, when Marcus gets the bill for this stuff, he is going to explode. Herbert told me I get a clothing allowance, but he didn't tell me how much. How can I find that out?"

"See Brenda in accounting. She can tell you about all of your accounts."

"I better hurry up and do that so when Marcus asks about the six thousand dollars I spent, I can at least tell him that the station is paying for some of it. Let me call Brenda."

"Okay Gina and good luck with your interview."

"Thanks, I need it."

After talking with accounting and discovering a very generous clothing allowance, Gina made her way to Herbert's office to go over the schedule.

He hurried her to make-up because Jeff Lee was already there. Jeff and Tommy were on the set when Gina arrived. They were introduced. Then Tommy, Jeff and Gina went over some of the questions that Gina would be asking.

When it was time to shoot, Gina felt pretty comfortable with Jeff and he seemed relaxed as well. Tiffany was right; the cameras did him no justice. He wore a nice fitting pair of jeans, a fitted leather shirt (open in the chest), his hair was in short twists, diamond earring in his left ear and he smelled good.

The interview went well. Herbert and Tommy were ecstatic. Gina talked to Jeff for a few minutes before he left with his entourage.

Tiffany was in Gina's office waiting for her after the interview.

"How was he?"

"He's a very nice guy. Not what I expected. Everyone is always talking about how he's a player and stuff, but I didn't sense that. He seemed kind of shy to me, but girl, he is one of the best looking men I have ever seen in my entire life."

"No offer for lunch this time, huh?"

"Naw, he was all about business."

"So who are you interviewing next?"

"Tommy is trying to get Jimmy Ross next week. He's another quarterback. I won't know until tomorrow."

Gina talked to Rick briefly about getting together when he returns. While she was going over some documents on her desk, Tommy came into her office to deliver a message.

"Jeff Lee wanted to know if he can call you. He asked me a thousand questions about you. I'm sure you can tell that he's shy and I guess he is used to women approaching him. He rarely has to make a move, but he is definitely interested in you."

"Really? I would have never known. Is he that shy that he was scared to ask me for my number?"

"Yeah, I guess so."

"Well if he wants to talk to me, he'll have to do it himself. He is gone, isn't he?"

"Yeah, he left with his entourage about an hour ago."

When Gina came out of the station, Jeff was leaning against her car waiting for her.

"Jeff, what are you doing here?"

"I wanted to ask you out to dinner. Are you available this evening?"

"I'm sorry, but I'm not."

"Okay, Gina."

"I'm available tomorrow though, if that's okay."

"Okay."

They made arrangements for dinner. Jeff planned to pick her up at the station and they would go from there.

Marcus was at the house when Gina came in.

"How was your interview today?"

"It went very well and how was your day?"

"Good."

"I'm going to have dinner with Tiffany tomorrow after work, so I may be a little late getting home. I'll speak to Mrs. Carver about it. I don't know how often you will be stopping by, so I don't want to put that on you."

"I'll come by when I get off from work until you get home."

"Mrs. Carver can stay."

"No, I'll do it."

"Alright, Marcus.

While Gina was looking for something to wear to work the next day and something for her date, she thought about Marcus being there when she came in. She didn't want to wear something that would make his antennas go up, but then she thought about it. He left her and she can dress however she wants and see who she wants to. She decided on a dress that she knew would get Jeff's attention.

Her work day went on without event. Jeff was at the station at six o'clock and they headed to the restaurant shortly thereafter. Dinner was great. She liked him, but he was shy. All of those stories she heard about him were not true. He wasn't forward in any way like the stories said. He hadn't been in a relationship in over a year, but was looking for someone to spend his time with. She told him that she was getting divorced and that she had been on one date. He has a three year old son who lives with the baby's mother. They are on good terms, so there is no drama there. He and Gina are the same age and he is from New York. He asked Gina if he could see her again the next day and she said yes, for lunch.

"I can't spend so much time away from my kids, so if we can do lunch that would be great."

"Okay, I'll see you at noon."

He took her back to her car. When she arrived home, it was eleven forty-five p.m. Marcus was in the family room watching TV. The kids were asleep.

As soon as he saw Gina he said, "That's what you wore to dinner with Tiffany?"

"Marcus, don't start please."

"Come on Gina, we said we would be honest."

"Okay, I went to dinner with Jeff Lee."

"I knew this job was going to be a problem. Every time you go to work someone is asking you out."

"That's not true. Just like with Rick, we only had dinner."

"But you said you were going to continue to see Rick."

"I don't know what I'm going to do, Marcus. I probably shouldn't have gone out with either of them, but I did and I had a good time. Let's leave it at that. I haven't said anything about your date."

"There is nothing to say, Gina. I told you I was dating Miranda. I'm not keeping anything from you."

"You haven't been sweating me for sex, so are you sleeping with her?"

He didn't say anything.

148

"I'll take that as yes, Marcus."

"Listen, Gina. You know what I need and you weren't giving it to me. What am I supposed to do?"

She started crying.

"Fine, Marcus."

"Gina, please don't cry. I tried to tell you what I needed, but you didn't care."

"I was giving you what you needed! I was doing all kinds of things for you to show you how much I loved you and wanted to satisfy you, but I'm not good enough for you Marcus, remember?"

"Come here, baby, I'm sorry."

She wiped her face, pulled away from him and screamed, "DON'T TOUCH ME!"

She ran upstairs, went into the bathroom and cried for the next ten minutes. Marcus was trying to talk to her, but she ignored him. She came out of the bathroom and asked him to leave so that she could get ready for work.

He eventually left. Gina found a pair of jeans and a top to wear. Most of the people at the station dressed in jeans unless they had to go on the air. She just didn't have the energy to find something dressy.

After her morning meetings, she went back to her office and there were flowers from Jeff on her desk. She was looking forward to seeing him.

At lunch she told him about last night with Marcus and that she went on a date with Rick Winters. He decided to tell her that he had been dating a well-known actress, but he broke it off about three weeks ago.

Her cell phone kept ringing, it was Marcus. She didn't answer. When she got back to her office, she had messages from Rick and Marcus. She called Rick. They talked briefly. He was on his way to the airport. He told her that he was looking forward to seeing her when he returned.

She avoided Marcus for the next few days. She didn't answer his calls and he left the house before she came home.

When Rick returned to town, he left tickets at Will-Call for Gina. She and Tiffany attended the game together. They arrived early so that Gina could talk to Rick before the game. They agreed to meet for dinner afterwards. Gina made arrangements with Mrs. Carver for the days she had to work late or was going out. Mrs. Carver had her own bedroom at their house that she could use to relax or if she wanted to stay overnight.

Rick's wife showed up and confronted Gina while she was talking to Rick.

"Excuse me, groupie, but this is my husband. I don't know what he told you, but he is still very much married."

"First of all, Mrs. Winters, I am not a groupie. Your "HUSBAND" invited me to this game. I don't chase men sweetheart, and secondly I suggest you get out of my face before some real drama jumps off in here. Rick, call me when you get this under control."

She went back to the stands where Tiffany was waiting and said, "Come on, let's get out of here."

"What happened, Gina?"

"Girl, I was talking to Rick and his wife showed up trying to start some drama, but I don't have time for that. I am not going to fight for a man."

"What did he say?"

"He really didn't have a chance to say anything. I told him to work that situation out with her and I walked away."

"Well, I guess we can go back to work."

"You can if you want to, I'm going shopping. You coming?"

"Yeah, let's go."

While they were at the mall, Jeff called and asked Gina if she was free for dinner. She said yes, gave him her home address and told him that she would be ready by seven o'clock.

Gina and Jeff started seeing each other exclusively. On their fifth date, Jeff chartered a plane and took Gina to New York to meet his family and to have dinner.

They stayed in New York overnight at the Waldorf and made love for the first time. Jeff may have been shy when it came to meeting people, but he wasn't shy at all in the bedroom. He was very romantic. He set the scene to perfection. He obviously had someone light candles throughout the suite before they returned from dinner. Rose pedals were sprinkled on the floors and furniture leading to the master bedroom as soft music played. When Gina saw this, she turned to Jeff and kissed him. He lifted her and held her in his arms as they continued to kiss. He then carried her into the bedroom where they made passionate love that night and then again the next morning.

After Gina and Jeff's first night of making love, they started spending most of their spare time together. Gina introduced Jeff and his son, little Jeff, to the kids. Marcus wasn't happy at all about Gina dating, but the relationship between Marcus and Gina was over.

When Marcus received the bill for the Black Card, he called Gina at work to get an explanation. She told him that she would pay half of the bill. He responded by saying, "Are you going to get the money from Jeff?"

"No, I have a clothing allowance and I will give you the money out of that."

"Don't worry about it, Gina. I was just surprised when I got the bill. I'll cover it."

"Thank you, Marcus."

Although Jeff was in training camp, they spent as much time together as possible. Gina asked Jeff if he would like to go with her to Denver and he said yes. She didn't tell Michele, Stacey or Kellie that she was bringing him. She didn't tell them how close she and Jeff had become. They were all under the impression that Gina dated other people and that she and Jeff saw each other on occasion.

When September rolled around, Gina convinced Marcus to keep the kids while she went to Denver. When she and Jeff arrived at Stacey's house hand-in-hand, for the first time that anyone could remember, Michele was speechless.

Once she found her voice, they all hugged and the introductions were made. Gina took the baby and was so happy for Stacey. Robert was beautiful. Once she put the baby down, they continued with the tour of the house. They all stayed at Stacey's house until late in the night, talking, drinking and eating.

Friday, September 3 – Stacey and Richards New Home

Nick and Jeff really hit it off. They had a lot in common with both of them working in the entertainment industry. Kellie kept going on and on about how good looking Nick and Jeff were and how she couldn't believe that Gina and Marcus were over.

They talked about Kellie's baby and when the baby was due. Kellie told them that it was a girl and she was due in January. She didn't mention Arthur and she asked Michele not to mention him either.

Gina told them about how she met Jeff and her short dating experience with Rick Winters. The other girls still couldn't believe that Gina and Marcus were getting divorced.

Stacey told them about Charles and Richard making up. They would never be the way they were, but they were at least on speaking terms. Charles was not invited to the reception. No one told Carolyn why they fell out, which Stacey was thankful for.

Michele told them about running into Lust and that Nick was his manager. They were all so surprised to see Michele in a monogamous relationship. Nick and Michele were in love and it was obvious to everyone. She told them about all of the women she had to stave off and how well Nick handled it. He made sure they all knew that he was off the market and that he was in love with Michele. She also told them that she and Nick were going to Hawaii for ten days when they left Denver Sunday morning. Everyone told her that they could hear wedding bells.

When they all dragged back to the hotel, it was two thirty in the morning.

Saturday, September 4th

The reception was scheduled to begin at two o'clock in the afternoon.

Stacey

Stacey and Richard prepared for their reception. They had a lot of family and friends in town. This was a formal event. Although no one was invited to the wedding, the reception was a huge celebration. They had over three hundred invited guests. Stacey was wearing a formal gown, not a wedding dress, but everyone would be dressed up.

Gina

Gina and Jeff spent the entire morning in bed, making love, but still made it to the reception on time.

Michele

Michele and Nick were excited about their trip to Hawaii. They played around in their room for a while, ordered breakfast in and made it to the reception on time.

Kellie

While in the shower, Kellie's cell phone rang. Craig had never answered her phone before, so he let the call go to voicemail. It rang again a few minutes later and again he let the call go to voicemail. When it rang the third time, he thought that it may have been something serious, so he answered it.

Arthur's name and picture appeared on the screen as he answered it.

"Man, why you calling Kellie?"

"I was calling to make sure y'all made it alright."

"Why didn't you call me? Why are you calling my wife?"

"Man, I was just calling her for some advice."

"You were calling for advice about what, Arthur?"

"I was having a problem with this chick and I was hoping Kellie could help me."

"Man, you calling my wife asking her about some of your shit while we're out here visiting? It couldn't wait until we got home or you couldn't ask someone else? You got what, five sisters; none of them could help you?"

"Man, come on, you know Kellie always got the answer."

"Listen, Arthur, man, don't call my wife again. I gave you her number in case of an emergency, not for you to call and chit chat. You feel me?"

"Yeah man."

Craig hung up the phone. He started going through Kellie's phone and discovered that there were lots of calls to and from Arthur along with text messages regarding getting together. Kellie came out of the bathroom just as Craig finished reading the last message when Arthur said that he was going to miss his babies and to have a safe trip...

When Kellie saw Craig holding her phone, she froze.

"What are you doing, Craig?"

He swiftly walked over to her, got in her face and asked, "Are you fucking Arthur?"

"No."

"Then why is he calling you, Kellie? Your phone was ringing off the hook. I thought it was an emergency, so I answered it and what did I find?"

He grabbed her face.

"Pictures of you and Arthur, phone calls back and forth between you and Arthur, text messages, Kellie. Text messages about my baby. Whose baby are you carrying?"

"Let me go, Craig!"

"Tell the truth! Are you fucking Arthur?"

"Yes."

He pushed her up against the wall and walked away. He stopped, came back and slapped her repeatedly.

"Is this my baby, Kellie?"

"I don't know."

"What do you mean you don't know?"

"I don't know, Craig!"

"Is it Arthur's?"

"I don't know!"

"So there is a possibility that this could be Arthur's baby?"

"Yes."

He slapped her so hard this time that she slammed into the wall and then crumbled to the floor. She crawled over to a corner and put her arms up defensively. He got down on the floor, got in her face and said, "You fucking bitch. Why would you do this to me, to us, Kellie? I gave you everything."

He reached over to his shaving kit which was on the bed, pulled his shaving knife out and put it to her stomach.

"I should kill you and this baby."

"Craig, please don't do that. This might be your baby."

"Might be! It might be Arthur's baby too, you fucking whore. I can't believe this shit. That's why you didn't want to tell me that you were pregnant because you were doing so much fucking you didn't know who the daddy was. Is there anybody else, Kellie?"

"No. Craig, please move that knife away from my stomach."

He got up, walked over to the bed and started packing his things.

"What are you doing?"

"I'm leaving. I can't stay here with you. I'm going home and I'm gonna kill Arthur's ass. I know you're going to call him and warn him, but I don't give a fuck. I'm gonna kill that bastard and if I have to go to jail for the rest of my life, fuck it, I'll go to jail, but he ain't shit and I can't let this level of disrespect go. As for you, bitch, I'm gonna make sure you never see C.J. again. You can stay in the house, I don't want to live there with you another day. I don't ever want to see your ass again. And if you are carrying my baby, too motherfucking bad, that's your problem, I don't want to have anything to do with it or you bitch."

As Craig walked towards the door, Kellie reached out and grabbed his arm. He stopped, turned around and grabbed her around the neck, pushed her

157

down on the bed, leaned over her and said, "Don't you ever touch me again, bitch or I promise you, I will kill your ass. You understand?"

She struggled to get the words out because he was cutting off her air supply, but she managed to say yes.

He took his bags and left for the airport.

Kellie first called Arthur and told him what happened, so that he could be prepared. She didn't want to mess up Stacey's big day, so she got dressed and went to the reception. Her face was swelling rapidly. She wore sunglasses to cover some of the bruising and swelling.

When Kellie arrived alone, everyone asked about Craig. Michele noticed that she hadn't removed her sunglasses and knew something was wrong by Kellie's body language. Michele excused herself and pulled Kellie into a private room.

"What happened, Kellie? And where is Craig?"

"He found out. We had a fight and he is on his way to Chicago."

"How did he find out?"

"Arthur called my phone while I was in the shower and Craig answered it. Then he went through my phone and found text messages and he looked at the sent and received calls."

"Are you okay?"

"No. After he kicked my ass, he told me that he never wanted to see me again and if this is his baby that it's too bad because he doesn't want to have anything to do with it or me and that he is going to kill Arthur."

Michele took Kellie's glasses off her face and gasped at the sight of her. She had two black eyes, a busted lip and her face was swollen. She could also see the redness around her neck.

"Come here, baby." She hugged Kellie and told her how sorry she was that this happened to her and promised her that she would be there for her and her babies. She then stepped back, looked Kellie in the eyes and said, "Kellie, this is serious. You know how Craig is. If he said he is going to kill Arthur, he is going to kill him."

"I called Arthur and warned him. Hopefully Craig will calm down before he gets there. I'm going to try to call him and talk to him. I'm going to get a flight out of here after the reception."

"Okay, let me know. If you need us to go to Chicago with you, we'll go. I don't want you walking back into trouble, Kellie. I know how upset Craig gets and I think he is going to try to kill Arthur for real and you have to be careful."

"I know. He put a knife to my stomach already."

"What?"

"Yeah. He threatened to kill me and the baby."

"Call him, Kellie. Please call him now and see if you can get through to him."

"Okay. Thanks, Michele."

Kellie called Craig, but he didn't answer the phone. She left a message.

"Craig, I'm so sorry for what I did. I never meant to hurt you. I just got caught up. I never stopped loving you and I never planned to ever be with another man. Arthur just happened. When I found out that I was pregnant, I was going to get an abortion, but then you found out and I knew you were ready for another baby. How could I tell you I wanted an abortion? I didn't have an explanation for it. Please call me Craig so that we can talk. If you do something to Arthur, you will go to jail and C.J. won't have a father. I'm not worth it Craig, I'm not worth you giving up your life for. I'm the one that did wrong and I'm the one that should suffer. I love you and I'm sorry. I wish that you could please forgive me. Please don't leave me Craig, I need you. I can't have this baby without you. Call me please, I'll be waiting."

Craig didn't call her back. Michele took her to the airport to make her flight. When she got to the airport, Craig was still there waiting for the same flight. When he saw her, he got up and walked away, Kellie followed.

He went to an empty waiting area and sat down. Kellie sat next to him. Neither of them said anything for a while. Kellie was crying.

"Craig, I'm sorry. I never meant for this to happen. I'm sorry that I hurt you and if I could take it back, I would."

Craig got up and walked over to the window and looked out towards the mountains. Kellie knew he was crying. She had only seen him cry once and it was when his father died, but she knew he was crying now. She wanted to go to him, but he would probably try to kill her if she touched him.

He came back and sat down. He wiped his eyes and sniffled.

"Kellie, when we get home, I'm moving out. What you've done is unforgivable. I'm not going to touch you again or try to hurt your baby. I listened to your message and you're right, you're not worth it. I'm not going to jail for the rest of my life and leave my son without a father because of what you've done. I don't know what I'm going to do about Arthur."

He was silent for a few minutes. "How could the two of you smile in my face everyday? I trusted both of you, but all of this time you were fucking both of us. A lot of things make sense to me now. I trusted you so much. I trusted both of you and I left you alone with him all of the time. He was welcomed in our home. We spent time at his house, I thought he was my friend and all along he was fucking my wife. Did you fuck him in our house?"

"No."

"You know what, Kellie, it ain't important. I'm not going to dwell on it. I'll get a transfer to another district."

"Arthur already did that."

"When?"

"Last week."

"Cool. I won't deal with him any longer. I won't take C.J. away; I'll take care of him. As far as the baby you're carrying, I don't want to deal with it, Kellie. If she's mine, I'll pay you child support, but I don't ever want to see her."

Kellie started crying then.

"Why, Craig? She didn't do anything to deserve that. If you're her daddy, why don't you want her?"

"Because I won't be able to look at her knowing how she got here."

"Craig, please don't do that to our baby."

"We don't know if she's our baby, Kellie. So don't ever say that she's mine until we have a paternity test done. Until then, I don't want to see you. I'll come by the house tomorrow and get my things. I'll stay at my mother's until I can get an apartment."

"Craig, I'm sorry."

"Yeah, you are."

He got up and walked away. The plane started boarding. Craig was two rows in front of Kellie and across the aisle. She cried almost the whole flight. The man next to her asked if she was alright and she said that she was.

When they arrived at O'Hare, Craig wouldn't help Kellie with her bags, a stranger got them off of the carousel for her at baggage pick-up. Craig walked away and left her behind as he went to the car, but he had forgotten that Kellie had the car keys. If she hadn't caught the same flight with him, he would have been stuck at the airport.

He waited fifteen minutes before she caught up with him at the car. She was tied down with three bags, but he stood by the car and watched her struggle. When she caught up to him, she handed him the keys. He threw his bag in the back of the truck, got in on the driver's side and left her standing there to put her bags in the truck. He knew her bags were too heavy and she shouldn't have been lifting that kind of weight in her pregnancy, but he didn't care. He sat in the car and waited while she struggled. After five minutes or so, a couple of guys walked by, saw her struggling and helped her with her bags.

They rode home in silence. When they got to the house, Craig pulled into the garage, got his bags out of her car and put them in his. He went into the house, got a few items and put them in his car.

Kellie sat in her car and cried while he got his things and prepared to leave. He ignored her and left her sitting there with her bags in the car.

As he was coming out of the house she got out of the car and asked Craig not to leave her. He laughed, put his items in his car and left.

Kellie convinced Michele and Nick not to change their plans because of her.

Once she convinced Michele that everything was alright, she and Nick headed to Hawaii. Michele was very worried about Kellie, but Gina told her that she and Jeff would go to Chicago to make sure everything was okay.

When Gina talked to Kellie on the phone she couldn't get her to stop crying. She told her they were on their way and Kellie seemed to be happy that someone was coming to be with her.

Arthur had been calling Kellie's cell phone since she called and told him that Craig was on his way back to Chicago to confront him. Once she came into the house after Craig left, she called Arthur.

He answered the phone immediately.

"Hello."

She was crying so hard and he couldn't understand what she was saying. He did manage to find out that she was at home and he told her that he was on his way over.

When Arthur arrived at Kellie's house and she opened the door, he was furious at the sight of her.

She fell into his arms and continued to bawl like a baby. Arthur had a seriously dangerous tone in his voice when he asked her, "Where is he, Kellie?"

"He's gone, Arthur. He's gone to his mom's and he's not coming back."

"Good. I'll be back."

"No, Arthur. No! Leave it alone."

He took her by the arm and dragged her over to a mirror and said, "Look at yourself, Kellie! He beat your ass and I'm gonna beat his!"

"Arthur, we were wrong for what we did to him. I deserved this and now it's over, he won't hit me again."

"You're damn right he won't hit you again. I'm gonna give him the opportunity to take his frustrations out on a man. What the fuck is wrong with him beating on a pregnant woman. I'm gonna beat his ass, Kellie!"

She tried to hold him back, but he stormed out of the house, jumped in his car and sped off. Kellie frantically tried to call Craig, but he wouldn't answer his phone.

She also tried to call Arthur to reason with him, but he wouldn't answer his phone either.

When Arthur arrived at Craig's mother's house, he saw Craig in the garage which was located in the back of the house. Craig stopped what he was doing when he saw Arthur approach.

"What's up, man?"

"What you want, Arthur? You done took my wife, messed up my family, what do you want now?"

"Why you hit her, man?"

"That's between me and my wife."

"Naw man, she's my woman and I don't appreciate you putting your hands on her, jeopardizing the life of my babies. If you feel like you need to release some anger, take it out on me. I caused all of this. Fight a man, not a defenseless pregnant woman."

"You ain't no man! You're a fucking snake, fucking my wife and any woman you can get your dick in."

"Man, that's where you're wrong, I wasn't touching them other women. Once I got Kellie, I was faithful to her."

"Yeah, well she wasn't faithful to you because I was fucking that bitch too. But that's your ho now and I hope y'all will be happy together."

"Man you got one more time to call her a ho or a bitch. And if you ever think about putting your hands on her again, I'm gonna beat your ass."

"You talking big shit, Arthur. I'll beat the fuck out of you right here and now."

Arthur took his jacket off and said, "Let's do this."

Craig walked up to him and hit him in the jaw. They went at it for a few minutes before Craig's gun fell out of his waistband. When Arthur saw it, he thought Craig pulled it on him and he pulled his out and they stood face to face pointing their guns at each other when C.J. came into the garage and said, "Hi Uncle, Arthur."

They looked at C.J. and back at each other and put their guns away. Kellie saw them pointing their guns at each other when she pulled up. She ran up to C.J. and dropped to her knees and grabbed him.

"What is wrong with y'all?"

Kellie saw the look of shock on Craig's face when he saw her. He apparently didn't realize that he had beaten her so badly. C.J. asked, "Mommy, what happened to your face?"

"I had an accident honey, but I'll be okay."

Craig's mother came to the door and told C.J. to come in the house.

"Arthur, let's go."

He picked up his jacket and headed for his car.

"Craig, when can C.J. come home?"

"I don't want him to see you looking like that again. I'll keep him for the next week or so and then I'll bring him home."

"Okay."

Shortly after Kellie and Arthur returned to her house, Gina and Jeff arrived and Kellie was still a mess. She had on the same clothes that she wore to the reception. Gina gave her a long tight hug. Arthur was introduced and Kellie explained everything that happened. Gina helped her get cleaned up and got her to lie down and relax. They stayed with her for four days until she was stable.

Michele

When Michele and Nick arrived in Hawaii, they retrieved their luggage and found their way to the car rental counter.

The lady behind the counter said, "Good afternoon, how may I help you?"

Nick said, "I reserved a car in the name of Nicholas Malloy."

The customer service lady keyed Nick's information into the computer. Shortly thereafter, she handed Nick keys to a Lexus and told him where he could find the car. Nick excused himself to the restroom and upon return told Michele that he was ready to go.

When Nick and Michele stepped outside into the warm air and sunshine, Michele was surprised to see a group of children holding a sign which read, Michele will you marry me? Nicholas.

Michele turned to Nick, threw her arms around his neck and kissed him.

"Yes Nick, I love you and yes, I will marry you." He placed a ring on her finger and everyone started clapping.

Once everyone settled down and Nick and Michele were in their car heading for their villa, Nick turned to Michele and said, "I'm so happy that you said yes, Michele. I know that we haven't been dating very long, but I've found everything I'm looking for in you. I wasn't looking for a wife when I met you."

"I wasn't looking for a husband when I met you, but I knew there was something special about you the moment I saw you. I can't wait to tell everyone that we're getting married."

" can't wait to see people's expressions when I tell them we're getting married. My parents are anxious to meet you. They will be in town a few days after we return. Is that okay with you?"

"Of course it is, sweetheart. I'm looking forward to meeting them too. So, how soon can I start planning?"

"Immediately. I want to get married as soon as you're ready."

"I'm ready now, but it will probably take about six months or so to plan it the way I want."

"Whatever you want, baby, that's what we'll do."

"Okay. I love you."

"I love you too."

They arrived at the private cottage where they planned to spend most of their time. This beautiful cottage sat in a valley, with a seasonal stream running through it. The unmanicured tropical jungle gardens with palms, mangoes, avocadoes, bananas, coffee, wildflowers, and more surrounded the cottage with breathtaking views from every room.

"Nick, this place is even more beautiful than the pictures."

"I know. The scenery is unbelievable. I want to make love to you, Michele."

"Where did that come from, baby?"

"Just looking at you and how beautiful you are in these beautiful surroundings, it all makes me want to make love to you. I need you."

"I need you too."

"Come here, baby."

Michele walked into Nick's waiting arms and they began to kiss.

"Nick, let's not go inside, let's make love out here in the middle of all of this natural beauty."

Nick said, "I was thinking the same thing," as he helped her out of her clothes.

They found a spot by the waterfall which could best be described as their backyard. Michele dove in the water naked.

When she came up for air, Nick said, "I wanted to check out the view a little longer before you jumped into the water."

"This stream looked so inviting that I couldn't wait to get in. You'll have the opportunity to look at me naked for the next ten days. I didn't bring anything to wear that would obstruct your view of any part of my body."

"Oh yeah."

"Yeah."

Nick dove in and joined Michele. They played in the stream for a good while and eventually made it to the lush foliage surrounding the shoreline and made passionate love to each other.

They enjoyed every day of their vacation and knew they eventually had to return to reality. They began making plans for an extravagant wedding to take place in six months.

After returning home and getting settled, Michele first called Kellie to see what was going on with her, Craig and Arthur. She spoke briefly to Kellie while vacationing, but Kellie kept telling her that they would talk when Michele returned to L.A.

"Kellie, girl, how are you and everything?"

"Hey, Michele. First tell me about your trip."

"Kellie, I can't until you tell me that everything is okay and give me a status on what's going on."

"Alright. Well, when we got back home, Craig and Arthur got into it, pulling guns on each other and shit."

"What!"

"Yeah, scared the shit out of me. If it hadn't been for C.J. walking up to them while they were having their so-called face off, I don't know what would have happened."

"So what's going on now?"

"I've been staying at Arthur's house since the incident. Craig has C.J., but we're working on custody."

"Are you okay, Kellie?"

"Not really. I love Arthur and I'm happy to be spending time with him. I just didn't want things to happen like this."

"I know you didn't. Things will be okay. How's the baby doing?"

"She's fine. Very active, though. It's killing me not knowing who the father is. Arthur keeps his hand on my tummy, kissing and rubbing on me; I just don't know how he's going to react if this isn't his baby."

"How are you going to feel if Craig is the father?"

"I don't know, Michele. I miss Craig. I haven't seen him in over a week and I miss him. I know he hates me and doesn't care if I live or die, so I'm ashamed to say that I miss him."

"Why are you ashamed?"

"Because I knew what the consequences were when I got involved with Arthur. I knew if Craig found out about us that I would loose him for good and I took that chance anyway."

"Maybe that says how much you love Arthur."

"Yeah, I guess. I just wish that it didn't happen the way it did. I wish that I could continue to have a relationship with Craig or at least us be friendly towards each other, but that will never happen. He's going to let me see C.J. today. He knows that I haven't been staying at home. He told me not to have C.J. at Arthur's house. Arthur can't be at our house until we sit down and talk to C.J. about what's going on. And I have to explain my situation with Arthur to C.J."

"Damn, Craig's making you do that?"

"Yes. He said that it is my fault that our family is torn apart and that I should explain to C.J. why we aren't a family any longer."

"Good luck with that. When do you plan to have that conversation?"

"I guess when Craig says. I just need to get C.J. home so that I can move forward in my life. All of the bruises and swelling are gone, so C.J. can come home. I didn't want him to see me like that. He freaked out when he saw me briefly at Craig's mother's house the day we came home from Denver, but both Craig and I agreed that he shouldn't see me like that again."

"Call me if you need to talk, or if you need me there to help you with anything, Kellie."

"I will, Michele, and thank you for being here for me. So now, can you please tell me about your trip to Hawaii?"

"Well, in about six months you'll be calling me Mrs. Malloy."

"What?"

"Nick asked me to marry him."

Kellie started screaming...congratulations, girl! I saw how Nick had that loving look in his eyes every time he looked at you or talked to you, but I had no idea he was that far gone."

"Girl, neither did I. I was surprised when he asked me to marry him, but I quickly said yes because I love him, Kellie. I'm so in love with Nick and I had the time of my life while in Hawaii. He's so attentive and passionate. I hope that you'll be able to be my maid of honor, Kellie."

"Really, Michele? Of course, you know I'll be honored. You set a date already?"

"April 10, so clear your calendar."

"Consider it done. I'm looking forward to all of the planning and parties that are involved. Congratulations to both of y'all. Make sure you tell Nick I said so."

"I will. I'm glad to hear that you're doing okay, Kellie and please remember you can call me anytime to talk."

"Okay, I'll be talking to you soon."

"Alright. Good luck with seeing Craig."

"Thanks, I need it."

Michele called Gina and Stacey on a conference call to get their take on what was going on.

Gina

When Gina returned from Denver, there was a package waiting for her from Megan, her attorney. Before she could open it and go over the contents, the door bell rang. She was expecting Marcus to bring the kids home, but was surprised to see him standing at the door alone. He looked in her hand and saw the FedEx envelope and asked her if they could talk.

She stepped aside and said, "Yes, come in, Marcus. Where are the children?"

"They are with my mother. I'll pick them up shortly. I wanted to talk to you about the divorce papers. I don't know if you've had a chance to look them over yet. Come on and sit down, Gina."

"I'm just getting in, so please excuse me for a minute while I put on some sweats."

"Alright. I'm going to fix a glass of wine, if you don't mind."

"No, of course not."

When Gina returned, Marcus was in the family room channel surfing. Gina took a seat on the couch next to Marcus.

Marcus leaned forward, rested his arms on his thighs and said, "I was up all night thinking about you coming home today, signing those papers and not being my wife any longer. I thought it was what I wanted because I was so mad at you, Gina. Now after the dust has settled, I don't know if this divorce is something I want to go through with. I know there have been some changes in both of our lives and believe me I know you're dating Jeff Lee and that's not why I'm having second thoughts. I love you, Gina. I love you and it's very hard for me to let you go. I guess I need to know how you feel about me."

He sat back, relaxed and listened to Gina's response.

"I love you, Marcus. I don't think that will ever change. I think we've gone through too much to ever get back what we had and that's my fault. I had everything. You gave me the world, two beautiful children and a lavish lifestyle that I could only wish for and I threw it all away for a fantasy."

Tears were pouring out Gina's eyes while she spoke.

Marcus handed her his handkerchief and she took it. It took Gina a few minutes to compose herself before she began speaking again.

"I think about you everyday, Marcus. Some mornings I wake up and forget that you're not mine anymore and I start crying. I've cried so much these past months that I'm surprised I have any tears left. I'm stupid, period."

"You're far from stupid, Gina. I guess I'll never understand how you did what you did, but I was unable to turn off my feelings for you. I miss you. I've been out of the house for months and it's been a very hard adjustment for me too. Are you in love with Jeff?"

Gina hesitated before she said, "Yes."

"Oh. Is he in love with you?"

"Yes."

"I know that was a silly question, I mean look at you and knowing you, what man wouldn't fall in love with you."

Gina turned towards Marcus, placed her palm along the side of his face and said, "Marcus, baby, what's wrong?"

"I love you, Gina. I love you and I'm having trouble letting you go."

"Marcus, so much has happened since Vegas. I'm not the same person anymore and neither are you. When you met me, I was a virgin. You never had to think about me being with another man. Now, after what you found out about me and since you know I've been dating Jeff, you won't be able to deal with knowing that I've been with other men."

Marcus stood up and walked over to the fireplace. He leaned against the mantel, put his head down and said, "I know that I would have a hard time with it, Gina. That's what has gotten us to this point, but I'm wondering if I'll be able to get over it." He looked at her and said, "I love you and I don't want to let you go."

"Why now, Marcus? This happened months ago."

"Because I felt like I had time or a chance to get past it and that within that time we could work things out and be together, but I'm not ready yet and you're about to sign those papers and all of my chances will be gone. I guess knowing that you're in love with Jeff should snap me back to reality."

"Are you and Miranda serious?"

"Not really. She wants more than I'm able to give."

Gina walked over to the fireplace where Marcus was standing, wrapped her arms around his waist and laid her head on his back.

"I love you, Marcus. I'm sure you know that and I wish that we could have spent the rest of our lives together, but we can't because of what I've done."

He turned around to face her and they began kissing.

Gina pulled away and looked into Marcus' eyes when he said, "I need to make love to you, Gina. I need to know how much you love me before you sign those papers and I have to accept that what we had is over."

Gina didn't say a word, but Marcus knew from the look in her eyes that she wanted him as much as he wanted her. Marcus helped her remove her clothes and quickly removed his. He lowered her body onto the rug that lay in front of the fireplace and made passionate love to her. Gina couldn't control the tears that flowed out of her eyes. Marcus knew what the tears represented and continued to please Gina the only way he knew how.

Once they were both satisfied, Gina said, "I'm so sorry, Marcus about what I did. I love you, baby, and I want you. I'm so afraid that I won't be faithful in my next relationship because I still desire you."

"Why don't we give ourselves a chance then, Gina? Tear up those papers and we can work towards being together because I don't think we made a real effort to be together, do you?"

"No."

"Well, can we?"

Just as Gina started to answer Marcus, her phone rang. She rolled over and picked up the handset and saw that Jeff was calling.

She looked at herself and the situation she was in before answering the phone.

"Hello."

"Hey, baby. You get yourself situated?"

"No, not yet. Marcus stopped by to discuss the divorce papers, so I haven't had a chance to unpack, but I'll get to it soon. How about you, are you settled?"

"Yeah, I'm unpacked and repacked. I need to get in the right frame of mind for these upcoming meetings. I know you're probably tired and you'll have the boys back home today, but I want to see you again before I hit the road tonight."

"What time is your flight?"

"I don't have to be at the airport until ten, so if you have time, maybe we can have a late dinner after the boys are in bed."

"Okay, baby. I'll put a little something together, a going away present."

"Alright. I'm looking forward to it. I'll be there about seven."

"Okay, I'll see you then."

"I love you."

"I love you too."

When Gina hung up the phone, Marcus was looking at her with so much hurt in his eyes.

"How could you talk to him like that, right in front of me and I'm your husband? Your fucking pussy is still wet from my nut and you telling another man that you love him."

He got up and started dressing. "I guess I needed this, Gina. Thank you. I guess I can move on now."

Gina got up and started slipping her clothes on. "What was I supposed to say, Marcus? Oh, let me call you back, Jeff. Marcus and I just finished fucking and we need to finish our pillow talk before I can talk to you?"

"Yeah, that would have been better than what just happened. Since you made plans to spend time with your man tonight, I'll bring the kids home in the morning."

"No. I want to see them, bring them today. Jeff will only be here for a couple of hours and they will be in bed shortly after he arrives."

"And I guess you and Jeff will be in bed shortly after the kids go to sleep."

"I don't fuck him here, Marcus."

"Alright, Gina. I'll bring the kids home shortly."

"Thank you."

Gina showered and got dinner ready for the boy's arrival. Marcus called at six thirty and said the kids were having dinner at his mother's and that he would have them home once they were done eating.

Shortly after talking to Marcus, Jeff arrived.

"Hey, baby. I didn't want to leave town without seeing you again."

"Come on in, Jeff. Are you hungry?"

"Yeah, I guess I can eat something, what you got?"

"I fixed some chicken, mac and cheese and broccoli. Sit down, I'll fix you a plate."

"Where are the boys?"

"Marcus was supposed to bring them home hours ago and then he called about twenty minutes ago and said that they were eating at his mother's house and that he would bring them home once they're done eating. He knew I was cooking dinner."

"Don't worry about it, baby. Now you have lunch ready for them tomorrow. Are you going to work tomorrow?"

"Yeah. I have an interview Thursday that I need to prepare for."

"Who are you interviewing?"

"Victor Newcastle, New England."

"I'm sure he's gonna pushup on you, baby."

"You know I'm not interested in anyone but you, Jeff."

"Alright, I guess I needed to hear that."

They went into the family room and put on some music. Shortly after they sat on the couch and began kissing they heard voices. Jeff and Gina turned towards the entryway as Marcus, Jr. came running towards her and jumped on her lap.

"Hey Mommy! I miss you."

"I've missed you too, baby and I'm so happy to see you. Where is your brother?"

"Sleep. Daddy took Michael upstairs to bed. He was sleep in the car."

Marcus, Jr. looked over at Jeff and said, "Hi, Jeff. Are you going to bring your son over to play with us again?"

"We can all go out and do something together when I return from my trip."

"Okay."

Marcus walked into the room.

"Marcus, did I leave the door unlocked?"

"No. I still have a key. It was in my hand and Michael is heavy. I put him to bed.

Marcus walked into the room. Hey, what's up, Jeff."

Jeff stood and extended his hand. "How are you, Marcus?"

"I'm all good. Hey, Gina? Did you see my watch laying around anywhere? I must have misplaced it earlier."

Gina gave Marcus a serious evil eye as he walked over to the ledge in front of the fireplace and picked up his watch.

"Here it is. Let me get out of here. Come on Marcus and walk your daddy to the door."

Marcus, Jr. hopped off of Gina's lap and ran over to his father. Gina got up and said, "I'll walk with you so that I can lock the door. Excuse me for a minute, Jeff."

When Gina got to the door, Marcus was sending Marcus, Jr. up to bed.

When Marcus, Jr. was out of sight, Gina turned to Marcus and said, "What are you trying to do, Marcus?"

"This is still my fucking house and my fucking pussy, Gina. How you gonna sit up in here kissing this man on my fucking couch. Isn't that disrespectful?"

"You left, Marcus. This is where I live. Like I told you earlier, I don't fuck him here. I thought I was being respectful and if you hadn't walked in unannounced, you wouldn't have seen us kissing on your couch."

"I guess you're gonna give him some going away pussy after I just had you. That's just two, Gina, I know how you like to fuck three men."

"Bye, Marcus."

Gina pushed him towards the door.

"I'm not done with this conversation, Gina. I will be calling you later tonight so that we can finish talking."

"Whatever, Marcus."

Gina went upstairs and made sure both the boys were tucked in before she made her way back to the family room. Jeff didn't stay much longer as he had to make it to the airport in time, but promised to call once he was settled in his hotel room.

Stacey

After making sure everyone made it to their destinations and that Kellie was safe, Stacey decided to return a phone call to Charles. He called her on her cell phone a few days ago leaving a message asking Stacey to call him. Since Richard was at work and Robert was asleep, Stacey decided that this was the best time to call.

"Good afternoon, Charles. How can I help you?"

"Stacey. Thank you for returning my call. You'll be happy that you did. I don't like to open old wounds, but this is something I think you should be aware of."

"What is it, Charles?"

"I didn't know at the time, but I was told that the bachelor party you danced at was taped. They had cameras in the living room and the bedroom."

"What!"

"From what I've been told, one of Roger's boys thought a DVD would be a nice wedding gift."

"What the fuck!"

"It gets worse, Stacey. Roger's wife found the DVD and confronted him. She also heard you and I talking to each other on the DVD and she knows that I know you. She knows your name and that you live in Denver. She is determined to find you."

"Why? Why does she want to find me? They weren't married and she has to know what happens at these parties."

"I'm just warning you that she is looking for you. Her sister is a cop and I think she is helping her track you down."

"What does she want from me? It doesn't make any sense. It's not like I was having a relationship with the groom, it was part of the night. That was it. I wouldn't know him if he walked up to me."

"I don't know why she is looking for you, or what she wants to say to you, Stacey. I just wanted to warn you."

"How did she find out?"

"The idiot had been watching the DVD and left it in the machine. His wife went to watch a movie and found the DVD in the machine and watched it."

"Damn. That had to be hard watching the man you love fucking another woman. I can only hope and pray that she never finds me. Thanks, Charles."

After Stacey hung up the phone she started replaying the events of that night. She had been content with Richard believing that she slept with Charles, but if he ever saw the tape, he would know that she lied and had sex with the groom also. Every time the phone rang, after Stacey's phone conversation with Charles, she became nervous. When Richard came in the next morning, Stacey was cooking breakfast. He walked up behind her and wrapped his arms around her waist. He kissed her behind her ear and said, "I love you, baby."

Stacey turned to face Richard. They kissed deeply and once they parted Stacey said, "I love you too, Richard. I missed you while you were gone. How long are you in town for?"

"Two days."

"Breakfast will be done soon. Can you check on Robert for me? He was still asleep when I last checked on him, but he's not going to sleep much longer."

"Alright. If he's awake, I'll change him and bring him down with me."

"Okay, I'll put the toast in the oven when you come back down."

"Okay."

Stacey set the table and got everything ready for Richard to return with Robert. He was taking a while, so she knew that he was getting the baby cleaned up. When Richard came into the kitchen, Stacey put the toast in the oven and began fixing Richard's plate. Once he was seated, Stacey put a plate in front of him and took the baby. She had been heating a bottle for the baby.

"I'll hurry and finish eating so that I can feed the baby and you can eat." Richard said.

"No, baby. Don't worry about it. I snacked on some bacon while I was cooking. I can wait. Take your time."

"Hey, do you know someone named, uh, shit I can't remember the name. It will come to me. Anyway, she called yesterday right after you left to take Robert to his doctor's appointment. I meant to tell you when you returned, but I got distracted."

"What did they want?"

"It was a woman. Sandra, her name was Sandra."

"No. I can't say that I know anyone by that name. Did she say what she wanted?"

"No, but she left a number for you to call. I left it on the notepad by the phone."

"I really need to pay attention to the notepad."

"Yeah, you do. I leave important stuff there sometimes."

Richard began walking towards the stairs to get some sleep when he stopped and said, "Why don't you come and lay down with me, Stacey. We'll never get a brother or sister for Robert unless we work diligently to make it happen."

"Okay. I'd be surprised if I wasn't already pregnant the way we've been going at each other."

Richard said, "Is that a complaint?"

She smiled at him and said, "Not at all. I'm looking forward to the work ahead of me."

Richard was due back last night, but was caught in bad weather and cancellations and was unable to fly. He slept uncomfortably in the pilots' lounge. Because of the wet and icy conditions, he wasn't able to make it to a hotel.

After making love to Richard and making sure Robert was sleeping comfortably, Stacey decided to return Sandra's call to see who she was and what she wanted.

Kellie

Gina and Jeff stayed with Kellie for a few days, but Kellie insisted that she was fine and that they go home. They felt assured that Kellie was stronger, so they returned to Memphis. Kellie was afraid to be alone and began spending all of her time at Arthur's house. After being at Arthur's house for almost two weeks, she was ready for C.J. to come home. She decided to call Craig and make arrangements to get C.J. and bring him home.

"Craig, I'm ready for C.J. to come home. It's been almost two weeks."

"Are you still staying at Arthur's house?"

"Yes."

"Once you go home and explain to C.J. why we aren't together anymore he can come home."

"How am I supposed to explain that to him?"

"Tell him you're a whore."

"I guess today isn't a good day to talk to you. I'll try again tomorrow." She hung up the phone.

When Arthur came in from work, Kellie had dinner waiting for him. When they sat down to eat, she said, "Arthur, Craig is still very angry at me and I don't know what to say to him anymore. I'm ready for C.J. to come home, but Craig always has an excuse. This time he told me that I had to go home and explain to C.J. why we aren't a family anymore."

"Maybe the two of you should say something to C.J. I'm sure he already knows something is wrong."

"Like what? Give me an example."

"Tell him that you love him and that the three of you won't be living in the same house anymore."

"He'll have a thousand questions."

"Don't worry about it, Kellie. Just explain it to him in a way a five year old will understand. You're smart, Kellie. You'll find the words."

"Okay, I'm going home tomorrow after my doctor appointment and I'll tell Craig to bring C.J. home so that I can explain to him what's going on."

"I've gotten used to having you here and I'll miss not seeing you every evening. How are we going to spend time together?"

"I guess we really need to talk about what we're going to do, Arthur. While we were sneaking around, I never really thought about what to do if we had the opportunity to be together. I don't know what you want from me."

"I love you, Kellie and I want to continue having a relationship with you."

"What if Craig is the father of this baby?" She rubbed her tummy. "How are you going to feel about that? What are we going to do?"

"Let's just take everything one day at a time. I won't love you or the baby any less if she isn't my natural child. You and I will have time to have our own children together. Let's get things resolved with you and Craig so that we can move forward. I love you, Kellie and I'm not going anywhere. I'll be here with you and for you so let's work towards you, me and the kids becoming a family, okay?"

"Yes, Arthur. Okay."

After dinner, Kellie and Arthur spent the night making passionate love to each other.

When she arrived at her house the next morning, Craig and C.J. were already there. She hadn't seen Craig or C.J. since the incident in the garage at Craig's mother's house. When she saw Craig's car in the driveway, she became nervous. She gathered her nerves, got out of the car, walked to the door and inside of the house.

"Mommy," C.J. cried out as he ran over to Kellie and wrapped his arms around her legs.

Craig walked into the room when he heard C.J. calling out to Kellie.

She bent over, picked C.J. up and said, "Hey baby. How are you?"

"Hi Mommy. Where you been, at Auntee Michele's?"

Kellie looked at Craig and said, "No baby, I wasn't at Auntee Michele's. I was staying with a friend, but I'm home now. You ready to come home?"

"Yeah."

Kellie put C.J. down and walked over to the couch. She patted the seat cushion next to her and told C.J. to come and sit with her. Once he was seated she said, "Listen, baby. When you come home, your daddy isn't going to come back with you to stay with us. It will just be the two of us."

"Why, Mommy? Why, Daddy? You don't like us anymore?"

Craig walked over to the couch, sat next to C.J., put him on his lap and said, "Of course I like you, man, I love you. It's just..."

Kellie said, "It's just that your dad and I aren't really getting along anymore and we think it's best that we spend some time away from each other. You'll still see your dad all of the time. The only thing that will change is that your dad won't live here anymore."

"Where are you going to live, Dad?"

"I'm going to stay at Grandma's for a little while."

"But why? Dads are supposed to live at home."

"I know man, but I need to stay at Grandma's for a little while."

"When are you coming home?"

"I don't know."

"What about Mommy? She can't fix stuff and do daddy stuff. What about my baby sister? Is she gonna stay here with me and Mommy or go to Grandma's house with you?"

"She will be with you and Mommy."

"Oh. Can I come to Grandma's house?"

"Yeah, you can come and spend time with me there. As a matter of fact, you'll be there with me a lot. Don't worry, man, I'll see you everyday like I do now."

"Okay, Dad."

C.J. jumped down and started playing with his toys that were on the floor.

"Thanks for helping me explain that to him, Craig."

He stood and said, "I didn't do it for you, I did it so that C.J. could understand why I can't live in the same house with you. Listen, I found an apartment, but we need to discuss what were going to do about the bills here and what we're going to do with the house."

"We can sell the house."

"Why are you so quick to sell? Are you gonna move in with Arthur?"

"I don't know what I'm going to do. I haven't been able to concentrate on it."

"I don't want you moving my son into Arthur's house, Kellie. If that's your plan, expect to give up custody."

"I didn't say I was going to do that, Craig."

"When did you say your baby was due?"

"February 21st."

"Alright. When you have your baby, I want a test while you're at the hospital. I'm not gonna take care of you and your fuckin' punk ass boyfriend's kid, so I want to know immediately. What the fuck is wrong with you anyway?"

"Nothing."

"You look like shit."

"Craig. I'm sorry about what I did. I wish I could go back and change things, but I can't. I know you can't stand me, but I would appreciate it if you didn't constantly degrade me. I'm having a hard time with this pregnancy. I may have to go on bed rest because my blood pressure keeps rising and Dr. Hubbard is concerned that I may go into premature labor."

"You're telling me all of this because?"

"She might be your baby, Craig."

He got in her face and said, "Might be, Kellie, that is the key word, isn't it? Might be. Tell all of this bullshit to Arthur, I'm sure he'll take care of you. You fucking whore."

"Fuck you then, Craig. I won't bother you again about this baby and if she is yours, fuck you anyway. I don't need you to take care of her, or do anything for her. As a matter of fact, you can walk the fuck away and leave C.J. alone too. Me and Arthur can raise him."

Craig had been walking towards the door until Kellie said that last line. He walked over to her, got in her face again and said, "Bitch, I will beat the shit out of you if you ever try to keep my son away from me. Keep on talking shit and I will take C.J. away from you. I know one thing, you better not have that mutherfucker in my house and you better not have C.J. at his house."

"Craig, you can't control me. You can't tell me what I can and cannot do with my son."

"Alright, Kellie. Believe that if you want to. Let me catch his ass in my house and it's gonna be some shit. Let C.J. tell me that he's been to Arthur's house and it's gonna be some more shit."

"Why, Craig? Why can't C.J. go to Arthur's house?"

"Can't you fucking wait until we're divorced? If you feel like you need to fuck that punk ass mutherfucker that bad, bring C.J. to me."

"Whatever, Craig."

"Whatever my ass. Think I'm playing." Craig walked away from Kellie and called out to C.J. "C.J., come on and say bye, man."

When C.J. came into the room, Craig said, "I'm on my way back to Grandma's. I'll pick you up from school tomorrow."

C.J. said, "Okay, Daddy." He ran back into the family room and continued to play.

Craig said, "I'll pick him up from school as usual and drop him off at home everyday. If I can't do it, I'll let you know. When are you going back to work?"

"Next Monday."

"Alright."

Craig walked out.

After getting C.J. to bed, Kellie called Arthur to let him know the details of her conversation with Craig.

"Kellie, don't let him intimidate you. I know he is still angry as he should be, but I don't like him threatening you like this. Do you want me to talk to him?"

"No. It will just make things worse."

"What did the doctor say about you being so tired?"

"He said that my blood pressure is up and that I may have to stop working and go on bed rest."

"Was it like this with C.J.?"

"No. I guess I'm just so stressed. I'll try not to worry so much and maybe things will be alright after that."

"I need to see you. I miss you being here when I get home. We've got to make some decisions on how we're going to do this, baby."

"I know. I can't let Craig dictate how we're going to be together. I can see you tomorrow while C.J. is at school. I'll come by after I drop him off and we can spend the day together, okay?"

"Alright, baby. When are you filing for divorce?"

"I'm waiting for the papers from Craig."

"Ask him if he's filed. If not, you need to do it. I'm ready for us to be a family. I really would like for us to be married before the baby is here."

"Married?"

"Yeah, baby. I want to marry you. I don't want to date or shack or any of that bullshit. I love you and I want to spend the rest of my life with you. I didn't do all of this for nothing. I wanted you and now that I have the chance to have you, I'm not letting you go. So let's do what we need to do to be together the right way, okay?"

"Okay. I'll ask Craig if he's filed. If not, I'll do it."

"I love you, Kellie."

"I love you too, Arthur. I'll see you in the morning.

Michele

After talking to Kellie, Gina and Stacey, Michele checked all of her messages and got herself organized to get back into her routine. Nick came by later that evening. They spent a quiet evening sitting in front of the fireplace, listening to music and discussing their future.

"Michele, we didn't talk about children. I know you have a strong career, so do I, but I'm willing to take a step back and raise a family. Are you?"

"I've thought about it, Nick. I've thought about babies, especially since I've met you. I never thought I would be a good mother because I've always only had to worry about me and didn't think that I would ever want to give up my lifestyle for a child. But to have your child, I'd give it all up in a heartbeat. Yes. I want to have children with you."

Nick smiled at Michele and then attacked her by pushing her on her back, pulling her tee-shirt over her head and saying, "Let's practice."

After making love they slept on the floor in front of the fireplace.

Over breakfast the next morning, Nick said, "My parents, my sister, brother and aunt will be here today. Please tell me you can have dinner with us this evening."

"I thought they weren't coming until tomorrow."

"That's what I thought too, but I got the days mixed up. I made reservations at Beau Rivage. My mom loves French Cuisine. I just want you to meet my family so that we can move forward. Have you thought about calling your mom?"

"Yes, baby. I have and I'm going to call my mom within the next few days. I hope that I can talk to her without getting angry."

"Be positive, baby. Things will be fine."

"We'll see."

Michele and her mom, Linda, had been estranged since Michele was fifteen years old. After Michele's father's death, her mother met and married Don. Don moved her mom to Santa Barbara, but told her that he couldn't accept Michele, so her mom left Michele with Michele's Aunt Dee Dee and moved away with Don.

Michele didn't see Linda again until Dee Dee's funeral two years ago. Michele refused to talk to Linda and returned every letter Linda sent to her. Linda had been trying to have a relationship with Michele, but Michele wasn't interested. Nick thought it was time she forgave her mother and work on having a relationship. Michele recently heard that Don died and she felt that was the only reason Linda was interested in a relationship with her now.

"Nick. I'll call Linda tomorrow and let her know that we are getting married. Then we'll take it from there."

"Alright, baby. I just want to share our happiness with everyone. I've got to get to the office, but I'll be by here to pick you up at six. We are going to meet everyone at the restaurant."

"Okay, baby, I'll be ready."

Michele spent the whole day getting ready to meet Nick's family. She was very nervous and decided to call Gina, Stacey and Kellie for advice.

"Hey girls. I have an issue."

Gina said, "What's up, Michele?"

"I'm meeting Nick's family tonight and I'm nervous."

"Why are you nervous?"

"It's his, mother, father, sister, brother and aunt. They are from Jackson, Mississippi and they probably are going to think I'm weird 'cause I'm pure L.A."

Kellie said, "You're not weird, Michele. Stop tripping and let these people see why Nick fell so hard for you."

"I'm trying to be strong, but I don't know. I don't know what to wear."

"Stacey said, "Where are you going? Out or staying in?"

"We're going to a French restaurant. I can really dress up for this place, but I don't want them to think I'm flashy."

"But you are flashy, Michele. Please just be yourself and you won't have anything to worry about," Kellie said.

"I guess that's true. I just want his mom to like me."

"Nick loves you and that's who you're marrying. Yes, it would be wonderful if they all love and accept you, but don't worry yourself to death if they don't. Just be cordial and respectful and everything will be fine," Gina said.

"Thank you for that, Gina. That's just what I needed to hear. I'll let you guys know how it went as soon as I can."

They all said their goodbyes. Michele was ready to go when Nick arrived to pick her up. While in the car, Nick said, "Why are you so quiet?"

"I guess I'm just a little nervous about meeting your family."

"Don't be nervous, Michele. They are loving people and they will love you just as much as I do."

"Okay, Nick."

Nick helped Michele out of the car and they walked into the restaurant holding hands.

Nick's family was seated at the bar waiting for them. The Maitre' D directed them to their waiting party.

Nick's mother saw them approaching and jumped up to greet them. She threw her arms around Nick's neck and said, "Nicholas, oh, I'm so happy to see you, baby."

"Mom, I'm so happy to see you too." He hugged and shook hands with everyone, then turned to Michele and said, "Michele, this is my mother, Eva, my father, Greg, my sister, Beverly, my brother, Jesse and my aunt Cheryl. Everyone, this is Michele."

"It's so nice to meet you all," Michele said.

The hostess came over and escorted them to their table. After everyone was seated, they engaged in small talk and the conversation eventually turned to Michele.

Eva said, "So, Michele, tell us a little about you. Nick told us that you sell real estate."

"Yes. I've been a broker for about four years now and my business is doing very well. I like my job very much."

"How do you like being a part of Nick's world? I mean, all of the celebrities and traveling and stuff."

"I like it. I have lived in L.A. all of my life and I'm used to this lifestyle. We had already shared some of the same friends and we seem to fit perfectly into each other's world."

Nick's sister, Beverly, said, "Have you guys set a wedding date?"

Nick said, "April 10th falls on a Saturday and it's the day Michele and I met, so we're going to get married that day."

"That's only seven months away." His aunt said.

"We know, but we'll have everything in place by then. We are very happy with each other and are anxious to begin our lives as husband and wife," Nick said.

Nick's mother said, "Well, I want to congratulate both of you and welcome Michele into the family. Please let me know what I can do to help you plan this wedding. Although we are in Mississippi, there is plenty that I can do to help you from there. I brought a list of the family members who should be invited to the wedding. We'll get a chance to go over this list while we're in town."

After dinner, while in the car headed to Michele's place, Nick said, "See, baby, that wasn't bad, was it?"

"No, baby, not at all. Your family is very nice. How long are they going to be in town?"

"Seven days. They will be here until next Tuesday."

"I was hoping to spend time with you soon. I need you."

"I'll get away tomorrow. I won't be able to spend the night, but I'll make the time we spend together memorable."

"I know you will."

"My mom was talking about having a cookout at my house."

"When?"

"Saturday."

"That sounds good. I have a few properties to show that morning, but I'll be there afterwards. What do you want me to bring?"

"How about some beverages?"

"Beverages? I can cook a dish or something a bit more significant than beverages."

"My mother likes to cook everything. This will be her last hurrah in my kitchen, so let's let her have it. Once we're married it will be your kitchen and you can run things the way you like."

"Okay, baby. When should we begin looking for a house?"

"Whenever you're ready."

"Let's talk about it in detail Saturday when we can relax."

"Okay. Did you call your mother?"

"No. I'll call her this weekend."

The next morning, Eva called Michele and asked her to meet her at Roscoe's on Pico for lunch. Michele gladly accepted.

Michele waited on the bench outside of the entrance door for Eva and was surprised to see Beverly and Cheryl coming towards her too. She thought that it would only be Eva. She stood as they approached.

Michele extended her arms for a hug from Eva, Beverly and Cheryl.

"Good afternoon, Michele. Girl, you are beautiful."

"Thank you, Cheryl. Come on y'all, they called our name as you guys were approaching."

They went inside and were seated in one of the booths.

Beverly jumped right in by saying, "Michele, we wanted the opportunity to spend some time with you without Nick. You know, girl time."

"I understand, Beverly."

"So, you and Nicholas met in Las Vegas?"

"Yes. I was on vacation with three of my girlfriends at the time. We've been inseparable since then. I'm very happy that we met and fell in love. Nick is a great guy and I love him."

"He loves you too, Michele," Cheryl said.

Eva said, "Are you planning a big wedding?"

"Not really big. Both Nick and I have lots of friends and know that we aren't going to be able to invite everyone. We decided on no more than one hundred guests each. We would like to keep it to family and close friends."

Eva picked up her list and put it back in her purse. She then said, "Let me make some adjustments to my list and I'll get it to you soon."

"Okay."

Beverly said, "Do you have a big family?"

"Not a big immediate family. I'm an only child, but I have lots of cousins, aunts and uncles. I also have lots of friends I would love to invite. I'll have to make many adjustments to my guest list, too, I'm sure."

"Are you and Nick planning to have children?" Eva asked.

"We actually had that talk a few nights ago and we both want children."

Beverly said, "How soon?"

"We didn't make a decision on when, but we'll make some adjustments and figure out when it's best for us."

Eva said, "There's never gonna be a good time. It's hard to plan a time to have a kid. It's best to just let it happen. Do you have a home church where you'll get married?"

"Yes, Nick and I have been attending services together at my church."

"Let me know what I can do to help out, Michele. I'm sure you'll put together a beautiful ceremony."

"I will, Eva."

"I'll see you at the cookout tomorrow, Michele."

"Yes. I'm sure we will have a great time."

After they finished their lunches, Michele left Eva, Beverly and Cheryl at the entrance of Roscoe's. They were deciding where they wanted to go next. Michele was a little ahead of them when she saw Eddie. He called out to her and ran across the street to see her.

"Michele. Damn, baby. I haven't seen you in a couple of months. You still seeing dude?"

He grabbed her hands.

"Yeah, Eddie, we're still together. He asked me to marry him."

"Damn. Y'all are serious."

"Yeah. He really makes me happy. What about you? How are things?"

"Better. We're working towards doing something permanent."

"That's great. It's time you settle down."

He slid his hand across her face and said, "I guess I should since I can't have you anymore."

He put his hand under her chin, tilted her head upward and kissed her on the mouth. "I miss you, Michele."

"I miss you too, Eddie."

"Any chance of us getting together?"

"Naw, I'm being faithful. I'm in love with Nick, Eddie. I don't want to mess this one up."

"Congratulations, Michele. You deserve happiness. Where are you coming from?"

"I just had lunch with Nick's mom, sister and aunt. It was interesting. I'm starting to meet the family and stuff like that."

"Well, I wish you the best and I'll expect an invitation."

"You'll definitely get one, Eddie."

They kissed each other again. I'll talk to you soon, Eddie."

"Where is your car?"

"Around the corner."

"Come on, I'll walk with you."

Eddie walked Michele to her car and they held hands while walking and talking.

When Michele saw Nick later that evening his first question to her was, "What happened?"

"What happened when?"

"When you had lunch with my mother?"

"We talked about the wedding and children and stuff. It was nice."

"Really?"

"Yeah. Why?"

"She said that I'm making a mistake. She said that I'm too young to get married. I thought something must have happened between the two of you."

"So she doesn't like me, does she?"

"I don't know what's going on, Michele. She thought you were wonderful before lunch. I'll find out what's up. But don't worry, baby.

There is nothing that anyone can say to change my mind about you. I love you and that will never change.

Gina

After getting the kids to sleep and talking to Jeff before boarding his flight, Gina poured a glass of merlot and relaxed on the couch. Shortly after getting situated the phone rang. It was Marcus.

"Yes, Marcus."

"You can quit acting like it's such a problem to hear from me, Gina."

"How may I assist you, Marcus?"

"We need some resolution to our situation. If you plan to entertain your man at my house, maybe you need to move and get your own place."

"I'm not going anywhere, Marcus. You told me that I can have this house. I can see already that I won't be able to stay here without you always popping by and being all in the middle of what I'm doing."

"My kids are there and I pay the mortgage."

"You'll continue to pay the mortgage and when you receive the divorce papers with the changes, you'll still pay the mortgage, but you won't be able to walk in and out of here whenever you want."

"Why does it bother you if I'm there? I only come in to pick up the kids or drop them off."

"Because I don't have any privacy. I'll never be able to entertain as long as I'm in this house. I was thinking that I should find a new house for me and my kids."

"Your kids? Maybe I should take custody of the kids and you can get an apartment or whatever you can afford."

"Whatever, Marcus. I'll have my attorney make changes to the documents, present them to you and your attorney, then we'll take it from there."

"Okay, Gina. What happened to what I said to you earlier today before Jeff showed up?"

"Well, first you tell me you want to work on us being together and then you said that you guess that you can move on now, after you heard my conversation with Jeff. I think its best that we continue on the course we're on, Marcus. We are never going to be able to get past what happened."

"You keep saying that. Are you sure it isn't because you'd just prefer to be with Jeff than to be with me?"

"I just know how you are. You are saying now that you want to be with me and that you'd hopefully be able to get past what happened, but I know you, Marcus. You won't ever be able to trust me and things will never be the way they were. Don't get me wrong, I love you. If I could take it all back, I would, but it happened and I messed this up and it will never be the same. I hope that we can be friends, especially for the kids."

"Damn, Gina. This is real, ain't it?"

"Yes, Marcus. I came to terms with it when we first separated and you began dating Miranda. It hurt so bad knowing that you were spending your time with another woman and that you couldn't stomach the sight of me. I couldn't be mad at you though, you had every right to get on with your life. For a long time I hoped that we could get together again, but as time went on I realized that we could never get back what we had. We shared a trustful and beautiful life together, but we'll never be able to recapture that lifestyle together again."

"I love you, Gina. I enjoyed making love to you today. It felt like old times. It felt like we were together and nothing had changed.

I can't promise that I'll always be okay with you and Jeff or whatever man you end up with, but I'll do my best to be respectful."

"Thank you, Marcus."

"Work things out with your attorney and we'll move forward with the divorce."

"Okay, I should be able to get something to you soon."

After her phone conversation with Marcus, Gina called Stacey to see how things were going with her and motherhood. When Stacey answered the phone, Gina knew there was something wrong."

"I'm sorry to call you so late, Stacey, but you were on my mind and I wanted to make sure everything was okay with you."

"Girl, you are not going to believe the new drama in my life."

"What now?"

Let me call you tomorrow. I don't want to talk while Richard is in the house. Although he is sleep, this isn't something I want to talk about with him having a chance of overhearing."

"Damn, Stacey. This must be big."

"It is. I'll call you in the morning after he leaves."

"Alright."

When Gina met with her attorney the next day, a new clause was added asking Marcus to purchase a new home for Gina and the kids within two years after finalization of the divorce. Her attorney, Megan, suggested they all meet to go over everything.

Gina received a call later that afternoon confirming a meeting with Marcus and his attorney to be held the next afternoon for mediation.

Stacey

Stacey pressed *67 on her cell phone keypad before dialing the number Sandra left with Richard when she called.

When Sandra answered the phone, Stacey was hesitant, but was anxious to know what this woman wanted from her.

"This is Sandra."

"Sandra, this is Stacey. My husband told me that you called."

"Yes, Stacey. I'm the wife of the man that you fucked at a bachelor party in Vegas."

Stacey didn't say anything.

"I wanted to talk to you to try to understand what type of woman would fuck another woman's man the night before his wedding. Especially a married woman. Would you be okay with someone doing that to you?"

"I don't know what you're talking about."

"I saw the DVD. I saw Roger trying to be true to me, trying to be strong, but you couldn't keep your ass out of his face or stop grinding on his dick until he had to fuck you. Then, you turn around and fuck the other dude, Charles."

"I think you have me mixed up with someone else. I don't know who you're looking for, but it ain't me."

"Don't you live in Pheasant Cove, right outside of Denver?"

"How did you get my phone number?"

"I'm just trying to find out why you would do something like that, Stacey. Does your husband know you strip?"

"Like I said, you have me mixed up with someone else. Good luck with your search."

When Stacey hung up the phone, her heart was racing. The phone rang again before Stacey could put it on the receiver. She looked at the caller ID and Gina's name appeared.

Stacey told her that she would call her later when she was able to talk.

Later that afternoon when Richard was up and about he asked Stacey about the phone call from Sandra.

"I called the number you left and she was looking for another Stacey. I didn't know her."

"Oh. I'm going to go to Larry's house this evening to watch the game. You cool with that?"

"Yes. That's cool. Go on and have a good time with your friends."

191

"I can stay home with you and Robert if you'd like, since I didn't make it home last night."

"Don't worry about it, baby. I'll see you when you get in."

"You'll probably be sleep when I get in."

"As long as you come home, I'm cool."

"Alright."

After Richard left to hang out with his friends, Stacey called Gina.

"What's up, Stacey."

"I've got big trouble. You know the bachelor party I danced at that Charles attended?"

"Yeah."

"Someone taped it, gave it to the groom as a wedding gift and the groom's wife found it. Now she's looking for me."

"What? Was there audio?"

"Yes. Of course there was audio. She knows my name and that I know Charles. But that's nothing compared to the fact that she called my house."

"What!"

"Yes. I don't know how she did it, but she has my home number."

"Do you think Charles gave it to her?"

"No. He's low down, but I don't think even he would do that. He's the one who warned me that she was looking for me. She called him first."

"Damn, Stacey. Shit, what are you gonna do?"

"I don't know. I denied knowing anything about what she was saying, but she has audio and video. She knows where I live."

"How do you know?"

"She told me. If she sees me, that's it. She'll have a positive ID. She already talked to Richard the first time she called and left a message. If she ID'd me, what would stop her from telling Richard, or even giving him a copy of the DVD."

"What's all on the DVD?"

"I slept with the groom and Charles. Plus, all of the bumping and grinding I was doing with the other guys. I just don't want Richard to see me acting like that and I really don't want him to see me fucking two other men. Especially after I told him it was just one."

"Damn, Stacey. If there is anything I can do to help, please let me know. I'll say or do anything you need to get through this."

"Thank you, Gina. I'll let you know. I've got to get the baby. I'll talk to you later."

When Richard came in later that evening, Stacey had fallen asleep on the couch. He picked her up and carried her to the bedroom. Stacey opened her eyes and smiled at Richard while enjoying her ride.

The next morning while out running errands, Stacey was pulled over by the police. She was talking to Gina on the cell phone. "Girl, I am being pulled over by the police."

"What did you do?"

"Nothing. I know I wasn't speeding, I have Robert in the car with me. I didn't run a light or a stop sign. Hold on, Gina, here she comes now."

Stacey laid the phone on the empty passenger seat and rolled down her window.

License, registration and proof of insurance, please."

Stacey pulled her wallet out of her purse and said, "May I ask what this is about, officer?"

"You were traveling 46 mph in a 35 mph zone."

"No I wasn't. Can I see your radar?"

"Listen," she looked at my driver's license, "Mrs. Shaw, I'm going to let you off with a warning, since you have a baby in the car and you have all of your credentials in order. Slow it down as you travel through here. There is a school zone ahead and you don't want to be distracted while talking on your cell phone."

"Thank you."

The officer handed Stacey's documents back and walked back to her squad car.

Stacey picked up the phone and said, "What the fuck! She said I was speeding when I know damn well that I wasn't."

"It's always your word against theirs. At least she let you go."

"Hell, she didn't have a reason to stop me."

So what are you going to do about this Sandra situation?"

"What can I do? I have to wait until she shows herself and hopefully I can get it resolved without Richard finding out about it. Shit, I thought this was all behind me."

"So did I. Listen, I know you've got a lot on your mind, but I need to talk about something."

"Sure, Gina, what's up?"

"I slept with Marcus. How can I tell Jeff that I love him and so easily sleep with Marcus?"

"He is still your husband. Feelings and desires don't just go away no matter the circumstance. Are you saying that you want Marcus back?"

"He asked me and I assured him that we didn't have a chance of being together again, but the possibility of it has my attention."

"Don't you love Jeff?"

"Yes. I do love him. Being in love with him and him with me creates another possibility of a great life...do you think that Marcus and I can be together and get past what happened?"

"Only the two of you can answer that question. Maybe you need to sit down with Marcus and talk to him and not put up the brick wall that you're so good at building and see if it can work."

"Maybe, Maybe...I should probably do that while Jeff is out of town."

"How long is he going to be out of town?"

"Four days. Damn, this is unfair to Jeff. He has been supportive and loving towards me, but I stab him in the back like this. What is wrong with me, Stacey?"

"There is nothing wrong with you. You were just lucky enough to meet and marry a great guy. Then love found you again, but this time it's not so easy. You have to really think about what you want and need for you and your kid's future. See how Marcus truly feels and take it from there."

"I guess this is a situation where I want to have my cake and eat it too. I really want both of them."

"Do you think they would agree to that?"

"Hell naw!"

"I hope you make the right decision. Either way, I'm here for you."

"Thanks, Stacey."

"You know what I just thought about?"

"What?"

"Charles said that Sandra's sister is a cop. What if that was her trying to ID me?"

"I guess that's a possibility because that traffic stop was bogus."

"Damn, Gina. This is really getting scary."

"Don't worry yourself to death about it, Stacey. Just let it run its course and we'll take it from there."

"I wish I could sound half as confident as you, but I can't. I'll be strong though. I'm at the store. I'll keep you in the loop and thanks for listening, Gina."

"You're welcome and thank you for listening to me. I'll talk to you soon."

When Stacey finished shopping and returned to her car, she noticed a huge scratch along the side of her car. She looked around to see if she could find who did it, but everyone continued with their routine as if nothing happened. She was pissed. After getting the baby situated in his car seat, she called Richard.

"Hey, baby. You're finished shopping already?"

"No. When I came out of Ross', I noticed a huge scratch on the driver's side of my car. I can tell it was deliberate. There is no way this could be an accident."

"Why would someone do that to your car?"

"I don't know. People make me sick."

"Don't worry about it, Stacey. We'll get it buffed out..."

"Buffing won't get this scratch out."

"Just don't worry about it. I'll take a look at it when you return then run it over to Ritchie at the shop and see what he can do about it. Okay, baby?"

"Yes. Thank you. You always make me feel better about things."

When Stacey pulled into the driveway of their home, Richard came out and met her at the car to take a look at the damage. Just as Stacey opened the car door a black SUV pulled into the driveway behind her car. Two women got out and were walking towards Stacey and Richard.

"Hello, Stacey. I'm Sandra." She turned to Richard and said, "You must be Stacey's husband."

"Yes, I am."

"Do you know what your wife does to earn money?"

"She's a housewife. She doesn't work outside of the home."

Sandra handed Richard a DVD and said, "Take a look at this DVD and you'll see that yes, she does work and it's not a very honorable job. Isn't that right, Stacey?"

Stacey just stood there staring.

"Cat got your tongue, Chocolick?"

Richard turned to Stacey and said, "What's this all about, Stacey?"

"The tape won't lie. I don't know what your wife told you about Vegas, but I bet she didn't tell you about what she did on that tape."

"Stacey, get the baby out of the car and let's go inside."

Stacey walked around to the other side of the car in a trance-like state. Once she unstrapped Robert, she grabbed her purse and Robert, and then headed into the house. She never looked back to see if Sandra and her sister were still in the driveway. Yes, the other girl was the cop from the earlier traffic stop.

Kellie

The next morning while C.J. was still asleep, Kellie called Craig. He didn't answer his cell phone, so she decided to call his mother's house. Eleanor answered the phone.

"Good morning, Eleanor. I'm sorry to call so early, but I tried calling Craig on his cell phone and he's not answering. Can you ask him to come to the phone, please?"

"I'm sorry, Kellie, but Craig ain't here?"

"Did he have to work?"

"I don't know. Maybe you should try to get him on his cell phone again."

"Okay, Eleanor, thanks."

Kellie tried calling Craig a couple more times, but didn't get an answer. Finally, about forty-five minutes after the initial call, he answered the phone.

"Hello."

"Craig, I've been calling you for almost an hour. What if there was an emergency."

"Is it?"

"No.

"Then what's up?"

"I wanted to talk about our situation."

"Let me call you back when I wake up."

"Are you at work?"

"Why would I be sleep at work?"

"I don't know, Craig. You're not at your mom's house and I didn't know you slept anywhere else."

"Things have changed, Kellie."

"Are you seeing someone?"

"Look, I'll call you when I get home."

"How long have you been seeing her, Craig? I mean, y'all fucking already and we've only been broke up for a couple of weeks. Were you seeing her before we broke up?"

"I'll call you later, Kellie."

"Alright, Craig, I'll be waiting."

Kellie woke C.J. and got him ready for daycare. After dressing him and dropping him off at school, she drove to Arthur's house.

Arthur greeted her at the door. Kellie walked past him and into the kitchen and had a seat.

"What's up with you, Kellie? No hug, no nothing?"

"I'm sorry. I'm tired, baby."

"Come on in here and lay on the couch, or would you rather lie in the bed?"

"I can lie on the couch."

"Did you talk to Craig?"

"I called him this morning, but he couldn't talk. He said he would call me back."

"Alright."

Just as Kellie got situated on the couch, her cell phone rang. It was Craig.

"Hello."

"What's up, Kellie?"

"So where were you, Craig?"

"Excuse me?"

"You weren't at your mother's and you weren't at work, so where else are you sleeping?"

"I don't answer to you anymore, Kellie. I'm sure you know that."

"I just didn't know that you were seeing someone."

"I didn't have to tell you either."

"So you are?"

"Yes."

"Is this someone you've known for a while? I mean, you're sleeping with her already, Craig?"

"Why do you care, Kellie?"

"I don't. Whatever."

"Why were you looking for me? Is C.J. alright?"

"Yes, he's fine. I called to ask if you've filed for divorce."

"I told you I would do it and I will."

"I was going to do it if you hadn't."

"What's the rush? Believe me, I want it as bad as you, if not more, but my attorney was out of town and won't be back for a couple of days. Once he's back, I'll ask him to put a rush on it. Does that help?"

"Yes."

"We've got a lot of stuff to sort out. The house, custody of C.J. and we need a paternity test on your baby, bills, the cars all of this. As a matter of fact, I'd like to get this done as soon as possible. When I bring C.J. home this evening we'll talk. Is that alright with you?"

"Yes. I'll see you then."

When Kellie hung up the phone, Arthur said, "What was that about, Kellie?"

"He hadn't filed yet because his attorney has been out of the office, but will be back tomorrow. He said that we will discuss the bills, house, cars and kids this evening when he drops C.J. off. I just want to get everything resolved and move forward with you, baby."

"That ain't what I'm talking about. I'm talking about the interrogation you gave Craig about who he's seeing. You have a problem with him seeing someone else?"

"Yeah, I guess I do a little bit. I mean, I'm feeling bad because I cheated behind his back and felt guilty about it. I'm just wondering if he had been cheating on me all of this time too. He's sleeping with this chick already."

"It doesn't take that long, Kellie. How long had I known you before we were intimate?"

"Not long at all. I'm sorry that I was tripping, baby. This is something I'm going to have to get used to."

"What?"

"Craig and another woman and the relationship this woman will have with my son. I somewhat understand Craig's issue about C.J. coming over here. It's hard to have another man or woman spending family time with your kid. What's harder about our situation is that C.J. already knows you and it's going to be very confusing for him when we tell him that you and I are going to be together."

"Yeah. When are we going to tell him?"

"I'll discuss it with Craig tonight. I didn't sleep well. It was hard sleeping without you. I've gotten used to having you next to me."

"I was at work most nights while you were here. How was last night any different?"

"All of the other nights I knew you were coming home. Last night, I knew you wouldn't be there and I was lonely."

"That's why we need to hurry up and do what we're going to do so that we can be together all of the time. You know, if you move here with me, we can be together all of the time."

"I'd love to be with you everyday, but I've got to get things resolved with Craig before I can take that step. Let's take our time and do this right."

"Alright. I'm a patient man. Come on and lay down with me. It was a long night and I need a massage. Don't you?"

"You know I do."

Kellie began undressing as she walked towards the bedroom. Arthur came up behind her and began grinding against her bare ass. He kissed her on her neck and placed both hands on her stomach as he continued to grind. Kellie pulled away and continued to undress as she walked to the bed.

Arthur was fully nude when he met up with Kellie at the end of the bed.

"Damn, baby. You still look good, even with the baby. I think you look better."

"Thank you, Arthur. I was feeling a little self conscious because I put on some weight."

"Don't be. Every pound went in the right place. It looks like your tits are a full cup larger and your ass, damn, Kellie, my dick gets hard every time I look at you. Lay back, relax, let me make you feel good."

"Okay, Arthur."

After making love they fell asleep. Kellie's alarm went off at three thirty. She had to get home and prepare dinner for C.J.

She turned the alarm off, slid under the covers and began massaging Arthur's dick. He shifted his body to give her access to what she wanted. She took him in her mouth then sucked and massaged him until he was ready to come. They discovered one of the most comfortable positions during Kellie's pregnancy was doggy style.

He felt the urgency in Kellie's stroke and turned her around, sat her on his lap and let her ride him to a climax, just the way she liked it.

"I have to get out of here, Arthur. I planned to cook dinner before I left. I didn't plan to sleep so late. I'll bring some food by here tomorrow, okay?"

"Alright, baby. Call me after your talk with Craig."

"I will."

Kellie started dinner as soon as she came through the door. Craig brought C.J. home shortly thereafter. Craig sat at the table while Kellie cut up lettuce for the salad.

"Would you like to stay for dinner, Craig?"

"What are you cooking?"

"I'm baking Chicken, au gratin potatoes, green salad..."

"Yeah. That sounds good. Listen about the house. If you want to keep it, you can. I'll continue to pay the mortgage in lieu of child support.

That way, things will not change. You take care of C.J. and I'll continue to take care of the house. If and when you decide to move, we'll sell the house and split the profit."

"That sounds like a good and reasonable compromise. What will we do once I move and the house is sold? Will we need to go to court or should we include something about that in the divorce papers?"

"Do you plan to move soon?"

Kellie stood and walked over to the sink.

"Arthur wants to get married as soon as we're divorced."

There was a long moment of silence.

Craig said, "Alright. We can do this until you're ready to move out of the house. After that, I'll pay child support for C.J."

"If the baby I'm carrying is yours, will I have a problem getting child support from you for her, especially if Arthur and I are married?"

"Naw, Kellie. I'll take care of your baby, if I have to. I paid your car note for this month, but you're going to need to pick it up from this point on. I have to pay rent for my apartment and I need furniture and stuff."

"Why don't you take some of this stuff? There is enough furniture in this house for both of us. You can get the bedroom set out of the guestroom, I'll put together a package with linens, kitchenware, whatever you need let me know, Craig."

"Alright. Can you pay the utilities, take care of C.J. and pay your car note without my help?"

"Yes. I should be able to handle that."

"I'll be moving into my apartment over the weekend. So whenever you can get that package together will be great."

"Okay. Can you help C.J. get cleaned up for dinner and y'all come on and sit down."

Craig helped C.J. wash his hands while Kellie set the table. When they returned to the kitchen the food was on the table waiting.

After saying grace, they all began eating. During dinner they listened to C.J. talk about his day.

After dinner, Kellie began cleaning the dishes and Craig got up and helped her. It was like old times.

"Kellie."

"Yes."

"I wanted to tell you that you are carrying your baby very well. I know you said that you were stressed and tired, but you look good. I didn't mean it when I said you look like shit."

"Thank you, Craig."

As they cleaned the kitchen, they kept bumping into each other. Finally, Craig came up behind Kellie, and stood so close to her that she could feel his breath on her neck.

"I've got to get out of here, Kellie. I can't do this."

She stood still and said, "Okay. I'll let you know when I have that package ready for you."

He walked out. She heard him saying bye to C.J. After cleaning the kitchen, Kellie got C.J. and herself ready for bed. She talked to Arthur briefly about what happened. He was upset with Kellie for inviting Craig to dinner. He told her that he was working overtime in the morning and would not be home until after four.

"I guess I won't see you tomorrow then."

"Not unless you can find a sitter and come by later."

"I don't know. I'll see and let you know."

Shortly after Kellie's conversation with Arthur, Craig called.

"Hello, Craig."

"Kellie, I'm sorry about what I did earlier. I've been with you for six years and it's hard for me to be around you without touching you. I hope that I didn't add to your stress."

"No, not at all. I'll have some things for you tomorrow when you drop C.J. off."

"Okay, thanks."

"You're welcome."

After talking to Craig and Arthur, Kellie got C.J. ready for bed and then went to bed herself. Kellie slept very well that night.

Since Arthur was at work during the day the next day, Kellie worked on separating some of the household items for herself and Craig. She talked to Arthur a few times during the day, but knew she wouldn't be able to get away to spend time with him. The situation with Craig was still too fragile and she didn't want to ask him to watch C.J.; he'd know why.

Kellie ran to the store for some essential items for dinner and when she returned to the house, Craig's car was in the driveway.

When she came inside, she heard a commotion upstairs.

"Craig?"

He stuck his head around the corner from the top of the stairs and said, "Yes. I'm dismantling this bed and getting stuff together. I'll be by here Saturday morning with a truck."

"Where is C.J.?"

Craig came down to the bottom of the stairs.

"He's at my mother's. He was eating dinner and I didn't want to pull him away."

"I got a few things for you that you can take today. Where is your place?"

"In Alsip. Not too far from here. I need to stay close to C.J."

"Are you going to be able to pay rent there and the mortgage here?"

"Yes. I should be okay. I'll get C.J. and try to finish up after I bring him home, if you don't mind."

"Okay."

After Craig left, Kellie started dinner.

* * *

Craig returned with C.J. about an hour later. Craig went upstairs to the guest room and began bringing things down to the garage.

Kellie asked Craig if he wanted to join her for dinner, but he passed. He had been working diligently in the basement boxing and gathering his things.

After giving C.J. his bath, Kellie took a shower and dressed for bed. She had a few movies that she wanted to watch before returning to work, so she popped one in the machine in the family room, got herself situated on the couch and pressed start on the remote. Shortly after the movie began, Kellie fell asleep. She wasn't sure how long she'd been sleep, but woke up when she felt herself being lifted. When she opened her eyes, Craig was staring at her. He carried her upstairs and laid her across the bed. They stared at each other until Kellie shifted her eyes.

"Can I make love to you, Kellie?"

When Kellie looked at Craig again, she saw the passion in his eyes, but she was afraid to say anything. She wanted him physically, but the consequences...

"That's okay, Kellie. I understand. We're not together anymore, I just miss you." He began to walk away.

Kellie grabbed Craig's hand, pulled him down on the bed with her and kissed him. She pulled away, stood in front of him, pulled her gown over her head and stood in front of him nude.

His hands went to her stomach. He started rubbing her stomach then laid his head on her stomach and said, "I miss you, Kellie."

"I miss you too, Craig. I'm sorry for all of this."

He pulled her down on the bed and then undressed himself. Before entering her, he looked her in the eyes and said, "I still love you, Kellie."

Craig knew how to please her during her pregnancy; he made sure to be gentle with her and to hold her stomach while riding her from behind. She pulled away from him and straddled him.

Her stroke wasn't as smooth as he remembered, but she was a little further along in her pregnancy, so he helped her. He gave as much of himself as she could handle. Craig knew that Kellie always came in such a dramatic way and was looking forward to seeing that look and passion in her eyes. He knew it was close when Kellie began moaning.

"Umm Craig, that feels so good."

"You miss big daddy's dick?"

"Yes. Damn, baby, this feels so good."

"Ride it, Kellie. Let me take care of what you need."

Kellie moaned and groaned herself into a hard climax with Craig following closely behind.

Kellie laid her head on Craig's chest and fell asleep. When Kellie opened her eyes the next morning and was staring into Craig's face, she was a little nervous. She slid off of him and went into the bathroom to shower.

While Kellie was showering, the phone rang and out of habit, Craig answered. It was Arthur.

"Hello."

There was a long pause.

"Hello."

"Where's Kellie?"

"In the shower."

"Tell her to call me."

"Man, I know you want to know what's up, so I'm gonna tell you. I fucked your woman last night."

"Yeah, right."

"Why do you think I'm here so early in the morning? I tapped that ass and it was just as good as I remember. I'll tell her to call you."

After hanging up the phone, Craig got out of bed, grabbed a towel out of the closet and went into the bathroom with Kellie. She let him join her in the shower where he made love to her again.

Michele

Michele and Nick spent quality time together, but Michele wondered why Eva didn't like her. She wanted Nick to find out immediately.

"Baby, why don't you call your mother and ask her why she doesn't think I'm right for you."

"Okay."

"I mean now, Nick. It's really bugging me not knowing. We had a great lunch and good conversation. She even offered to help with the wedding. There were no signs of her not liking me and now this? I need to know what it is."

"Okay, baby, I'll find out."

Michele just stared at him.

"Okay, I'll find out now. Don't say anything because I don't want her to know that I'm with you and having this conversation."

"Okay, I wont' say anything."

He dialed Eva's number.

"Hey, Mom. What y'all up to?

Nick talked to his mother for at least twenty minutes before hanging up. Most of his conversation consisted of um's and oh's.

When he hung up the phone, Michele said, "Well?"

"Were you talking to and kissing some guy outside of Roscoe's today?"

"That was Eddie."

"Eddie. The guy you were seeing when we first met."

"Eddie is a friend."

"Oh, that's right. He was your sex buddy."

"Yes and that's all it was. But after meeting you, I didn't need him anymore."

"When is the last time you were with him?"

"The time you asked me if I was on a date and I told you that I was. After that you and I were getting pretty serious, so I didn't need him any longer."

"Well, my mom said she saw you kissing him and that you two left together holding hands. She said that you can't be trusted and that you're a flirt."

"I am not a flirt."

"Yes you are, Michele."

"Okay, I am a little, but isn't that one of the things you love about me?"

"Yes. She's convinced that you slept with Eddie yesterday."

"Baby, you know where I was yesterday evening. I was with you and you were working your magic on me. I don't want your mother to think that I would disrespect you in any way. You've got to tell her that Eddie is just a friend of mine. Someone you know."

"I don't know him."

"Nick. Nothing happened with Eddie and I. I came home after lunch with your family. You know that."

"Yeah, you're right. Why did you kiss him?"

"It wasn't a kiss, it was a peck on the lips."

"My mom made it sound so passionate. She said that he tilted your head up to him and he planted a big juicy kiss on you right on the mouth."

"He did, but it didn't mean anything sexual. It's just how we are with each other."

"Michele, please don't ever kiss another man like that. When my mother was telling me about it I was getting sick to the stomach. All kinds of horrific thoughts were running through my mind. I don't know if I could handle it if I lost you to another man."

"There is no other man that comes close to you, Nick. I will never give up what we have for anything in the world. I would never jeopardize what we have. I love you, baby."

"I love you too. I'll get my mother straight. I don't want there to be any misunderstandings. I want you and my family to get along. You're going to be my wife and I want nothing more than to have a warm and loving family."

"That's what I want too."

"Alright, let me get out of here. I need to make sure everything is in order for the cookout tomorrow. My mom has invited a few people and I've invited a few people, so it should be nice."

"Okay, baby. Let me know if you need me to bring more than beverages. I can definitely contribute more."

"Don't worry about it. I've got it covered."

***

The next afternoon when Michele arrived at Nick's place, his family was there.

Nick greeted her at the door.

"Hey, baby."

"Hey, Michele. They are all in the back cooking, in the pool, they got the music going and everyone is really having a good time."

"You've got a full house."

"Yes. It looks like everyone made it. Come on."

"Did you talk to your mom?"

"Yes. She's cool now."

"I still want to talk to her and reassure her that I'm faithful to you."

"Don't worry about it, baby. It's all good."

When Michele saw Eva, she said, "Eva, can I talk to you for a minute?"

"Of course, Michele."

Michele began walking towards Nick's office.

"Come in here so that we can have some privacy."

Michele closed the door behind Eva and sat at Nick's desk.

"Eva, I just want to explain what you saw yesterday. Nick told me that you thought I was flirtatious, which is true. I am a flirt, but I would never do anything to jeopardize what I have with Nick and he knows that. The guy you saw me talking to yesterday. His name is Eddie. We go way back and yes we used to date. As a matter of fact, I was seeing Eddie off and on when I met Nick."

"So Eddie is an old boyfriend."

"Yes and no. He's a friend. After Nick and I had our second date, I told Eddie that I couldn't see him any longer. I knew early on that Nick was the man for me. I didn't want anyone or anything to jeopardize my chances of being in a relationship with Nick."

"So you broke things off with Eddie, yet when you saw him yesterday, you kissed him, passionately I may add."

"There was nothing sexual about our kiss. I kissed him and we held hands. It was loving, not sexual. I love Eddie as a friend, a friend who will always be there for me and look out for me. Nick knows this and he is comfortable with it."

"Do you think Nick would be comfortable if he saw how Eddie kissed you?"

"No. I promised Nick today that would never happen again. Before Nick, I'd always been so independent, not tied down to any guy in particular and I'm still adjusting my thinking. Nick told me he didn't want me doing it, so I won't do it."

"It looked like you were leaving with Eddie."

"He walked me to my car which was parked around the corner."

"I'm sorry for the interrogation, Michele. You're beautiful and I love my son. I just don't want him to be blinded by your beauty and accept anything you say just to be with you."

"You sure don't have to worry about that, Eva. Nick is very confident and to be honest, he's the true catch. I'm the lucky one that has his eye and his heart and I won't do anything to take the focus off of that."

"I'm very happy to hear that, Michele. I'm not one to get involved in Nick's personal business, but he is talking marriage and I want nothing more than love and happiness for my son."

"That's what I'm giving him."

"Thanks for that, Michele. I see why he loves you so much."

"I love him just as much."

When Michele saw Nick after she and Eva rejoined the party, she winked her eye at him and smiled. He smiled back.

Gina

Gina walked into the conference room with confidence. She was determined to go through mediation and not think about working things out with Marcus. When she saw Marcus all of those strong feelings came flooding back. He looked so good in his Navy blue pinstriped suit.

She sat next to Megan across the table from Marcus.

Megan said, "I'm glad that we all could make it today and hopefully we can make progress with this agreement. Gina has a new proposal which includes a new or another home for her and the kids within two years of the finalization of the divorce. She will be allowed to stay in the current home until the time that the new home becomes available."

Marcus' attorney said, "Is my client expected to continue to pay the mortgage at the current home and if so, for how long?"

"The mortgage, utilities and an allowance are what my client needs to maintain the lifestyle that she and the children have become accustomed to. Your client will continue to pay the mortgage and the attached bills until it is deemed unnecessary and a new arrangement has been agreed upon."

Marcus' attorney said, "Doesn't your client work? She has her own income now and from what I understand, it's fairly lucrative."

"Yes, she does work. Her income isn't sufficient enough to cover the household expenses, nor maintain the children's activities. She has agreed to pay for childcare and some of the children's activities."

"Marcus' attorney began to protest, but Marcus put his hand up and said, "Okay. If Gina will pay Mrs. Carver and Karate classes for the boys, I'll cover everything else."

Marcus' attorney looked at him like he was crazy.

Marcus said, "Let's discuss visitation. I would like to have the boys with me every other weekend and a few days during the week."

"Okay, and we'll discuss special occasions and holidays as they come up," Gina said.

Marcus' attorney said, "Gina, Marcus would like to continue storing his personal items at the house until he is able to find suitable living conditions."

"Okay."

Megan said, "Is there anything else we need to discuss?"

Marcus said, "Can I have a private moment alone with Gina, please?"

The attorneys excused themselves and left Gina and Marcus in the conference room. Once the door closed it was silent for at least a minute before Marcus said, "Gina, I love you and I want to stay married to you. I don't want a divorce. I don't want to share the kids at different households. I don't want to lose you to another man. I don't want anyone else to have you, baby. You're mine and I don't want to let you go."

"Marcus, you won't be able to get over what I did."

"I have to. I won't be able to get over losing you forever. I can't go through with this. Yes, I was very upset about what you'd done. It's still upsetting, but the pain of not having you in my life hurts more than what you've done. I promise you, Gina, I will do everything in my power to put that incident behind us if you're willing to give us another chance."

Gina sat in silence for what seemed an eternity before she spoke.

"When you made love to me the other day, I knew that I wanted to be with you for the rest of my life. I've been a fool trying to convince myself that I could be with another man when in reality there is no other man for me. I love you and I always will. I hope you can forgive me for what I've done in the past and I'm hoping we can start anew right now this minute."

Marcus walked around the table, reached for Gina's hand and as she stood to face him, he kissed her passionately. When they parted, Marcus said, "You're my wife Gina and I don't ever want that to change. Promise me that we'll never come to this table again."

"I promise, Marcus. I love you and I'll make sure you know it everyday for the rest of our lives."

They were kissing when the attorneys entered the room. Megan cleared her throat and said, "Okay guys, do we have an agreement?"

Marcus said, "Gina and I have decided to reconcile."

Megan said, "Really? Gina, what happened?"

"We love each other and we want to be together."

"Alright then. I wish you two the best of luck and I'm really happy that you found the courage to speak up before it went any further than it has."

"Thank you, Megan."

Marcus took Gina's hand and said, "Come on, baby, let's go home."

* * *

When Gina and Marcus arrived home, Mrs. Carver was serving lunch to the kids. Marcus told Mrs. Carver that he would finish serving their food. After she made sure everything was situated, she left the kitchen.

Marcus and Gina sat down with the kids. Marcus began by saying, "Listen guys, I've been gone out of the house for a while now and I'm ready to come back home. Do you want me to come back home?"

They both jumped up and started screaming, "Yes, Daddy! Yes!!!"

"Okay, we'll be together again. Gina, let's go out to dinner this evening. All four of us."

"Okay. I'll find clothes for the boys to wear."

"I'll make reservations at Chez Philippe for six o'clock. How is that?"

"That's great. Can I see you upstairs, Marcus?"

"Sure, baby."

Marcus went upstairs ahead of Gina. Gina walked into the family room and asked Mrs. Carver if she could make sure the kids finished their lunch while she went to find clothes for them for dinner and if she could bathe the boys and have them dressed by five thirty.

She said that she would.

When Gina walked into the bedroom, she closed the door behind herself. She began undressing and told Marcus to do the same.

"I can't wait any longer, Marcus. I need you. When I walked into that conference room, it was love at first sight all over again. I wanted you so bad at that moment and I didn't think I would ever get the opportunity to have you again. I need to make love to you."

Marcus walked over to Gina, pulled her into his arms and they kissed passionately. They were hungry for each other. They quickly undressed and were clawing at each other trying to get as close to one another as possible.

After making love, they showered, dressed for dinner and made their way downstairs.

Mrs. Carver had the boys ready to go. After seeing Mrs. Carver out, they headed to Marcus' car and then to the restaurant.

Marcus, Jr. said, "When are you coming home, Dad?"

I'm already home. I'll go to the apartment and get my things tomorrow, but I'm coming home with you guys tonight."

Both Marcus, Jr. and Michael screamed, "Yippee!"

Michael said, "Mommy, can I sleep with you in your bed tonight?"

Marcus and Gina looked at each other and said, "No."

Dinner was nice. It was one of the nicest evenings Gina and Marcus had had together or apart in a long time. After arriving home and getting the boys to bed, Gina poured a glass of wine for herself and Marcus then they sat together on the couch in the family room.

"Jeff called me earlier, but I haven't had a chance to tell him that you and I are together again. I don't want to tell him over the phone. It just wouldn't be right."

"I agree. When is he due to return?"

"Tomorrow. I'll meet him for lunch and tell him."

"Why do you have to have lunch with him?"

"I don't want to do it here or at his place. I think a public place is best so that we can go our separate ways afterwards."

"That makes sense."

"Do you need to tell someone that you're committed to your marriage?"

"No. I already told Miranda that I didn't want to see her anymore a month or more ago."

"Really? Why?"

"She's not you."

Gina smiled and slid closer to Marcus.

"What are your friends going to say when you tell them that you and I are back together?"

"They will be happy for me. That's the type of friends I have. They want me to be happy and they knew that I was very happy with you."

Marcus held Gina's hand and said, "Can we work on that baby girl we've been talking about for years?"

"Yes. I'm ready."

"What about your job?"

"I really like my job, Marcus. I want to continue working."

"My real concern about your job is that every time you go to work, you end up dating someone new."

"I needed the attention. I felt rejected by you and after you slept with Miranda, I really needed attention from someone. Now that I have you again, I don't need anyone else."

"Will you stop working when you become pregnant?"

"Not immediately. I like working, Marcus. Let's take it one day at a time. Okay?"

"Okay. Will you go with me tomorrow to get my things?"

"Yes, of course. What are you going to do with your condo?"

"I'll rent it out. We can use the income for the kids' college fund or something."

"Okay, whatever you say. Would you like another glass of wine?"

"Yes, thank you."

Stacey

When Stacey went inside, Richard was putting the DVD in the player. Stacey tried to go upstairs.

"Don't go upstairs, Stacey. We need to watch this together."

"I want to put Robert to bed."

"Put him in his playpen in here."

Stacey turned around and came into the family room and put Robert in the playpen.

She plopped down on the couch with tears in her eyes.

"Do you want to tell me what's on this DVD, Stacey? I can tell that you know what it is."

"When Sandra called yesterday, she was trying to find me to confront me about dancing at the bachelor party in Vegas. Charles called me and warned me that Sandra was looking for me. I didn't believe that she would find me, so I didn't worry about it too much."

"What's on the DVD?"

Long pause.

"What's on the DVD, Stacey? I can press play and watch you dance and get mad and walk out of here or you can tell me and I won't have to watch you shake your ass in the faces of all of those men. There must be more to it than what you told me. Does it show you having sex with Charles?"

"Yes. I don't want you to watch me fuck another man, Richard."

"I know that's not all. Is it? Why was this woman so determined to find you because you had sex with Charles?"

"I guess she was mad that I danced for her husband."

"What kind of dancing did you do?"

"You know how it is at a bachelor party, Richard. I did what I needed to so that the groom was satisfied."

"You fucked him, didn't you? That's why his wife is so upset. You fucked the groom the night before his wedding, and you fucked Charles at this same party. How many more were there, Stacey?"

"That was it."

"So you did fuck the groom?"

"Yes."

He stood, faced Stacey and said, "Why did you lie to me? You told me that you only danced and that you fucked Charles because he blackmailed you."

"That's partially true. I did sleep with Charles because he blackmailed me, but I also slept with the groom."

"So you were not just a dancer, you were a prostitute too."

"I wasn't a prostitute."

"I've been to bachelor parties, Stacey and every ho that sleeps with men at the party are always considered prostitutes. Why is it different for you?"

"It was one time, Richard."

"How many other men did you sleep with?"

"No others."

"Charles was telling the truth and I chose to believe you.'

"I'm sorry that I lied to you, but I couldn't tell you that I slept with the groom. I wish I had, but I would have lost you for sure. Are you going to look at the DVD?"

"I don't know, Stacey. I want to watch it and find out the truth so that nothing else comes out later. I don't want to see you fucking another man and I especially don't want to see Charles inside of you, Stacey."

He walked over to the DVD player and took the DVD out and went upstairs. Stacey sat on the couch frozen, scared to move. A few minutes later, Richard came downstairs, got his coat out of the closet and walked out the door. When the door closed, Stacey broke down and cried.

Stacey was awake all night waiting for Richard to call or come home. He did neither.

Richard bought a bottle of Jack Daniels, got a hotel room and watched the DVD featuring his wife and two other women dancing nude in a room full of men. He then watched Stacey having sex with the groom and then with his best friend, Charles. He watched the DVD several times before passing out.

The next morning when he woke, he went to the hotel lobby and bought a bottle of Aleve. He knew he had to get himself together because he was flying out that night. He had to get away. He decided to go home, pack and return to the hotel until he was ready to report for work.

Stacey had been calling his cell phone, but he had no desire to talk to her.

When he came through the front door at home, he didn't see anyone and was happy to not face Stacey. As he climbed the stairs he heard Stacey talking to the baby. He slid past the nursery and into the bedroom he shared with Stacey and began packing his bag. He would be out for two days, but was packing enough for more. Just as he zipped his last piece of luggage, Stacey appeared in the doorway.

"Richard..."

Richard put his hand up to Stacey signaling that he didn't want to discuss it with her. He caught a glimpse of her out of the corner of his eye and was disgusted. He had a flash of her dancing, giving blow jobs, and fucking and it made him sick.

He grabbed his bags, pushed past Stacey, quickly descended the stairs and out the door. He needed some fresh air. He wanted to see Robert, but that would delay his departure and he had to get out of the house and away from Stacey.

Stacey looked out of the picture window as she stood at the top of the stairs and watched Richard drive away without letting her know where he was going and if he was coming back.

She called Gina.

"Good morning, Stacey. How are you?"

Stacey started bawling immediately.

Gina let her cry it out. Once Stacey settled down, she asked, "What's wrong, Stacey?"

"Richard left me."

"What do you mean he left you? Did he tell you he was not coming back, or was he upset and walked out the house?"

"That bitch Sandra found me and came to my house. Oh yeah, the traffic stop was bogus. It was her sister. I'm tempted to report her to her superiors. But anyway, I know that bitch keyed my car too. When I came in from shopping, Richard came out to the car to see the damage and Sandra and her sister pulled in the driveway behind me and gave Richard the DVD.

He didn't watch it in front of me. He questioned me about the contents and I had to admit that I had sex with the groom and Charles because he had the evidence in his hand. He got mad and stormed out yesterday. He didn't come home last night, he didn't call nor would he answer my calls. He came in a little while ago and packed a couple of suitcases. I know he has to travel tonight, but that is just a two day trip. He had enough stuff for at least a week.

He didn't say anything to me or the baby. He just walked out."

"Okay. Just give him some time and let him come to you, Stacey. I'm sure he has watched the DVD and he has to make a decision about what he wants to do. Richard is very level headed, I'm sure he will be back."

"I don't know this time, Gina. I lied when I had the opportunity to tell him the truth and he forgave me and married me. Now he finds out that not only did I have sex with Charles, I also had sex with the groom and all of those guys were groping and squeezing, slapping and feeling all over me and I let them. How difficult do you think that was for him to watch?"

"Maybe he didn't watch it."

"He watched it. If he hadn't, he would at least be talking to me right now."

"Do you need me to come out there to be with you?"

"No, that's okay, Gina. I'll get through this. Just be there to listen to me."

"I'll definitely do that."

After talking to Gina, Stacey took the baby downstairs and began cleaning the house. She didn't hear from Richard at all that day.

The phone rang early the next morning.

"Hello."

"Hello, Stacey, it's Richard."

"Good morning."

"I think it's only fair that I let you know when I come back in town that I'll be staying at a hotel for a couple more days until I can sort out my feelings."

"Okay."

"How is Robert?"

"He's doing well. I'm sorry about all of this Richard."

"Not right now, Stacey. I'm not ready to discuss this with you yet. Like I said, I need to sort through some things, but once I'm ready to talk, we'll talk."

"Okay."

Richard didn't return the next day, nor did he call. Stacey tried to keep herself busy, but she couldn't concentrate. When nightfall arrived and she hadn't heard from Richard, she cried herself to sleep again. Although she was only able to sleep for a couple of hours, she was happy to get any sleep at all.

After almost a week of waiting and wondering, Richard walked into the house in the middle of the afternoon. Stacey heard him come in, but was afraid to greet him. She heard him when he came into the kitchen.

"Stacey."

She turned to face him. "Yes, Richard."

"I need to talk to you. Can you come into the family room?"

She took Robert out of his swing and brought him into the family room with her.

"Give him to me."

She handed the baby to Richard and had a seat on the sofa.

"I watched the DVD."

Stacey knew not to say anything.

"I couldn't believe my eyes, Stacey. There was no shame in what you did. You were dancing like a professional. Where did you learn to do that?"

"I bought a tape and practiced before we went to Vegas. Once I was there and the music was going and I had a few drinks, I just went into another state of mind."

"How could you tell me that you love me and then do that? I'm having a big problem trying to accept this and move forward with you. Now we have Robert to consider, this house, you not working anymore and the chance of you being pregnant again."

Stacey looked up and said, "I'm not pregnant."

"You don't know that yet, Stacey."

"Yes I do. My period came this morning."

"Isn't it early?"

"Yes, a few days or so. I guess it's just stress."

"Well, that will make this a little easier. I can't look at you right now without thinking about what you've done. I've got to get out of the house for a while. I got a room at an extended stay hotel a couple of miles from here. I reserved the room for a month. I need this time to get the anger out of my system. I don't want to desert you and I need to see Robert. I'm not sure how we're going to work that out, but this is something that I must do.

I'll leave my work schedule on the dresser so that you'll know where I am and you can reach me on my cell phone."

"Again, I'm sorry about what I did, Richard. I thought that whole episode was behind me. It's all out now and we won't have to revisit it again."

He slid the DVD across the table to Stacey and walked out of the room and up the stairs.

Kellie

Kellie fixed breakfast while Craig got C.J. ready for daycare. When they all sat down for breakfast, Craig said, "I'll be here early Saturday to pick up the stuff I packed. I want to get moved early and not make it an all day ordeal."

"Alright. I'll have everything else ready for you. Can you drop C.J. off at daycare this morning?"

"Yeah, no problem. As a matter of fact, why don't you let him stay with me tonight? I'm off work tomorrow and he can help me around the house."

"Okay, I'll get his things together."

Kellie packed C.J.'s things and shortly afterwards Craig and C.J. were heading out the door.

Craig stopped at the door and said, "Kellie, thanks for last night and this morning. Making love to you felt good and I really got what I needed."

"It was good, Craig."

"I'll talk to you later."

After Craig and C.J. left, Kellie began cleaning the kitchen. A few minutes later the door bell rang. When Kellie opened the door, Arthur was there.

"Hey, baby. What a nice surprise."

"Is it really, Kellie?"

"Yes, of course it is. Come on in."

She stepped aside and Arthur came inside.

She tried to kiss him, but he turned away.

"What's wrong?"

"Did I just see Craig leaving?"

"Yes. He took C.J. to daycare."

"Why didn't you call me back?"

"When?"

"When you got out of the shower this morning."

"I didn't know you called."

"I knew Craig wouldn't tell you that I called, but he was happy to tell me that he fucked you last night."

Kellie was speechless.

"What's up, Kellie? You still fucking Craig?"

Kellie was totally dumbfounded.

Arthur turned and walked towards the door and said, "Call me when you find your voice."

She ran up behind him, grabbed his arm and said, "Arthur, I'm sorry. I got caught up in the moment of guilt and familiarity. I think he planned this. He's been extra nice to me, helping with C.J. and just spending a lot of time around me and I got caught up in it. Please, Arthur, don't leave. I'm sorry."

"Listen, Kellie. I'm gonna give you a little time to decide if you're serious about being with me. I love you and I'm serious about being with you for the rest of my life. I thought you felt the same way, but if it's so easy for you to sleep with Craig, then maybe you aren't as serious about us as I am. I love you, Kellie. I risked my life and yours to be with you and now you do this."

"I can't make you understand how it happened. The guilt of how it all went down made me weak. I was a fool for falling for it. Craig knew what he was doing. He doesn't want me and I'm sure he hates me. I think he just wanted to get back at you and me. I promise, it will never happen again, Arthur. I love you and I want to be with you for the rest of my life. Please don't let this drive a wedge between us."

"I've got to go home and get some sleep. We'll talk this evening."

After Arthur left, Kellie tried calling Craig, but he wouldn't answer his phone. Her call went to voicemail.

"Craig, why did you tell Arthur that we slept together? You know what? I don't want your answer to that question because I already know what it is. It's alright, Craig. I understand why you did it and it will never happen again. I deserved it, Arthur deserved it. Yes, it hurt and it hurt Arthur, so you accomplished your mission. I was weak for you, but I see you had a motive. You didn't desire me. You wanted me so that you could tell Arthur that we slept together.

I hope that we can now move forward, Craig. You got what you wanted. I won't mention anything about this to you again and there is no need for you to explain yourself.

I hope to hear from your attorney soon. If I don't hear something by Monday, I'll file for divorce. I did love you, Craig, whether you believe that or not, I don't know. That's why it was so easy for me to give myself to you last night. So let's be adults for C.J.'s sake and we'll see what happens with the baby I'm carrying. If she's yours we'll deal with it. If not, we'll take care of C.J. together in an adult and civil manner. Have a good day."

Craig never returned her call and she didn't expect to see him again until the next evening when he brings C.J. home.

Kellie packed a bag and headed to Arthur's house. She stood on his porch for what seemed an eternity. She didn't want to use her key because she didn't know if she was still welcome at his house.

When Arthur opened the door, he stood and stared at Kellie for a few seconds before he opened the screen door and let her in.

After he closed the door they stood in silence for a few seconds before Arthur opened his arms and Kelly walked into them.

"Come on and lay down with me, I had a long night and I'm really tired. I couldn't sleep after this morning, but maybe I'll be able to sleep with you here. How long can you stay?"

"C.J. won't be home until tomorrow evening."

"I want you to move in with me, Kellie. Craig is going to have to get over himself and accept that we're going to be together. After he gets his stuff out of the house this weekend, we'll start packing yours and C.J.'s things and y'all will move in here. Once we're married, we'll have a house of our own built. I've been planning for a new home to share with you and the kids so that's what we'll work towards together. Okay?"

"Yes, Arthur. Yes."

"Come here." He pulled her into his arms and they both drifted off to sleep."

Michele

While Michele sat on one of the chaise lounges positioned around the pool, she watched Nick's family and friends interact. She decided that it was time for her to call her mom and let her know that she was getting married and work towards mending their relationship.

Michele went into Nick's office and sat at his desk. Inside of her wallet was the phone number her mother wrote inside of a card that she gave Michele at her Aunt Dee Dee's funeral.

This is Michele's first time using the number. She hoped that her mother wouldn't show much interest and wouldn't ask to attend the wedding. She just wanted to let her know that she was getting married and move on from there.

Linda answered the phone with a cheerful sound in her voice.

"Hello."

"Good afternoon, Linda. This is Michele, your daughter."

There was a slight pause before Linda said, "Michele, what a pleasure it is to hear from you. How are you? I'm so happy to hear from you"

"I'm doing great. I called to let you know that I'm getting married."

"Congratulations! Who is the lucky man?"

'His name is Nicholas Malloy."

"That's a nice name, Michele. I'm sure he's a wonderful man. I hope to meet him one day soon."

"I'm sure you will. How is everything with you?"

"Fine. Things are good. I was thinking about moving back to L.A."

"Really. Why?"

"All of our family is there in L.A. and since Don's passing, I'm here alone. I have friends here, but...I don't know, Michele, I was just thinking about it. Maybe if I do, you and I can spend time together."

"Maybe. I have to go, Linda, but I'll talk to you."

"Bye, Michele."

Michele ended her call with Linda and sat in silence for a little while until she got her emotions under control.

The office door opened and Nick stuck his head in.

"Are you alright, Michele?"

"Yes. I just called Linda and told her that we're getting married. She said congratulations."

"What else did she say?"

"She said that she was thinking about moving back to L.A., but nothing much more than that."

"Did you invite her to the wedding?"

"No, but I did tell her that I will be in touch with her. I'll send her an invitation when the time comes."

"That's a start. Come on and join the party, people are asking about you."

Upon joining the party, Michele was introduced to family and friends in the L.A. area. They had a great and relaxing evening.

Later that evening when Michele returned home, she called Kellie to see how things were going. No one answered at Kellie's house, so she called Kellie's cell phone.

When Kellie answered the phone she said, "Michele, I've been calling you for a few days. Why has it taken you so long to return my call?"

"Girl, Nick's people are in town and I've been running around with them, running back and forth between here and Santa Monica and work never ends, I'm sorry."

"So how did the big meeting go?"

"It was cool. His people are nice although I had a moment with his mother."

"What type of moment?"

"I had lunch with Nick's mom, sister and aunt and after lunch, I ran into Eddie."

"Your ex-fuck buddy?"

"Yes. Anyway, Eddie greeted me with a kiss and his mother saw it and labeled me a flirt and said that Nick needs to reconsider marrying me."

"Damn. You are a flirt, Michele."

"I'm not really a flirt. I'm just not shy and I like to talk to men."

"How does Nick deal with your personality?"

"He's cool with who I am. He did tell me not to kiss Eddie again. I think he would have been upset had he saw the kiss, so to keep him happy, I won't be kissing any other men."

"That sounds like a good idea. Did you get everything ironed out with his mom?"

"Yeah, we got it resolved and everything is fine now. What's going on with you and your life?"

"I'm going to be moving in with Arthur soon."

"Really, when did this come about? I remember that Craig was totally against that."

"It's not Craig's decision where I'm going to be living, so C.J. and I will be moving soon."

"Have you told Craig?"

"No. I will when he brings C.J. home tomorrow."

"That should be an interesting conversation."

"I don't care what Craig thinks about anything anymore after what he did to me."

"And what's that?"

"I'm so ashamed of myself. Michele, don't tell everybody."

"Oh hell, here we go again."

"Michele. I mean it this time."

"Alright, what happened?"

"Craig seduced me and I fell for it."

"Damnit, Kellie! I'm sorry, but damn, girl, can't you keep your legs closed."

"Fuck you, Michele."

Kellie hung up on her. Michele decided to wait a few hours before calling Kellie back. She needed time to calm down.

In the meantime, she went into her office and worked on the listings for her and Nick.

Before she could call Kellie, Kellie called her.

"I'm sorry about hanging up on you, Michele. I understand why you said what you said and yes, I can keep my legs closed. I should have been able to see through what Craig was doing, but my guilt got the best of me."

"How do you know that he didn't do it to get back with you."

"He told Arthur."

"What?"

"Yeah. Arthur called early this morning and Craig answered the phone and told him that he was at the house because he slept with me and spent the night."

"So what's going to happen now?"

"I had to confess to Arthur. It's going to be rocky for a little while, but we'll get past this. He told me that he wants us to move in with him and that we'll have a house of our own built and ready for us when we get married."

"Married?"

"Yes, Michele, married. He wants to get married as soon as possible. I love him and he loves me and we want to be together. I'll tell Craig that C.J.

and I are moving and I don't care how he feels about it. I'm not going to live my life to satisfy Craig."

"Good luck with that, Kellie."

"So tell me, what can I do to help you get this wedding planned?"

"It sounds like you have a wedding of your own to plan."

"Not yet. I have to get divorced from Craig first. Hopefully, he won't contest. I definitely won't. I just want to get it over with."

"Well, good luck with that, Kellie. It sounds like things will work themselves out. Once you get through this next conversation with Craig everything will be out in the open and you can move forward."

"We'll see. Have you talked to Gina or Stacey?"

"Naw. Do you want to get them on a conference call?"

"Yeah, I guess I can talk for a few minutes. I need to get dinner done for Arthur. I need to wake him up in a little while so that he can eat and get ready for work."

"Girl, you know you be taking care of your man. That's why Craig is so mad. He knows that he lost a good woman."

"As long as they take care of me, I'm going to do what I need to do to make him happy."

"I'll need to talk to you about being a good wife. I've been independent for so long, I need to start thinking more about us and not me."

"You're absolutely right, Michele. You love Nick and you'll want to take care of him, so I really don't think it will be a big adjustment for you. You'll learn what he likes as you get to know each other better and then you'll do what's necessary to keep him satisfied. I'm sure he'll do the same for you."

"You're right. Let me call Gina and Stacey to see what's going on with them.

When Michele got Gina and Stacey on the line, she reconnected Kellie.

Michele said, "Hey everybody, what's going on?"

Gina said, "Let me start. My husband and I are back together."

Kellie and Michele said, "WHAT!" in unison.

"Yes, ladies. My husband is back home and we've reconciled. I'm so happy."

"I'm happy for you, Gina," Michele said. "I'm really happy for y'all because I don't think y'all really wanted to be apart. Marcus just needed time."

"Yeah. We were actually in mediation trying to get everything settled and we both just stepped up and said how we felt."

Kellie said, "I'm happy that you did it before signing the divorce papers, or else there would be three weddings instead of two."

Stacey said, "Three? You're getting married, Kellie?"

"Arthur asked me to marry him once my divorce is final from Craig."

"He's serious about you, isn't he?" Stacey said.

"Yes, and I'm serious about him. Hopefully, we'll get through the divorce in a timely manner and we can all get on with our lives."

"Wow, Kellie. Congratulations," Gina said.

"Thank you, Gina and congratulations to you too."

"Thank you."

Michele said, "What's going on with you and that beautiful baby, Stacey?"

"Where do I begin? Well, Robert is fine."

"What's not fine?"

"The wife of the groom at the bachelor party I danced at which Charles was at."

"Yeah."

"She tracked me down at my house and confronted me about dancing for her husband and having sex with him."

"How does she know you had sex with him?" Kellie said.

"Apparently, someone thought it was a good idea to tape the event and give the DVD to the groom as a wedding gift. The wife found the DVD, watched it and set out to find me, which she did."

"Hell naw, Stacey," Kellie said.

"Yeah."

"So what's going on with Richard? Did he watch it?"

"Yes. He reserved a room at the extended stay hotel not too far from here for a month. I don't think he's going to leave me. He said he can't stand the sight of me and has to get away from me for a while."

"Damn, Stacey, I'm so sorry that you're going through this."

"Thanks, Michele. I'm sorry too. I'm not going to dwell on it. I'm just going to continue to take care of Robert and wait for Richard to return. What's up with the wedding plans?"

"We're working on things. I met Nick's family. We had a rocky moment, but things are great now. I'll have some information for you guys soon. Y'all already know the date, so start planning to be here that week."

"A week," Kellie said.

"Yes. Y'all know I'm gonna need a lot of help and I'll need y'all here with me."

"We'll see about a week, Michele," Gina said.

"Alright ladies, get off my phone. We'll talk next week. Congratulations again, Gina. Kellie and Stacey, I'm sure everything will work out for you guys. In the meantime, if you need anything, please call me."

"Alright, Michele and everybody, I'll talk to y'all soon," Stacey said.

Everyone said goodbye and got off the phone. Stacey called back a few minutes later asking Michele if she could come out to visit for a few days. Of course Michele said yes. It would give her something to do while Nick's people were still in town.

Michele prepared her home for Stacey's visit.

Gina

Gina was a little nervous about seeing Jeff and telling him that she and Marcus were a couple again. When she talked to Jeff on the phone, she hadn't given him any indication that anything was wrong.

When Jeff walked through the restaurant door and saw Gina sitting at the bar waiting for him, he smiled in a way that reminded Gina of why she was so attracted to him. For a fleeing moment she had second thoughts about breaking things off with Jeff. She told herself to be strong and slid off the barstool to greet him.

Jeff greeted Gina with the hostess in tow. After a brief hug and kiss, they were escorted to their table.

Once they were seated and situated, Gina said, "How was your trip?"

"It was good. I got my business in order. I really missed you and I've been thinking a lot about us since our trip to Denver. In the off season, I spend a lot of time at my house in Nassau and I was hoping that you and the boys could spend time there with lil Jeff and I."

"Jeff, while you were gone, Marcus and I reconciled."

"Excuse me?"

"When we went to mediation, we discovered that we didn't want a divorce and wanted to be together."

Jeff sat back in his chair and stared at Gina.

"I'm sorry about this, Jeff. I don't want you to think that I don't care about you because I do. It's just that when Marcus and I cut out all of the bullshit, we admitted that we still loved each other and wanted to work things out and that's what we're doing. Marcus has moved back in the house and we're going to give our marriage another chance."

"I'm happy for you then, Gina. You're a good woman and Marcus is lucky to have another chance with you."

"Thank you, Jeff."

"Let's order lunch, enjoy the afternoon and we'll part as friends. Okay?"

"Yes. Let's order."

When Gina left the restaurant, she called Marcus at work and told him the details of her lunch with Jeff. Marcus was happy that it was over and that it ended smoothly. They were both ready to start making up for lost time.

Stacey

After Stacey called Michele back and asked if she could visit for a few days, she immediately got on the internet and booked a flight for herself and Robert. Next, she called Richard.

"Hello, Stacey."

"Good afternoon, Richard. How are you?"

"Okay. How is Robert?"

"He's doing great. He misses you. I miss you."

Richard didn't say anything.

"Richard. I'm lonely here without you and I was hoping that you would be coming home soon."

"I'm not ready, Stacey. I want to be with you, but I can't right now. I want to see Robert though."

"I'm taking Robert with me to L.A. for a few days. I'm leaving in the morning and we'll be back Monday."

"What's in L.A.?"

"Michele. We're just going to visit for the weekend. It's been boring around here without you and I need a change of scenery. You can see Robert this evening if you want to."

"I'll be there in an hour or so."

"Okay."

Stacey packed a bag for the weekend for herself and Robert. She heard the garage door as it went up, but she stayed upstairs and continued packing.

Richard appeared in the door of the nursery. He walked over to the bassinette and picked Robert up.

"Hey man, your dad really misses you." He kissed him.

"Hello, Stacey."

"Hello, Richard."

Stacey walked out of the nursery and went into her bedroom and continued packing from there. Richard walked into the bedroom and said, "How long did you say you were going to be in L.A.?"

Stacey kept her head down and continued putting items in her suitcase. "We're just going for the weekend. We'll be back here Monday afternoon."

"I've been lonely. I miss you and Robert. I'll be here when you return."

Stacey looked at Richard for the first time since he came in the house. He smiled at her and she smiled back.

"I love you, Richard and I promise, I promise you that nothing like this will ever happen again."

"Okay, Stacey. I have a flight in the morning and I'll be back in town Sunday. Like I said before, I'll be here when you return Monday. Do you need me to pick you up from the airport?"

"Yes. Our flight arrives at two twenty."

"Okay, I need to get some sleep, but I'll see you Monday when your flight comes in. I'll call you in the morning. As a matter of fact, what time is your flight in the morning? I can take you to the airport."

"Ten thirty-five. What time is your flight out?"

"I need to be at the airport by nine, so I'll come by and pick y'all up on my way."

"Thank you, Richard."

He started walking towards the door and said, "I'll see you then, Stacey. Have a good night."

"You too."

"The next morning, Richard was at the house at seven thirty. Stacey had breakfast ready when he arrived. He came in the kitchen while she was feeding the baby. Richard took over the feeding while Stacey finished breakfast.

"Do you want some coffee, Richard?"

"Yes, thank you."

"I'm going to get the rest of our things and bring them down and we can leave after you finish your breakfast."

"Okay. Just put your bags in the hall and I'll bring them down to the car."

The ride to the airport was a little tense, but they were both happy to be together. Richard made sure Stacey and Robert reached their gate before reporting to his gate.

* * *

Michele was at the gate waiting when Stacey and Robert disembarked from the plane.

Kellie

The next evening when Kellie returned home, Craig was in the garage. He tried to ignore her, but she stood in the door until he acknowledged her.

"Alright, Kellie, I'm sorry about what I did. Okay?"

"No, it's not okay, Craig. But like I said on the message, I don't want to talk about it. You know what you did and why you did it so there is no need to discuss it further."

"Okay."

"I'm moving in with Arthur."

"You're not taking my son with you."

"Yes I am."

He stood up, walked over to her and said, "No you're not."

"Yes I am. Look Craig, I know you're not happy about the way things have turned out with us, but I have to live my life and you have to live yours. I'm going to be with Arthur and C.J. is going to be a part of my life with Arthur."

"I'm telling you now, Kellie. Do not move my son to Arthur's house or there will be trouble for real."

"Why Craig? You'll eventually be with another woman. I'm sure you'll get married again. Would it be fair of me to tell you who you can have around C.J.?"

"He's going to be confused, Kellie. He's been calling Arthur his uncle all of this time and now you want him to see you sleeping in the same bed with Arthur every night and kissing and touching each other. It's confusing for a five year old."

"He's seen me with Arthur, Craig. He's seen me kissing Arthur, he's seen Arthur touching me and he's seen Arthur and I sleeping in the same bed."

"What the fuck! When, Kellie?"

"A couple of weeks ago. We spent the night at Arthur's house and he's okay with it. He understands that you and I are not together anymore and that I'm going to be with Arthur."

"Ain't that a bitch. You decided to change the dynamics of my son's life without telling me? You and Arthur took it upon yourselves to introduce my son to your new lifestyle. Fine, Kellie. If you need to be with that punk ass bitch that bad, then you be with him."

"Where is C.J.?"

"My mother took him to McDonald's. She's going to drop him off when they are done."

Kellie walked past Craig and into the house.

Craig came inside shortly after and sat down at the table. Kellie was in the kitchen.

"When are you talking about moving?"

"I don't have a definitive date, but soon."

"Before you have your baby?"

"Probably."

"Alright. I'll stay in the house after you leave. I'll pay you out in the divorce settlement and I'll keep the house."

"Okay. Any word from your attorney?"

"Yeah. Your attorney should have something by tomorrow. I'll call him in the morning and have him add the details of the house.

You know, Kellie. I want to try to keep things civil, but you make it hard for me. First, I can't believe that you did this and now you're going to take my son and move him into this man's house. I'll have to come to this man's house to get my son?"

"It doesn't have to be that way, Craig. I know you picking C.J. up from daycare everyday will probably change, but we can work out a schedule that is conducive for both of us. You will still be able to get C.J. from school on the nights that he stays with you. I don't want to keep your son from you. On the contrary, I want the two of you to spend as much time as you can together. I don't want to do anything to jeopardize the relationship the two of you have. I promise to do everything I can to keep yours and C.J.'s relationship strong."

"Let me know when you're going to move out of here. I did a month to month lease at this apartment, so I'll at least know how many months I'll be there."

"Is it too late to cancel your lease?"

"I didn't give it back to the landlord yet. Why?"

"I'll be moving soon and I don't want you to move all of your things just to move them back."

"Why didn't you tell me all of this before I made all of these arrangements, Kellie?"

"I didn't plan to move so soon, but things changed."

"Is Arthur that insecure?"

"Yeah, I guess he is after what happened with us the other night. He wants me there with him. I was going to wait until after we're divorced, but I don't want to be here by myself."

"You didn't have to be here by yourself."

Before Kellie could respond, the doorbell rang. Kellie opened the door to let C.J. and Craig's mother in.

"Mommy!"

"Hey, baby. Give Mommy a hug and a kiss."

C.J. ran over to Kellie and hugged and kissed her.

"How are you, Eleanor?"

"I'm doing well, Kellie. C.J. has played himself silly. All he needs is a bath and he'll be ready for bed."

She looked at Kellie's stomach and said, "When is the baby due, Kellie?"

"Two months."

"Craig, I left C.J.'s bag in the car, can you get it for me?"

"Yeah. Is the door open?"

"Yes."

Kellie said, "C.J., I need you to get your toys off of the floor in the family room. I'm going to give you a bath in a minute, okay?"

"Okay, Mommy."

Eleanor said, "Kellie, what's going on with you and Craig?"

"We're getting divorced."

"He's very unhappy and I'm really concerned about his state of mind. He's been functioning like nothing has happened and that bothers me. I know he spent the night with you a few nights ago, C.J. told me. That couldn't be a good thing if you're getting divorced."

"I know. It's just hard to let go. I was wrong for what I did in our marriage and I just got caught up in the moment. But Craig didn't want me, nor did he want to reconcile. His motive was to hurt me and Arthur."

"C.J. has been talking about it all and I don't think he fully understands what's going on. He'll have to get older before he does. My concern is my son and my grandson, Kellie. Craig didn't deserve this."

"I know he didn't. He has been a great husband and father and I messed that up."

"And what about the baby you're carrying. What if Craig is the father? This child will never share a home with both of her parents. How are you going to explain your actions to your children when they are old enough to understand what happened?"

"I don't know, Eleanor."

Craig walked in the room and said, "Mom, please. Kellie and I are trying to work this out. Let us take care of this. If I'm the father of her baby, I'll take care of her and we'll have a great father/daughter relationship. It's been done for many years. I'll have joint custody of the kids and they will be with me as much as with Kellie."

"I'm just concerned about my grandchildren."

"Your grandchildren will be fine."

"Fine. C.J., come and say bye to grandma."

C.J. ran into the room and hugged Eleanor. I'll see you tomorrow right?"

"Yes."

He ran back into the family room to play.

After Eleanor left, Craig said, "Since you're moving in with Arthur, what are your plans for this furniture here?"

"I guess I won't need most of it. I'll take C.J.'s bedroom set. I want him to sleep in a bed he's familiar with. I don't really know what else I'll take. We're having a house built."

"Really? Where?"

"I'm not sure. It won't be far and as you know, it will be within the city limits.

Alright, Kellie. I'll be here early to get some of these things. I won't take much since you're moving.

After Craig left, Kellie called Arthur.

"Hey, baby."

"I told him."

"And?"

"He clowned a little initially, but he got over himself and we're cool."

"So when can I expect you?"

"Soon. I need to pack and sort through this stuff. Craig is going to stay here after I move and pay me out in the divorce settlement."

"Did he mention anything about filing?"

"Yes. He said that I should hear something tomorrow."

"Cool. We're on our way, baby. How's my baby doing?"

"She's really active, Arthur. I could swear that I've gotten bigger since yesterday."

"Our baby is growing inside of you. She'll be here soon, Kellie. I can't wait to meet her. I can't wait to hold her."

"Me either. I hope she looks like you. You're so gorgeous."

"Nope. I hope she looks like you. You're so beautiful, Kellie. Everything about you is beautiful. I want all of our children to look like you."

"All of. How many kids are you thinking about, Arthur?"

"Well, I know you love children as much I do and I was thinking maybe four."

"Four? That means two more pregnancies."

"I know, baby, but four is a good number. C.J. is already five. He's not going to want to be bothered with the other kids. If we can just have two more after this baby within, I say, three years, we'll be set."

"Two more kids within three years, Arthur? I'll be pregnant all of the time."

"Don't you think it will be fun getting pregnant?"

"Yes, of course, but, baby, I can't be pregnant like that. I won't be able to work."

"I don't want you to work anymore. Listen, Kellie. When my dad died nineteen years ago, I received a hefty life insurance policy which my mom invested. My wife won't have to work. To be honest, I don't need to work, but I do because I want to. We'll talk about everything in detail tomorrow when I see you. Can you spend the weekend with me?"

"I'll see if Craig can keep C.J. over the weekend. But yes, baby, I'll be there with you."

"I love you, Kellie."

"I love you too, Arthur. I'll talk to you in the morning."

"I miss having you here with me and I hope that it won't be much longer before you're here with me permanently."

"It won't be."

Kellie called Craig and asked if he could keep C.J. for the weekend and he said yes.

* * *

When February rolled around, Kellie had the things in the house she was taking with her packed. Her plan was to move to Arthur's house after the baby was born. Craig was due to pick C.J. up from daycare and drop him off at home. Craig called earlier and told Kellie that he had the final divorce papers and that he would bring them with him for her to sign that evening. She had been having very mild labor pains for about three hours now and decided that she would call Arthur and let him know after Craig left.

Kellie was a bit nervous when the doorbell rang. Although the divorce was truly what she wanted, she was scared to break the bond that she shared with Craig. After she signed those papers, he would no longer be her husband.

When she opened the door, C.J. came running through. Craig walked in and took a seat on the couch.

"C.J., honey, put your coat and book bag up and I'll get your dinner in a minute, okay, baby?"

"Yes, Mommy."

Craig said, "Well, Kellie. I have the final papers here in my hand. Once we sign these papers, you won't be my wife any longer."

"And you won't be my husband."

"Are you ready to do this?"

"Not really, but I guess I have to."

C.J. came into the room and said, "I'm ready to eat, Mommy."

"Craig, did you want to stay for dinner?"

"No. I'm not hungry."

"Do you mind if I fix his plate before we go over this?"

"No. Please do."

While Kellie was standing at the stove putting food on C.J.'s plate, she had a sharp labor pain and dropped the plate. Craig ran into the room to see what happened and found Kellie on her knees in a pool of water.

"What happened, Kellie?"

"My water broke."

"Damn. You're about to have the baby?"

"Yes."

"How long have you been in labor?"

"For a couple of hours."

"Why didn't you say anything?"

"Because the pains have been very mild and very far and in between."

"And now?"

"They are stronger."

"Are you ready to go to the hospital?"

"Yes."

"Do you have your things ready to go, or do you want to call your boyfriend to take you?"

"No, Craig. I need to go now. Can you please take me?"

"Of course. C.J., you'll have to eat at Grandma's. I'll wrap your plate and you can take it with you."

"Why are we leaving?"

"Mommy has to go to the hospital to have the baby."

Craig helped Kellie get her things together and they headed for the hospital. They first dropped C.J. off at Craig's mother's house. While Craig and C.J. were inside, Kellie called Arthur to let him know that she was headed to the hospital. He didn't answer his phone, but Kellie left a message telling him what was going on and that Craig had been at the house and was taking her to the hospital.

When Craig got in the car, he asked Kellie if she called Arthur and she told him that she did.

The baby was ready when they reached the hospital. Kellie was prepped for delivery immediately. Craig was ushered into the delivery room with Kellie. He tried to leave, but was caught up in the moment.

"Craig, please stay with me. I'm scared."

"Why are you scared, Kellie? You've done this before and you were great. You'll be okay."

"Please, Craig."

She grabbed his hand.

She said, "It hurts. Oh, it really does hurt." She asked the doctor if she could have an epidural."

Kellie's doctor said, "No, the baby is on her way out, Kellie and you're too far along."

"Shit! I need something."

Craig said, "Relax and breathe, Kellie. You can do this. Just relax."

He took a cloth and wiped the sweat off of her forehead.

"Come on, baby, you'll be alright. It will be over before you know it and our beautiful baby girl will be here. You've been waiting for nine months to see her and she is moments away. Be strong baby, she's almost here."

Kellie was able to relax and Craig held her hand as she gave birth to a 7lb. 8 oz. baby girl.

After getting the baby cleaned up, she was handed to Kellie. She looked a lot like C.J. and they both knew it, but neither said it out loud. Craig held the baby and eventually the nurse took her away. Craig was told that they needed to finish up with Kellie and the baby and once she was in a room, they would let him visit them both in the room. When Craig came out of the delivery room, Arthur was waiting.

Michele

Stacey arrived with Robert in tow. Michele was really looking forward to spending time with both of them. When Stacey and Robert walked off the plane, Michele rushed over and took Robert out of Stacey's arms.

"Hey, baby. Your auntee has missed seeing you. I think you're even more gorgeous than you were the last time I saw you."

"Yeah, he has a head full of hair now."

Stacey leaned over, hugged Michele and said, "Hey, girl. You're looking good. How you doing?"

"I'm doing great. I'm just so happy to have y'all here with me. You doing okay?"

"Yeah. Just knowing that Richard will be home when I return makes me feel a whole lot better than I've been feeling for a while now."

"I know that's right. Come on, let's get your bag and head back to my place."

When they got to Michele's place and put Robert down for a nap, Michele and Stacey sat on the balcony with a bottle of Chardonnay.

Michele said, "So are things better?"

"Yes. Richard brought us to the airport and he's picking us up Monday. He said that he will be home when we return."

"For good?"

"Yes. I can't wait to spend time with him and get back on track. We were planning to have another baby and I swear this Vegas shit keeps coming up. It was the worst thing I could have ever done."

"I think that I'm the only one out of all of us who had a positive life changing experience stemming from that Vegas trip. I mean, if we hadn't gone, I would have never met Nick."

"Yeah, but look at what happened to everyone else."

"Not Kellie. She changed her own life and it had nothing to do with Vegas. I wish she would go on and have this baby so that we'll know who her baby daddy is."

They both burst out laughing.

Stacey said, "Girl, it's got to be killing all three of them not knowing. And Craig is still trippin'."

"Wouldn't you?"

"Yeah, I guess I would. Truth be told, that was really foul how Craig got treated."

"Yeah, I thought for sure he was going to kill somebody. I'm glad he didn't, but he got them back the other night."

"What did he do the other night?"

"He played on Kellie's feelings and she slept with him. He ended up spending the night and the next morning when Arthur called the house, Craig answered the phone and told him."

"Damn. He did get them back, didn't he?"

"Yeah."

"Are Kellie and Arthur alright?"

"Yeah, they both saw what Craig was doing. He told Kellie that he wanted her to move in sooner than they originally planned and she said that she would."

"Michele, could you ever do anything like that? I don't mean just cheat on your man, but cheat on him with his partner. I can't imagine what that could feel like to be in the same room with two guys that you're fucking regularly, two guys who are spending most of their day together."

"I don't know if I could be comfortable with it. Arthur knew that she was still sleeping with Craig and he was pressuring her to leave him. The worst part is when she turned up pregnant and not knowing which one is the daddy. She has a mess on her hands. She said she's done with Craig's crap and she and C.J. are moving in with Arthur."

Stacey said, "Did she tell Craig that she was moving, yet?"

"I don't know. She said she would call and tell me when she did. I'm going to call her in a little while and find out what's up."

"How are things with you and Nick?"

"Couldn't be better. I love him, he loves me, we're getting married and it's all good. As a matter of fact, he'll be by here in a little while to see you guys. Well, he really wants to see Robert."

"Good. I wanted to see his fine ass anyway. So tell me, Michele, how does it feel to be in a real relationship?"

"I love it. If I had known it could be like this, I would have been looking for a husband before now."

"Nick really is a good catch. He loves you, girl."

"I love him too. He'll be here shortly. He's supposed to be taking his brother out to a few clubs tonight. I'm really happy that you're here. I've been spending all of my spare time with him and I would have been lonely if you weren't here."

"Don't you go out anymore?"

"Not nearly as often as I used to. I go out with the girls from the office sometimes. We'll stop at a bar and have a drink. I've gone to birthday parties at clubs, but straight out clubbin', I only do that with Nick."

"Wow, Michele. Nick has turned you into a different woman. How does it feel?"

"Actually, it feels wonderful knowing that I have a man, and a fine ass man at that, who loves my ass. I find it incredible that someone loves me like this and will do anything to make me happy."

"You don't think anyone has ever been in love with you before now?"

"I'm sure someone has, not trying to sound arrogant. I mean, this is different. I know there are guys who were in love with me because of my appearance, that's what it had to be. You know that I don't let anyone get close to me and really know me. So, before when a guy would tell me that he loved me, I always thought to myself, yeah right. No one has ever had access to my heart the way Nick does. It seems the ones I wanted to give access to didn't want it and the ones who wanted access, I wasn't willing to give it. Then I met Nick and he wanted access and I gave it and it's a beautiful thing, Stacey."

"Listen at you, Michele. I've never heard you talk like this. I'm just happy that you found love."

"And I'm so happy that love found me."

There was a light knock on the door.

"Excuse me, Stacey."

Michele greeted Nick at the door. They shared a kiss and headed for the balcony where Stacey was sitting.

Nick walked out on the balcony and said, "Stacey, it's so wonderful to see you again."

She stood, reached out to Nick and said, "Nick, it's so good to see you too."

They hugged.

"Where's Robert?"

"He's right there in the living room sleeping in his carrier."

Nick walked into the living room and looked into the carrier. Robert was wide awake and smiled at Nick when he looked at him.

"Can I pick him up, Stacey?"

"Is he awake?"

"Yes and smiling at me."

"Sure. Go ahead."

Nick picked Robert up. "Boy, you sure are getting heavy and look at all of this hair on your head. Man, you're going to have to fight the women off. I can see that already."

He carried Robert over to the couch and sat down with him.

"Stacey."

"Yes, Nick?"

"Robert needs changing. I'll be happy to do it if you show me where his gear is at."

"I most certainly will show you where it's at."

"I can keep an eye on him while you ladies get caught up."

"Really, that would be wonderful, Nick."

"I told you that he was all that, Stacey, didn't I."

"Yes you did, Michele, and he is proving it over and over again."

Nick changed Robert, fed him and played with him until both Nick and Robert drifted off to sleep while lying in Michele's bed.

After spending hours on the balcony drinking and talking, Michele and Stacey both admitted to being sleepy and made their way inside to prepare for bed. Nick and Robert were sleeping soundly.

"Look at them, Michele. Your man is ready to be a daddy."

"You think so?"

"Yeah, I do. Are you ready to be a mother?"

"Yes. I don't think that it will be long after the wedding that I'll become pregnant. I'm ready to get married and for Nick and I to be together forever."

"Listen at you, girl. I'm happy that you're happy."

"And I'm very happy."

Stacey retrieved Robert, got him ready for bed and they went to sleep."

Nick and Michele stayed awake for a while to talk.

I thought you were going clubbin' with Jesse."

"He wasn't feeling too good. Probably something he ate. We'll do a little something together tomorrow."

"Oh, okay. Well, Mr. Malloy. You sure did look good holding that baby."

"It felt good holding him and caring for him. I'm looking forward to holding and caring for children of my own."

"So am I, Nick. I'm ready to be a mother. I have a lot of love to give."

"I know you do, Michele. That's why I love you so much. How much more do we need to do before the wedding?"

"Not much more. Everything is paid for, my dress is almost ready and all of my bridesmaids have their dresses.
All we really have left is for Kellie to have her baby so that she can get fitted for her dress and to send out the invitations, which we will be doing at the end of February."

"I can't wait, baby. Now we have to find a house. I've looked over the listings and there are a couple of places I want to see."

"Which ones?"

"Well, there's one not too far from my house. I love that area and would like to stay there."

"Is it on Mulholland?"

"Yeah. I drove by on my way over to take a look and it's incredible. The price is in our range too."

"One of my agents told me about it, so I ran by and had a look at it before I went to the airport to get Kellie and Robert. Wait until you see the inside and the grounds. They are incredible, Nick. It's close to Rodeo. I can walk to all of my favorite boutiques. My favorite shops are close by. It's really a good location."

"I didn't think you were interested in Beverly Hills."

"I really hadn't thought about it until Mia told me about this property and I saw that it was in our price range. I absolutely love it, Nick, and once you see all of it, you will love it too."

"Let's go by and take a serious look at it tomorrow. Have you seen any of the other properties on the list?"

"Yes, I've seen a few of them, but nothing has come close to this one."

"Is it kid friendly?"

"Yes, very much so."

"If it's what you want, Michele, we'll get it."

"I love you, Nick."

"I love you too."

The next morning, Michele, Nick and Stacey packed Robert up and rode over to the property that Nick and Michele were interested in purchasing.

"Wow, guys! This house is stunning and the location is great. You can walk to the shopping mall. Look at the landscaping."

As they walked around the outside, Stacey said, "And it has an in ground pool."

"Most of the houses in this area have in ground pools. Come on, let's go inside and see everything. I want to get a good look at the yard," Michele said.

They all ooohed and ahhhed about everything in the house. The marble flooring in the foyer, along the spiral staircase and in the master bathroom was breathtaking. The kitchen, dining room, great room, den and all bedrooms had beautiful polished hardwood flooring. The floor-to-ceiling windows give a breathtaking view of the hills and the city.

When they stepped into the yard, it was even more beautiful than what they were able to see over the fence. The pool had gold inlays in the tiles. The landscaping was incredible with the gazebo covered in a beautiful rose vine and a brick path that led to two hammocks under large palm trees. Everything about the house said yes.

When they stood on the balcony outside of the master bedroom, Michele turned to Nick and said, "I love this house, Nick. I want it."

He kissed her and said, "If this is the house you want, Michele, consider it yours."

"Thank you, baby."

They stayed at the house for another half an hour or more looking around, making plans and discussing what pieces of furniture would go in what room.

Nick dropped Michele, Stacey and Robert off at Michele's house and headed home to spend time with his family.

Michele and Stacey relaxed, talked, cried, drank and ate the next day before Stacey headed home to be with Richard.

* * *

Michele and Nick finalized the plans for their wedding. The invitations were mailed and the big day was fast approaching.

Gina

When Marcus came home later that evening, he was excited.

When Gina saw him she said, "Wow, baby, you're beaming. What are you so excited about?"

"Do you remember when I told you that Doug and Sara inherited a yacht from Doug's father?"

"Yes."

"They are going to Cozumel to retrieve it and they asked if we'd like to join them."

"Really? Tell me more."

"Well, we'll fly to Cozumel, spend a few days on the island and sail back to Florida." He pulled an itinerary out of his pocket and began reading from it. "Once we begin sailing, our first stop will be Georgetown, Grand Cayman where we'll spend the day, shopping, lunch, whatever you want, baby. From there we'll sail on to Labadee, Haiti, then to Ocho Rios then we'll be at sea for two days after those ports until we reach Miami. Once we arrive in Miami, we'll fly home."

"Does Doug know how to sail or will he hire someone?"

"He's already hired a crew."

"This is exciting, Marcus. Is this a trip for the kids too?"

"I would love to take them on this trip, but I don't think that this is for them. They are too small and I don't want to have them on the water for that long for the first time. I was thinking that if sailing is something we enjoy, maybe we can look into getting a boat of our own. We can keep it at our house on Kentucky Lake and use it while we're there."

"How long will this trip take?"

"We'll need at least ten days."

"I don't know if I can take that much time off from work already, Marcus. I haven't been on this job very long. When are they going?"

"They are leaving two weeks from Thursday."

"I definitely want to go. Let me see if I can get the time off without causing too much trouble."

"I'll tell Doug and Sara that we are going. Okay?"

"Yes. I'll work out my schedule. Are you able to get the time off."

"I haven't taken much time this year. We didn't go to Kentucky Lake this summer, so I didn't use the two weeks I usually schedule off for that time. It won't be a problem for me."

"We need to go to the Lake and check on the house. Let's at least try to get out there for a weekend soon."

"Okay. We'll do that after we return. It will be a great getaway for the kids too. I'm really looking forward to spending time away from everything with you, Gina. I want us to get back what we had and I think this trip will help move us in the right direction."

"I think so too, Marcus. I'm really looking forward to spending alone time with you in a romantic setting. Just how big is this boat?"

"It's not called a boat, it's a Yacht. Our stateroom will be on a different level than Doug and Sara's. Complete privacy."

They smiled at each other just thinking about it.

Later after dinner and after getting the kids to bed, Gina called Michele to see how her visit went with Stacey and to share her good news.

The next day at work, Gina found Tiffany to get her take on getting time off.

Tiffany said, "Herbert will do everything in his power to keep you from taking time off, but I'm sure they offered it to you in your contract. They will make do, so don't worry about it. Tell him what time you need off and then take that time off. What's up? Where are you going?"

"Well, first, Marcus and I reconciled."

"What! What about, Jeff? Y'all were getting pretty close."

"Yeah, I know, but when Marcus and I went to mediation, we talked and we both admitted that we still wanted to be together and decided to give our marriage another chance."

"I'm really happy to hear that, Gina. I don't know what went down with y'all and I don't want to know, but I never wanted to see the two of you apart."

"Well, I'm the one who messed things up the first time, but I'll never be a fool like that again. I've got a second chance with my husband and I plan to be with him for the rest of my life."

"What are you two going to do, take another honeymoon?"

"I didn't think about it like that, but we could consider it that. Friends of ours, Doug and Sara, inherited a yacht from Doug's dad who died while vacationing in Cozumel a couple of months ago. He sailed down from Florida and his yacht is still docked down there. Sara and Doug are going to sail it back to Florida and they invited us to join them."

"That's nice, Gina. I'm sure you'll get the time off."

"Marcus has an itinerary and I'm really excited about the stops we're going to make at a few islands where we can do some shopping and have dinner or lunch or whatever on those islands."

"A yacht, huh?"

"Yes. Then, Marcus was saying that if we enjoy our trip we'll look at getting a boat that we can use when we got to Kentucky Lake."

"That's a really nice house y'all have on that lake and putting a boat in the slip will complete the package. Darren and I have been looking at vacation homes."

"Why don't y'all look at Kentucky Lake? We have great neighbors and it would be great to have you guys in the community too."

"We're driving out there next weekend to see three houses in the area."

"Really? I hope you find something you like."

"Me too. I just saw Herbert go into his office, you'd better go on and tell him now so that he can have his tantrum and get it over with."

"Hopefully, it won't be that bad."

"If he doesn't clown, it will be a first."

"Well, let me go on and get it over with then."

Gina walked into Herbert's office and had a seat.

"Good morning, Herbert."

"What do you want, Gina?"

"Sheez. Alright, I need to take ten to twelve days off in about two weeks."

"That is absolutely out of the question."

"Herbert, this is absolutely necessary. As you know, I was going through a divorce. Well, my husband and I reconciled over the weekend. We need to get away to get to know each other again. I need this time off, Herbert."

"What is it you have to do that is going to take ten to twelve days?"

"We're sailing from Cozumel to Florida with some friends on their yacht."

"Gina, I can't just give you that kind of time off for you to go caravanning across the Caribbean. I'm going to have to deny your request."

"Herbert, in my contract it states that I'm entitled to four weeks vacation and I'm going to take two weeks starting two weeks from tomorrow."

"Who is going to do your job while you're out?"

"The same people who need me to cover for them while they're out. It can be done, Herbert. It's done all of the time."

"Alright, Gina. Make sure you get those dates to me as soon as possible so that I can make sure there is someone to cover your responsibilities while you're out sailing."

"Thank you, Herbert."

"Yeah, yeah and congratulations on your reconciliation. Maybe now you can stop dating all of our guests."

"That wasn't funny, Herbert."

"I know. I just couldn't help myself. But for real, Gina, congratulations."

"Thank you, Herbert."

Over dinner that evening, Gina told Marcus that she got the time off approved and they began planning for their trip.

* * *

The day before they left for their cruise, they received Nick and Michele's wedding invitation in the mail. The wedding was scheduled to commence three weeks after their return. Gina talked to Michele, Stacey and Kellie before her and Marcus set out to renew their marriage.

<u>Stacey</u>

Richard was at the gate waiting for Stacey and Robert when they arrived in Denver.

He greeted them both with a kiss.

"Welcome back, Stacey."

"It's good to be home, Richard. I've missed you so much."

"I've missed you too, baby. Come on and let's go home."

They engaged in small talk and chit chatted while in the car. Once they were home, Richard put Robert to bed and Stacey took a shower and waited for Richard in the bedroom. They hadn't been intimate since the discovery of the DVD. They needed each other.

When Richard entered the bedroom, Stacey was laying across the bed nude. He undressed as he walked towards the bed. Stacey got up on her knees, and met him at the edge of the bed then they began kissing. Richard laid Stacey on her back and explored her body. They stayed in bed for hours talking and making love until Robert started crying. After Stacey got Robert situated, she brought him in their bedroom and laid him in bed with her and Richard. They all slept together peacefully.

The next morning, Stacey told Richard about her trip and the time she spent with Michele.

Richard did his best at putting everything behind them. He seemed distant at times and Stacey knew to leave him alone during those times. She knew he was thinking about that DVD, which she destroyed.

* * *

Things seemed to be getting back to normal. Stacey didn't mention anything about getting pregnant since Richard had been back in the house, which had been almost two months now.

When Richard came down for breakfast and sat at the table, Stacey said, "Richard, are we still going to work on having another baby?"

"Yes. That hasn't changed, Stacey. Why do you ask?"

"Well, we haven't talked about it in a while and I didn't want you to be upset if I told you that I was pregnant."

"Are you?"

"Yes."

He stood and walked over to Stacey and hugged her.

"When did you find out?"

"Yesterday. I wanted to tell you yesterday, but I wanted to tell you face to face so I waited for you to return."

"I'm glad you did. How far along are you?"

"Seven weeks."

"This happened as soon as I came back?"

"I would say yes. I'm excited about this Richard and I hope that you are too."

"I am, I really am. Robert will have a sibling."

"We also received the invitation to Michele's wedding today. She is going to kill me."

"Why?"

"Because I'll be pregnant during her wedding. My dress was done and now I may have to get it altered again."

"I'm sure she'll understand, Stacey. She knew we were working on having another baby, didn't she?"

"Yeah. It will be fine."

"Will you be showing at that time?"

"Maybe not. I'll only be three months, so I'm probably making more out of it than I should. Both Michele and Nick are ready for children. I bet you anything she'll come up pregnant shortly after they are married."

"You think so?"

"Definitely."

"I thought Michele probably didn't want any children. To be honest, I never thought that she would get married. She is the most independent woman I've ever met and she seemed perfectly happy just dating and not answering to any man. Nick must have really laid it on her to get her to settle down." Richard said.

"I think it was mutual. From what I can tell, Nick planned to be a bachelor for the rest of his life. They swept each other off of their feet. They both needed to settle down and I think they are a great couple."

"I agree with that, Stacey. I'm looking forward to seeing both of them and dancing at their wedding."

Stacey decided to save her news about her pregnancy and share it with everyone while in L.A. for Michele's wedding which was a few weeks away.

Kellie

When Craig saw Arthur, Kellie's mother and his mother waiting, he walked over to where his mother and Kellie's mother were waiting and gave them the details. "Mom, where is C.J.?"

"He's with your brother. I wanted to see the baby, Craig. Is she yours?"

"Yeah, I think so. I'm still going to have the test done, but I do think she's mine. Let me get out of here, Mom. I'll see you at home."

He gave Kellie's mom a hug. He looked at Arthur, turned and walked out.

Craig found Kellie's doctor and told him that he wanted a DNA test taken immediately on the three of them. The nurse took a DNA sample from Craig before he left the hospital.

Once Kellie was situated in her room, her mom, Eleanor and Arthur were allowed to come into the room. They all stopped by the nursery to see Raven Marie before they came to the room to visit with Kellie. No one said anything, but Raven had a strong resemblance to Craig and C.J.

Arthur left the nursery and made his way to Kellie's room before her mother and Eleanor could get there.

He walked over to the bed and sat next to Kellie.

"Hey, baby. I'm so sorry that I couldn't get here in time to make sure you were okay. The baby is beautiful, but I think she's Craig's. She looks like him, baby."

"I thought so too. We're still going to get the test done. I want to be sure."

"So do I. She's beautiful and so are you. You look great."

"Thank you, Arthur. It was hard and I'm glad to have it over with."

"I'll have the baby's room done when you come home tomorrow. I'm ready to be a dad. Did you sign the papers?"

"I went into labor before I could."

'I'll sign them when I get home tomorrow."

"Does Craig know that you're moving next weekend?"

"Yes. The rest of our things are ready to go."

When Kellie's mom and Eleanor came into the room, Arthur kissed Kellie on the forehead and said, "I will be back later. I'll stay with you over night. That way, me, you and the baby can have some alone time and I'll be here to take you home once they release you. I love you, baby."

"I love you too."

Just as Arthur was leaving, the nurse brought the baby into the room. He waited and held the baby, talked to her and kissed her. After he left, Kellie's mom and Eleanor oohed and ahhed all over her. They spent a little over an hour with Kellie and the baby, but it was very late and they decided to go on home for the night.

Kellie's mom gave her a kiss and told her that she would see her at home the next day. Eleanor did the same and they told her that they had a lot of things for the baby that they would drop by the house once Kellie was home.

After they left, Kellie called Michele.

"Hello, Kellie. Aren't you ready to have that baby yet?"

"I had her a few hours ago."

"And you're just calling me"

"What was I supposed to do? Call you from the delivery room?"

"Yes."

They both laughed.

"So?"

"So what?"

"Arthur or Craig?"

"I'm 99.9% sure she's Craig's. She looks just like him, but I still want to have the test done to be sure. I don't want there to be any doubt, or give him any reason to deny her."

"Does he know you had her?"

"Yes. He was in the delivery room."

"What?"

"He was at the house dropping C.J. off from daycare and had the divorce papers for me to sign when my water broke. I had been in labor for a few hours, but it was nothing worth talking about."

"What does that mean?"

"I was having very mild pains and they were very far and in between. Then, suddenly my water broke and the pains became intense immediately. Craig was there and he took me to the hospital. I think he was caught up in it all and ended up in the delivery room."

"Where was Arthur?"

"At work. I called him, but he wasn't able to make it to the hospital in time. Craig was great. He comforted me, talked to me and he held Raven when she was born. He knows she's his and we'll get the test results to make it official. At least C.J. and Raven will be 100% brothers and sisters."

"When are you going to move in with Arthur?"

"Next weekend. I hope things will go smoothly. I don't know how Craig is going to be able to see Raven. He won't come to Arthur's house, so I'll probably have to take the baby to him for a while."

"That should work since he'll be at the house anyway."

"I like the idea of him being at the house that way C.J. will still have his home base. How is your wedding planning coming along?"

"All we have left to do is walk down the aisle. The best thing I've ever done is to hire a wedding planner. She is wonderful. When we first started I was trying to do everything myself and that wasn't working out. Now that Becky is on the case, it's a done deal. Nick and I have been talking about children, especially since Gina was here with Robert. You should have seen him. He took care of Robert while Gina and I got caught up. By the time Gina and I were ready for bed, we found Nick and Robert sleeping in my bed. It was so cute, Kellie."

"I bet it was. How soon are you talking about starting a family?"

"I guess we'll just let it happen. I haven't stopped taking my pills yet, but I will soon."

"You'll be great parents."

"I'll be there for a few days next week to spend a little time with you and see Ms. Raven and C.J."

"That's perfect. Arthur has to go out of town Tuesday, but he'll be back Wednesday and if you can stay with me that would really be great."

"Okay. I can do that."

"Thanks, Michele. Can you call Stacey and Gina and tell them that I've had the baby and I'll talk to them soon."

"Okay. I'll call them in the morning."

"Let me know when you're home and settled and I'll let you know when I'll be out."

"Okay, Michele. I'll talk to you tomorrow."

Arthur came back to the hospital with the baby's car seat and clothes for her to wear home. He held Raven, fed her, changed her diaper and talked to her until she was sleep again. They were all sleepy. Arthur slid in bed with Kellie. The baby was in the portable crib next to the bed. The nurse came by a little later and took Raven back to the nursery. Kellie and Arthur slept peacefully until the nurse came in with the baby the next morning.

"Good morning, all."

Kellie and Arthur stirred and he slid out of the bed and went into the bathroom to freshen up while the nurse checked on Kellie.

When Arthur came out of the bathroom, the doctor was in the room talking to Kellie, making sure she felt well and that everything was okay. He told her that she would be released shortly and that he would begin the paperwork. He also took a DNA sample from Kellie and Raven.

"Do you need Craig to come in to get a sample from him?"

"No. I retrieved a sample from Craig last night before he left. Someone will contact you in a day or two with the results."

"Thank you."

* * *

When Kellie and Raven were released from the hospital, Arthur took them home. Craig, C.J., Eleanor, Kellie's mom and dad and Craig's brother were at the house waiting for them.

Kellie and Arthur sat in the driveway for a few minutes talking before going into the house.

"Arthur, I know this is going to be very uncomfortable for you and I'm sorry. Hopefully, Craig won't stay too long. He knows Raven is his, anyone that looks at her knows she's his, so I can't deny him access to her."

"I know, Kellie. I'll help you to get situated, but I won't stay long. I'll give Craig time to spend with his daughter. We'll work on him having access to the kids once we move. The main thing I want you to focus on is to sit down with Craig, go over the divorce papers and sign them today."

"I will, Arthur. Today is a big day in our lives. After I sign the papers, the opportunity for us to begin our lives together as a family will truly be available to us. I'm looking forward to spending the rest of my life with you. I also want to say thank you for sticking by my side knowing that the chance of Raven being Craig's daughter was strong and that you accept her and C.J. and are willing to go on with me."

"I love you, Kellie. Nothing will ever change that. Come on let's go in and move forward."

Arthur carried the baby into the house. C.J. ran to the door to greet Kellie. She and Arthur spoke to everyone. Craig sat at the table in the dining room and watched. When Kellie got situated, Arthur handed her the baby. He whispered in her ear, "I'll talk to you later, baby. I love you and in two more days you'll be home with me."

She said, "I'm looking forward to it. I'll call you later."

After Arthur left, Craig came and took Raven from Kellie. He sat down next to her and said, "How are we going to do this, Kellie?"

"This is my daughter. I know that she is and I don't need the test to tell me that. How am I going to be able to see her, Kellie?"

"I'll bring the kids to you. We are moving the day after tomorrow and I'd like to have something set up that's comfortable for everyone."

"I'll keep C.J. with me for the next two days until you get situated with Raven. She's beautiful, Kellie."

"Yes, she is. Thank you for being there for me at the hospital. I'm glad you were there to see your daughter come into the world, Craig. I hope that we'll be able to share custody of the kids and give them as much of a normal childhood as we can. You're a great father to C.J. and I'm sure you'll be just as good to Raven."

"Thank you, Kellie. If you want your boyfriend to stay here with you tonight, that's okay with me. I don't want him in my bed though."

"Okay. Thank you, Craig."

The doorbell rang. Eleanor answered the door and let Craig's attorney, Steve, inside of the house. He was there to retrieve the divorce documents.

Kellie's mom came and took the baby from Craig. He turned to Kellie and said, "Are you ready to sign those papers now? I think now is the best time to move to the next phase of our lives."

"Yes. So do I."

They joined Steve at the dining room table and had a seat. Craig sat next to Kellie and they went over everything line by line. Once they reached the end of the document, Craig pulled a pen out of his shirt pocket, laid the paper on the table and signed his name. He handed the pen to Kellie and she stared at him for a few seconds, a tear dropped out of her eye, which she quickly wiped away, reached for the pen and signed her name too. Craig's attorney, who was a notary, notarized the document, told them both that they would get a copy in the mail in a day or two. He gathered the documents and headed out.

Craig stood and said, "I'll see you tomorrow. C.J. get your coat, we're leaving."

Kellie said, "C.J., come and say bye to me."

He gave Kellie a kiss, hugged his grand parents and left with Craig.

Kellie's mom helped Kellie get situated before she left and once Kellie got the baby to sleep, she called Gina, Stacey and Michele on a conference call. She was tired and didn't talk long, but told them that she would see them in six weeks at the wedding and she told Michele that she would see her next week when Michele was scheduled to arrive in Chicago for a visit.

Kellie told Arthur about Craig's offer for Arthur to stay at the house with Kellie and the baby that night. Arthur arrived with dinner later that evening.

"I brought some Chinese food. I remember you said that you wanted some a few days ago. I've had a taste for it too."

"Thanks, baby."

Once they were seated, Arthur moved his chair close to Kellie, took her hands and said, "Kellie, I love you and I'm so happy to have this opportunity to spend the rest of my life with you. I'm officially asking you if you will please marry me."

He pulled a ring box out of his pocket, opened it and inside was a beautiful diamond and platinum engagement ring. He took it out of the box, Kellie held her hand out and Arthur slipped the ring on her finger.

"Yes, Arthur. Yes I will marry you and I look forward to spending the rest of my life with you."

"Can we get married as soon as possible?"

"How soon are you talking about?"

"Next week. We can go to city hall and have a celebration at a later date. I just want you to be my wife, Kellie. I want to make everything official."

"Okay, we can do that. Maybe we can get married while Michele is here. She can be a witness for us."

"When will she be here? Tuesday. She can only stay for a few days."

"When is her wedding?"

"Saturday, April 10th. Exactly one year from the day they met."

"I'm looking forward to getting away from here for a while."

After dinner, they relaxed found their way to the guest bedroom where they slept in each other's arms. Arthur changed his schedule so that he could be with Kellie and the kids at night.

He left out and headed to work early the next morning.

When Craig and C.J. came by a little later to see the baby, he spotted Kellie's ring immediately.

"You're engaged already?"

"Yes. Arthur asked me last night."

"Where is Raven?"

"She's sleep."

Craig went up to her room and stayed in there with her for a while.

When he came downstairs he said, "Kellie, I'm having a hard time dealing with all of this. I mean, you fuck around with my partner, we go through all of this wondering who fathered Raven. Now I have a son and a newborn that will be raised by another man. I feel like you couldn't wait to be rid of me, Kellie. We signed the divorce papers yesterday and you're engaged to another man the same day. When is the wedding?"

She mumbled, "Wednesday."

"Excuse me."

"Arthur and I are getting married next Wednesday."

"Alright, Kellie. You're moving Saturday, right?"

"Yes."

"Alright. I'll move back in here Sunday and we'll get on with our lives. C.J., let's go."

Kellie didn't say anything. She knew Craig was upset and she didn't want to argue with him, so she let them leave without making a comment.

Saturday morning, Arthur and a few of his friends were at the house bright and early to move the remainder of Kellie and C.J.'s items to his house.

C.J. stayed with Craig over the weekend while Kellie and Arthur got situated. Kellie dropped Raven off with Craig the next evening. He wanted to get accustomed to spending time with the kids on his own.

The following evening, Kellie went to Craig's house to get C.J. and Raven to bring them home.

She was caught off guard when she entered the house and Craig had a woman in the house holding Raven.

Kellie walked over to the lady and took Raven.

Craig said, "Kellie, this is Joyce, Joyce this is my ex-wife, Kellie."

Michele

Michele received a call from Kellie at eleven thirty p.m. letting her know that Raven Marie was here. Michele planned a trip to Chicago to spend a few days with Kellie and the kids.

Nick, who was laying in the bed next to Michele when she received the phone call said, "Kellie had the baby, huh?"

"Yeah. She says she's 99.9% sure that Craig is the father. She says Raven looks just like him."

"Raven. That's a nice name. Does Craig know?"

"Yeah, he was at the hospital with her. I'll get all of the details when I see her next week. I'm going to go to Chicago for a couple of days next week and spend a little time with Kellie and the kids while Arthur is out of town."

'I'm sure she will be glad to have you there."

Nick dropped Michele off at the airport Tuesday morning. She rented a car while at the airport and drove herself to Kellie and Arthur's house. Michele used the navigation system in the car to find Arthur's house, which she found without a problem.

Kellie greeted her at the door.

"Come on in, Michele, girl, I'm so glad to see you."

Michele came in and they hugged.

Arthur came into the living room.

"Hello, Michele. It's good to see you again."

"It's good to see you too."

Kellie said, "Let me show you your room, so you can put your bags down."

"Girl, forget them bags, where is Raven?"

"She's in the bedroom. Come on and meet her."

They walked into the nursery and Raven was awake.

Michele said, "Oh my, Kellie. She is the most beautiful baby I've ever seen in my entire life."

"You said the same thing about Robert."

"Well, he was the most beautiful baby I had ever seen at that time, but look at this beauty laying here in front of me. She is absolutely gorgeous. Can I hold her?"

"Of course you can."

"Let me wash my hands."

"Like I said before, get yourself situated and then you can hold her."

"Alright. What time does C.J. come home?"

"Arthur will pick him up from school before he heads out this evening."

"Okay. I have some stuff for him."

"Don't you always."

Michele enjoyed her stay in Chicago, but was anxious to get back home to Nick. It was a little awkward seeing Craig, but she managed to get through it. Kellie told her that she met Craig's girlfriend and had the nerve to be mad that he had one.

When Michele arrived home and got back into her routine, she knew she had to finish all of the little details because the wedding date was swiftly approaching. She decided to call her mother and formally invite her to the wedding.

When Linda answered the phone, Michele was a bit hesitant.

"Hello."

"Hello, Linda. This is Michele."

"I recognize your voice, Michele. How are you?"

"I'm doing well. I wanted to invite you to my wedding on April 10th. I planned to send you an invitation, but I wanted to personally invite you and I hope that you'll be able to make it."

"Of course I'll be there, Michele. Thank you so much for giving me this opportunity to be a part of your life."

"You'll receive an invitation with the details soon and I'm looking forward to seeing you, Linda."

"I'm looking forward to seeing you too. Is there anything you need help with?"

"No. Nick and I have taken care of everything."

"If you find that you need help with anything, please let me know and I will take care of it."

"Thank you, Linda, I will. Look for the invitation in the mail and I'll see you in April."

After Michele ended her conversation with Linda, she felt that she had all of the loose ends tied up.

* * *

Kellie called two weeks before the wedding date to let Michele know that her dress was done. Everyone was expected to be in town Wednesday before the wedding. Nick and Michele decided that neither of them were going to have a bachelor or bachelorette party. They felt that unpleasant memories of Las Vegas would surface.

Gina, Kellie and Stacey arrived as scheduled along with their mates.

Gina

When Gina and Marcus arrived in Cozumel, they were giddy as school kids. They were all over each other and so happy with their reconciliation. During their flight, Gina thought about how stupid she had been to risk the beautiful life she enjoyed with Marcus over a Las Vegas fantasy. Vegas really did live up to its nickname for Gina. The city itself offered her the opportunity to do the things she would have never dreamed of doing anywhere else.

They took a cab to the pier where the Yacht, affectionately named Gloria, named after Doug's mom was docked. It didn't take Marcus and Gina long to find Doug and Sara. They were on the deck of the yacht waving at Marcus and Gina as they walked down the pier.

Doug yelled, "Marcus, Gina, over here."

He jumped onto the pier and greeted them both with a hug. Sara also greeted them with a hug and helped them to get their luggage aboard.

Once Marcus and Gina got everything in their stateroom and changed clothes, they met Doug and Sara on deck.

Doug said, "Welcome, guys. Sara and I have been here for two days and we don't ever want to go back to the states."

Marcus said, "Spoiled already, huh?"

"Man, this is the life. I can do this. Are you guys up to going into town? We saved a few locations for you guys to get here. Sara and I have been like maniacs. I had to stop her from shopping. We have more ports to visit and we'll need space to store all of the things she's buying. It's ridiculous."

Gina said, "Really."

"You've said the magic words, Doug. Shopping. That's all Gina needs to hear to get her adrenaline going."

They all laughed.

Gina said, come on then, let's go and check out this island."

Marcus, Gina, Doug and Sara went to dinner and then partied at club after club and finally made it back to the yacht about four thirty a.m. They were scheduled to set sail at four in the afternoon.

Gina rolled out of bed around noon and heard Marcus and Doug on deck. Her porthole in their stateroom was open and she could hear them talking. Marcus was telling Doug how difficult things had been for him while he and Gina were separated.

Marcus was saying, "It was very hard for me to be away from her and watch her date other men. The thought of another man touching her was driving me crazy. I tried to move on from her, but I couldn't. I tried dating, but I wasn't interested in another woman. I couldn't understand how she dated other men. She was dating Jeff Lee when we got back together."

"The quarterback?"

"Yes. She got a job at the local TV station. It was supposed to be for a staff writer, but after they saw her, they wanted to put her in front of the camera. Then she started meeting all of these athletes."

"Who else did she meet?"

"She was dating Rick Winters before Jeff. I mean, they were all over her. Every time she went to work she came home with a date with another man. I had to have a talk with myself and put my anger behind me and not let her go. I was so happy that she wanted to reconcile also. This trip is just what we needed. Let me thank you again for the invite. I'm going to do whatever it takes to make her happy."

"She had a good time last night man. She seems very happy and it shows. I think you guys will be fine, Marcus. I'm glad to see y'all back together."

Gina made her way up on deck and spoke to everyone. Sara came up shortly after. They all went in town for lunch and a little shopping before setting sail.

The entire trip was unbelievable. Marcus and Gina decided that they loved sailing and would look into getting a boat of their own. Nothing of the magnitude of Doug and Sara's yacht, but a respectable boat which they could dock at their vacation home on Kentucky Lake.

While in the limousine heading home, Gina said, "That was one of the best trips I've ever been on Marcus. Not only because I was able to spend eleven whole days with you, being happy and in love and making love all over the Caribbean, but everything about the trip made me happy."

"Me too. I'll never let you go again, Gina. Come here."

Gina leaned over and they kissed deeply and passionately. When they arrived home, Marcus' mother was at the house with the boys.

Gina and Marcus were like newlyweds. They were happy to be together again and they showed how much they loved each other every chance they got.

* * *

Gina and Marcus arrived in L.A. Wednesday April 9th. After checking into their hotel room, they made their way to Nick's house to see Michele and everyone else who had arrived in town.

Stacey

Richard and Stacey arrived in L.A. in the early afternoon on Wednesday. After checking into their hotel room, they made their way to Nick's house to meet everyone and to have an informal get together.

This was Stacey and Richard's first time leaving Robert with a sitter long-term and Stacey was trying very hard not to call every few minutes to check on him.

When they arrived at Nick's home, they were greeted at the door by Michele.

Kellie

When Kellie found her voice, she smiled at Joyce and asked Craig if she could see him in the kitchen.

"Excuse us for a minute, Joyce."

Joyce said, "Craig. I need to go home, but I'll call you later. Kellie it was nice meeting you. You have beautiful children."

"Thank you."

Craig walked over to Joyce. They whispered something to each other. Craig walked Joyce to her car. When he came back in, Kellie said, "You could have let me know that you were going to have women around my kids."

"You have got to be kidding me, Kellie. You're here to take my kids to the home you share with your fucking punk ass boyfriend. You're going to be laying up with this man in front of my fucking children and you've got the nerve to say something to me about who I spend my damn time with. You must have lost your mutherfucking mind, Kellie."

"I'm sorry. You're right, Craig. I guess I need to get used to you spending your time with another woman."

"Yeah. You should."

"Are they ready to go?"

"C.J. is taking a nap. I'll wake him and get him ready. Raven just ate and Joyce changed her. She'll probably sleep in the car. She slept about eight hours straight last night."

"Really? I hope she does it again tonight."

"Will you be able to keep the kids while I go to L.A. next month?"

"Yeah. Just make sure you give me the dates so that I can put in a slip to have the time off at work."

"I will."

Kellie pulled a piece of paper out of her purse and handed it to Craig.

"Here are the results of the DNA test that we took for Raven."

Craig took the paper, looked it over and said, "I knew she was mine, Kellie. I knew it the minute I saw her."

"I just wanted you to have scientific proof so that there would never be a doubt in your mind about her."

"There's no doubt."

Craig went upstairs and got C.J. and brought him downstairs. C.J. was groggy, but he walked over to Kellie and fell on her lap with his head down.

"He'll wake up shortly and talk you to death."

"I know."

Kellie helped C.J. into his coat while Craig got Raven ready for the ride home. He helped Kellie to get the kids in the car.

When she arrived home, Arthur met her in the garage when he heard the door opening.

After getting the kids settled into bed, Kellie and Arthur sat down and talked about their future over a glass of wine.

"We have a meeting with a builder tomorrow. We need to work on getting our house built. I don't want to be here this time next year."

"Where are you interested in building?"

"I've seriously been thinking about building in Orland Park."

"We can't move out of the city limits. Your job won't allow that, Arthur."

"Well, if I take this job with the FBI, I'll be able to live outside of the city limits."

"What job?"

"I've been offered a job with the FBI. I've been interviewing with them for a couple of months and the offer finally came through. I wanted to surprise you with this because it opens up lots of opportunities for us. I'll be much more flexible in my career with this position. Do you think I should take it?"

"Is it what you want?"

"Yes. I want this position very much."

"Then yes, please do accept the position, Arthur."

The next day Kellie and Arthur met with the builder and got started with having their dream home built.

When Michele arrived in town Kellie was very happy to have her there.

After Michele was situated, they sat down and talked about everything.

"Michele, Arthur and I are going to get married tomorrow and we want you to be a part of the ceremony. We're going to city hall and we'll plan on a reception or something down the line."

"What's the rush?"

"It's not a rush. We just want to be married so that we can do some of the things we've planned on doing since we've been together. We looked at plans for our house that we're having built. We've already met with the developer. Arthur went to Washington, D.C. today to accept a position with the FBI. There are a lot of changes happening in both of our lives and we want to be official as we make all of these changes."

"Well of course, count me in Kellie. I'm definitely on board for whatever you're going to do that will bring you happiness. From what I can see, Arthur is the one that brings you happiness."

"He does, Michele."

Arthur was due back in town the day that Michele was leaving. Michele's flight was at seven thirty p.m.

Kellie, Arthur and Michele made their way to city hall mid afternoon after dropping the kids off at Kellie's mom's house where Craig would pick them up after work that evening. Kellie and Arthur got married.

The three of them had a nice dinner before taking Michele to the airport. Kellie and Arthur spent the night in a downtown hotel on the first night as a married couple.

When Kellie went to Craig's house to get the children she told Craig that she and Arthur were married. He didn't have a comment.

*　*　*

Craig kept the kids while Kellie and Arthur went to L.A. for Michele and Nick's wedding. They checked into their hotel room early afternoon the Wednesday before the wedding. They found their way to Nick's home and were greeted at the door by Michele.

Wednesday, April 7th

Michele made a general announcement once everyone was together. She and Nick opened a few bottles of wine, filled glasses and everyone gathered around to listen to what Michele had to say.

"Welcome to Hollywood everybody. I am so happy that we are all here together again. Although there are a few different players in the game, everything is as it should be. All of my friends are happy and are with the ones they love."

"Nick and I are very happy and are looking forward to Saturday when we officially become husband and wife. We found a house that we love and will be moving into when we return from our honeymoon in Paris."

Kellie said, "Where is the new house?"

"It's around the corner from here. We'll go by and let you guys see it shortly. Stacey saw the house the last time that she was out here. It's a little different now, Stacey. We've put furniture in and added our touches. It's exactly what we wanted."

"Anyway, it's been a long and interesting year. This time last year, Kellie, Gina, Stacey and I landed in Las Vegas, a trip which has brought happiness and heartache to us all. I won't go into all of the details about the changes that have come about since that infamous trip, but I will say that things happen for a reason and I believe that we must go through things that may not always be pleasant to allow us to get to where we are truly meant to be."

"I'm happy that we are all still together and I'd like to welcome the new additions to our group. Stacey and Richard's beautiful son, Robert. Nick and I were lucky enough to have the opportunity to spend time with Robert recently. Ms. Raven Marie, Kellie and her new husband, Arthur's beautiful baby girl. Lucky me again, I was able to spend time with Raven and she is definitely a diva. Arthur, Kellie's new husband. It was a rough flight getting to that position, Arthur, but it was a smooth landing and we welcome you into our circle. Gina and Marcus are smiling, kissing and touching each other every time I look in their direction and that is wonderful. I'm really happy for y'all and last, but not least, Nicholas Malloy. The greatest moment in my life will be when I acquire the title of Mrs. Nicholas Malloy. I love you, baby."

Nick walked up to Michele and they kissed. Some were crying, but everyone was very happy.

Kellie said, "Okay guys, I need to say a few things too. I'm sorry that I took you all through my mess with Craig. You've all been really great friends helping me get through everything and for you to welcome my new husband, Arthur, into our circle of love lets me know that you all love me and are there for me no matter what. Thanks for not judging me for my behavior. I guess being in love makes you do crazy things. I'm just happy to have great friends like you ladies who have been here for me through thick and thin and I wouldn't trade any of you for anything in the world."

"Nick, good luck to you and Michele. I wish you both all the happiness in the world. You both deserve it and I know you will have a great life together."

Gina lifted her glass and said, "Here, here." They drank to Kellie's speech.

Gina said, "I'd like to also add that I've had a tumultuous year and I'm so happy to have a second chance with my husband, Marcus. If it hadn't been for my friends, I don't know how I would have made it. Thank you all for listening to me when I needed to vent and for being there and giving me hope. Michele, I wish you and Nick as much happiness as I have found with Marcus. I love you all."

A teary eyed Stacey stood and said, "I've been a fool and I too am very lucky to have the opportunity to have another chance with my husband. Thank you Gina, Michele and Kellie for helping me through my heartache and for being there to listen to me while I cried and cried and cried again. You guys are the absolute best.

"Nick you are getting a wonderful woman. Michele is the foundation of our circle. She is the one that we all run to for advice about everything. You're not only gaining a wife, you get the network, baby, because we're a package deal. Get used to us because we're going to be around forever."

Everyone laughed and drank to all of the toasts. Finally, Nick spoke.

"I would like to share my feelings about the past year with all of you. When I went to Vegas, my schedule was so full that I had lost track of the days. I had been running around like a fool for a few days and the day I met Michele had been a long day and I was dead tired when I saw her walking through the hotel lobby. Seeing her stroll towards me instantly woke me out of my stupor. Now I'm not a real forward type guy, but there was no way I was going to let this woman walk past me without saying something and hoping to get a positive response."

"I had so many things I had to do the next day, but I shuffled everything around to find time to get to know, Michele. I've been on cloud nine since that day and will continue to be the happiest man on earth as long as Michele is a part of my life. She brought me down effortlessly. I was the

guy who said that I'd never get married, but I knew immediately that I was going to ask Michele to marry me. I was a nervous wreck awaiting her answer when I asked her. I don't know what I would have done had she said no. I would have done anything she required to win her over. Michele is the love of my life and I can say that I am the luckiest man alive to have her as my wife. Thank you, Michele, for being you."

Michele stood, wrapped her arms around Nick and kissed him. Everyone clapped.

They didn't make it to see the new house until the next day. The women spent the day at Michele's condo and the guys hung out with Nick at his place. They planned to meet up for dinner later that evening.

Saturday, April 10th

Gina, Stacey and Kellie rode over to Michele's condo together at seven a.m. the morning of the wedding. Nick's mother and sister were already there. They were all introduced and began getting ready for the ceremony which was set to begin at one p.m.

For the first time that Michele could recall, Courtney, her hairdresser was on time. She arrived at Michele's condo at nine, along with two assistants to work on styling Michele and her bridesmaids' hair.

Michele was dressed and ready to head to the church by twelve thirty. A white horse drawn carriage was waiting outside of her building which she would ride in alone. The videographer had been at her apartment videoing the details of her morning and was now in the building lobby filming her descent from the elevator.

The church was approximately two blocks from her condo. Everyone from her condo was trailing the carriage in cars. When she arrived at the church, there was a big crowd outside awaiting her arrival. The first person she saw was her mother, Linda, with a tissue up to her eyes.

The groomsmen were outside waiting for Michele and her entourage. Her Uncle Earl was there to help her out of the carriage and walk her into the church.

Nick and his best man were inside waiting at the altar for Nick to take Michele's hand. The bridesmaids and groomsmen lined up and made their entrance. The carriage driver opened the door to the carriage and Uncle Earl helped Michele out and they marched into the church together.

Uncle Earl handed Michele off to Nick and they said their vows.

The ceremony was beautiful and perfect. Nick and Michele were officially husband and wife.

The reception immediately followed the ceremony at an oceanfront restaurant in Santa Monica.

It was a spectacular evening filled with laughter, crying, dancing and everyone having a great time. Michele, Gina, Stacey and Kellie snuck away from the crowd to have a private moment before Nick and Michele left the partygoers to make their flight to Paris.

Michele said, "Ladies, it's been a good year and it's been a bad year, but in the end, it's been a great year! I love each of you and thank you for being in my life. My husband and I are on our way out of here."

"Listen to you, my husband..." Kellie said.

"He is my husband. Can y'all believe it? I's married now."

They all laughed.

Gina said, "Congratulations, Michele. We love you and wouldn't change a thing about you. You go on with your husband and have a wonderful time in Paris. Hey, when Michele and Nick return, we need to work on plans for a group trip that will include our husbands and children."

"That's a great idea, Gina. In a year, I'm sure there will be more children added to this group, hopefully, one will be mine," Michele said.

"One will definitely be mine," Stacey said.

They all looked at her. Gina said, "What are you saying, Stacey?"

"I'm pregnant."

They all congratulated and hugged her.

Nick stuck his head in the door and said, "Come on, baby, it's time."

"Well, ladies, my husband is waiting for me so I must go. I'll call you all when we return to the states."

Everyone walked Nick and Michele out to the limousine that was waiting to take them to the airport. When Michele and Nick were situated in the limo, they opened the sunroof and stood so that they could wave to everyone as they were driven away.

THE END

Printed in the United States
108228LV00004B/48/A